SPECIAL MESSAGE TO READERS

THE ULVERSCROFT FOUNDATION
(registered UK charity number 264873)
was established in 1972 to provide funds for
research, diagnosis and treatment of eye diseases.
Examples of major projects funded by
the Ulverscroft Foundation are:-

- The Children's Eye Unit at Moorfields Eye Hospital, London
- The Ulverscroft Children's Eye Unit at Great Ormond Street Hospital for Sick Children
- Funding research into eye diseases and treatment at the Department of Ophthalmology, University of Leicester
- The Ulverscroft Vision Research Group, Institute of Child Health
- Twin operating theatres at the Western Ophthalmic Hospital, London
- The Chair of Ophthalmology at the Royal Australian College of Ophthalmologists

You can help further the work of the Foundation
by making a donation or leaving a legacy.
Every contribution is gratefully received. If you
would like to help support the Foundation or
require further information, please contact:

THE ULVERSCROFT FOUNDATION
The Green, Bradgate Road, Anstey
Leicester LE7 7FU, England
Tel: (0116) 236 4325

website: www.foundation.ulverscroft.com

After a peripatetic childhood, Denise Mina left school at age 16 before doing her law degree at Glasgow University. Her first novel won the CWA John Creasey Dagger for Best First Crime Novel in 1998. She has since been nominated for many more prizes, including the CWA Gold Dagger, and has won the Theakston Old Peculier Crime Novel of the Year Award twice. In addition to novels, Denise has also written plays and graphic novels, including the adaptation of *The Girl with the Dragon Tattoo*. In 2014 she was inducted into the Crime Writers' Association Hall of Fame, and was a judge for the Baileys Prize. She has also presented TV and radio programmes, as well as appearing regularly in the media. She lives and works in Glasgow.

You can discover more about the author at www.denisemina.com

CONVICTION

It's just a normal morning for Anna McDonald — until she opens the front door to her best friend, Estelle. Anna turns to see her own husband at the top of the stairs, suitcase in hand. They're leaving together, taking Anna's two daughters with them. Left alone in the big dark house, Anna can't think; she can't take it in. So she distracts herself with a story: a true crime podcast. There's a sunken yacht in the Atlantic, multiple murders, and a hint of power and corruption. But Anna realises she knew one of the victims in another life. This is a murder case she can't ignore. As she throws herself into an investigation, Anna's past and present lives are about to collide, sending everything she has worked so hard to achieve into freefall . . .

Books by Denise Mina
Published by Ulverscroft:

SANCTUM
THE FIELD OF BLOOD
THE DEAD HOUR
THE LAST BREATH
THE LONG DROP

DENISE MINA

CONVICTION

Complete and Unabridged

CHARNWOOD
Leicester

First published in Great Britain in 2019 by
Harvill Secker
an imprint of Vintage
London

First Charnwood Edition
published 2019
by arrangement with
Vintage
Penguin Random House
London

A catalogue record for this book is available
from the British Library.

ISBN 978–1–4448–4219–7

Published by
F. A. Thorpe (Publishing)
Anstey, Leicestershire

Set by Words & Graphics Ltd.
Anstey, Leicestershire
Printed and bound in Great Britain by
T. J. International Ltd., Padstow, Cornwall

This book is printed on acid-free paper

One [belief] is that violence is caused by a deficit of morality and justice. On the contrary, violence is often caused by a surfeit of morality and justice, at least as they are conceived in the minds of the perpetrators.

Steven Pinker
The Better Angels of Our Nature

Prologue

Just tell the truth. I've said that to my own kids. What a ridiculous thing to teach children. No one wants to hear it. There has to be a reason to tell the truth. I stopped some time ago and, let me tell you, it was great. Best decision I ever made. Lie and lie again, make up a name, a background, your likes and dislikes, just fabricate the whole thing. So much more rational. But I'm telling you the truth in this book. There's a very good reason for that.

I ruined my life by telling the truth. I was very young. My mum had just died. Men gathered in my garden at night to shout abuse at my house because I wouldn't lie. Everyone started discussing what was wrong with me, with people like me. Someone nailed a dead cat to my front door in protest. A man broke into my house and tried to kill me to shut me up.

So I shut up and I ran. I changed my name. I became secretive and careful and sealed off that part of my life; I never told it again. When anything even touching on that story came up — house fires, Gretchen Teigler, football — I went to the loo or changed the subject. I didn't feel as if I was lying, I just wasn't Sophie Bukaran any more. I was Anna McDonald and those things were nothing to do with me. I felt safe.

When you're tired and young and frightened and the whole world hates you, shutting up is luxurious.

But now I'm telling that story again. Why am I writing a whole book about it for you to read? What changed? I wouldn't be doing it if my life hadn't imploded that morning. I'm no hero. I'm not a whistle-blower of tremendous personal courage, content to be hounded to my grave because I will not be silenced. I'm truth-telling for a very different reason. It's less laudable but a bit more relatable, maybe. And it's the truth.

1

The day my life exploded started well.

It was early morning in November and I woke up without the use of an alarm clock. I was pleased about that. It was a concession to our couples counselling: I wouldn't wake Hamish at six with my alarm clock and he wouldn't play Candy Crush on his phone all evening while ignoring the children.

I was looking forward to my day. I had a new true crime podcast series waiting on my phone and I'd heard good things about it. I planned to listen to the first episode, get a taste for the story before I woke the kids for school, and then binge on it while I trawled through a day of menial tasks. A good podcast can add a glorious multi-world texture to anything. I've resisted an Assyrian invasion while picking up dry-cleaning. I've seen justice served on a vicious murderer while buying underpants.

I lay in bed savouring the anticipation, watching light from the street ripple across the ceiling, listening as the heating kicked on and the grand old dame of a house groaned and cracked her bones. I got up, pulled on a jumper and slippers, and crept out of the bedroom.

I loved getting up before everyone else, when the house was still and I could read or listen to a podcast alone in a frozen world. I knew where everyone was. I knew they were safe. I could relax.

Hamish resented it. He said it was creepy. Why did I need this time alone, sneaking around the house? Why did I need to be alone so much?

Trust issues, the couples counsellor called it.

I tried to reassure Hamish, *I'm not planning to kill you or anything*. But that was not reassuring, apparently. In fact, Anna, it might sound rather hostile to Hamish, if you think about it from his point of view. *Really?* (I said it in a hostile way.) *Does that sound hostile?* Then we talked about that for a while. It was a stupid process. We were both hostile and sad. Our relationship was in its death throes.

I tiptoed across the landing, skirting the squeakiest floor-boards and looked in on both of the girls. They were fast asleep in their wee beds, school uniforms laid out on chairs, socks in shoes, ties under collars. I wish I had lingered longer. I would never see them so innocent again.

I went back out to the landing. The oak banister curled softly from the top of the house to bottom, carved to fit the cup of a hand, grainy to the touch, following the wind of the stairs like a great long snake of yellow marzipan. It led down to a grand hallway with marble pillars flanking the front door and a floor mosaic of Hamish's ancestral coat of arms. The house was bought by Hamish's great-grandfather in 1869. He bought it new from Greek Thompson.

Hamish was very proud of his background. He knew *nothing* at all about mine. I must emphasise that. I'm not just saying that to

2

protect him, now that everything has come out. He was a senior member of the Bar, hoping to be appointed to the bench like his forebears. He wouldn't have risked that just to be with me.

When we met I was Anna, the new office temp from Somewhere-Outside-of-Aberdeen. I chose Hamish quite carefully. I did love him, I must say that, and I still do, sometimes. But I deliberately picked an older man with money and status. A declamatory man, full of facts and opinions. He was the perfect hide.

Hamish was born in that house and had never lived anywhere else. His family had been on or near the Scottish judiciary for two hundred years. He didn't much like foreign travel. He read only Scottish writers. That seemed so weird to me. I think I found it a little exotic.

It was cold in the hall that morning. I walked through into the white-gleaming, German-designed kitchen and made a pot of strong coffee. I picked up my phone. The true crime podcast series was called *Death and the Dana*. The description read 'A sunken yacht, a murdered family on board, a secret still unsolved . . . '

Oh yes: ponderous tone, secrets, murders, it had everything. And the case had happened while my girls were small, a time of little jumpers and waiting outside school, standing silently with the timeless phalanx of mothers, absent from the wider world. I didn't know anything about this murder case.

I poured a big mug of coffee, sat down, put my phone on the kitchen table in front of me and

3

pressed play. I expected an absorbing, high-stakes story.

I had no idea I was about to meet Leon Parker again.

2

Episode 1: Death and the Dana

Hi.

I'm Trina Keany, a producer here on the MisoNetwork. Welcome to this podcast series: *Death and the Dana.*

According to French police this strange and troubling case is closed. They solved it. Amila Fabricase was convicted of the murder of three members of the same family on their yacht. But Amila Fabricase could not have done it: the murders could only have been committed by someone on board and multiple witnesses, CCTV and passport checks place Amila on an airplane, flying to Lyon, at the time.

On the night in question a wealthy family — a father and his two children — were having dinner on board their docked private yacht, the Dana. The crew had been sent ashore at the father's insistence and the family were alone.

While Amila was in the air the boat motored out of port in the dark. No sails were set. Radio and navigation lights were off. Still, the Dana navigated the tricky sandbanks of the Perthuis Breton strait, changed course by thirty-two degrees and headed out into the Atlantic. Several miles

5

out to sea an explosion in the hull sank the ship. All three people on board died.

So what could have happened? Why were the authorities so determined to believe something that was provably not true? And why has there never been an appeal against the conviction?

Even before it sank, the Dana had a reputation for being haunted. Superstitious commentators immediately seized upon the sinking as proof that the boat was haunted. A month later, a bizarre underwater film of the wreck seemed to confirm tales of vengeful ghosts on board.

Trina Keany's south London accent was soft, her timbre low, intonation melodic. I put my feet up on the chair next to me and sipped delicious coffee.

But let's go back to the beginning and set the scene.

The Île de Ré is a chichi holiday resort off the west coast of France. It has a quirky history. It's a long, flat island, basically a sandbank between La Rochelle and the Bay of Biscay. For most of its history the island was cut off from the mainland and very poor. The economy depended on salt harvesting and criminal transportations. It was from the island's capital, Saint-Martin, that French prisoners left for the penal colonies of New Caledonia and Guiana. Dreyfus left for Devil's Island from Saint-Martin. The author of

6

Papillon, *Henri Charrière*, *left on a prison ship in 1931.*

Because it was poor and isolated the island remained undeveloped. It kept its ancient cobbled streets, pretty sun-bleached cottages with terracotta roofs, doors and shutters painted pastel green or blue. Tall pink hollyhocks burst from pavements in summer and it has become a UNESCO World Heritage site. But the population is very wealthy now and that's because of the bridge.

In the late 1980s, at great expense, a long road bridge was built linking it with La Rochelle. French holidaymakers slowly began to discover the unspoiled island. It became a low-key holiday resort, understated, modest in scale. The climate is pleasant, as sunny as the south of France but cooler because of a breeze coming off the Atlantic. The island is flat. There are cycle lanes everywhere.

Over the next couple of decades more and more people wanted a simple life in the bucolic setting. Movie stars, musicians, ex-presidents and captains of industry moved there. Competition for houses became intense. Even modest houses became expensive, then unaffordable. Poor fishermen's cottages stand empty, used occasionally by high-end holiday-makers who sail into the marina in the centre of town. Shops no longer sell horsemeat or hardware, they sell Gucci and Chanel. It has an air of wealth.

Locals have resisted. Holiday homes have

been burned to the ground. Incomers have reported harassment and prejudicial treatment. A family from New Zealand claimed they were chased off the island. But mostly it is peaceful.

As the Dana docked in Saint-Martin that day there were a lot of hobby sailors who recognised and admired her. She was a beautiful ship.

The Dana was not the kind of private yacht we tend to think of now: there were no plasma screens or helipads, no four storeys of white couches and minibars. She was a sailing ship, a schooner. Schooners are louche. In times gone by, pirates and privateers loved schooners for their speed. They have high sails and a curved bow that sits low in the water like a slick-hipped cowboy's gun belt.

So the Dana was beautiful and she was famous. Once dubbed 'the most haunted yacht afloat', a movie had been made about her in the 1970s in the tradition of The Amityville Horror. Like that film and other horror movies of that period, The Haunting of the Dana looks creaky to us now, but it was very successful at the time, as was the book that inspired it. The ship's notoriety followed it, creating a flurry of interest wherever she docked.

That afternoon, she docked in Saint-Martin, was tied up, bow and stern, and a gangplank was lowered.

A mismatched young couple were seen

8

approaching the ship. The girl was slim, tanned, blonde and looked very Italian. She wore a sleeveless, ankle-length Missoni dress and sandals. Her companion was a gangly teen boy dressed in baggy shorts, skater shoes and an oversized T-shirt. One eyewitness actually thought the boy was a lucky horror fan who had stumbled unexpectedly on the Dana, because his T-shirt had an image from the cult horror movie Drag Me to Hell. The witness remembered thinking that the boy must be very pleased to see the famous ship. He was surprised when a man with the same hair and face, obviously the boy's father, waved to the boy from the yacht. He wondered if the father had bought the yacht for the boy's entertainment or if the boy wore the T-shirt for his father's. It stuck in his mind.

I was relaxed, had my feet up on the table and I was drinking coffee so strong that it was making me break into a gentle sweat. My mind began to stray to the day ahead but then Keany said:

In fact, the mismatched boy and girl were siblings and had come to meet their father, Leon Parker, the yacht's new owner.

Startled, I sat up. I must have misheard. I was groggy, it was early. I thought it was sleepy mind tricks, that made me hear Leon's name. I hadn't thought about him for years and it surprised me that his name should come to me now.

He'd invited his two children to come to Saint-Martin to join him on board the Dana. They were celebrating the eldest, Violetta, turning twenty-one. The kids barely knew each other. They came from homes in different countries and from very different mothers. Leon had recently remarried and was making an effort to forge a family unit out of the mess of his past, an effort that may have been at the behest of his new wife. It was a marked change from his previous behaviour.

He meant to serve them a meal on board his yacht and present his daughter with a fabulous antique diamond necklace to mark her coming of age.

Sitting upright in the chill of the morning kitchen, I was still in denial, convinced I had heard the name wrong, but my heart rate rose steadily. It was as if my blood knew it was him before my mind could take it in.

As the gangplank hit the dock, a young woman rushed off the ship. She had a bag of clothes with her; she held one hand over her right eye and was being shouted after by the captain.

This was Amila Fabricase, the ship's chef.

Amila left fast enough to make a loud clang clang clang on the metal gangplank. The noise drew the eyes of multiple witnesses. She pushed through the crowds, ran across town and stopped to ask a waiter in a cafe where she could get a taxi to the airport. He later described her as holding a hand over her eye, face ashen, body trembling, tears rolling down the covered side of her face and dripping from her chin. The waiter made her sit down and called a cab. She seemed to be in a lot of pain, he thought she had hurt her eye and asked if she wanted him to take a look. She didn't. He helped her into the cab for the airport and she thanked him.

Back on the Dana the captain was furious. The family had gathered for a celebration meal but the chef was gone. He called Amila's employment agency demanding a replacement but it was the height of the season and no one was available. He left angry messages on Amila's phone, insisting that she give back her wages: the crew had all been paid in cash at the start of the voyage. This is very unusual practice and made the captain look bad. Amila had taken all of her money with her. She never called back.

The kids watched Amila leave, saw the captain shouting, but then their father came down the gangplank. They hugged and then all three set off for a walk while the captain fumed and made arrangements for dinner.

They walked up through the town and stopped at a café-bar for beer and Fantas. The café owner remembered that Leon smoked and talked a lot, that they all laughed together but seemed tense.

Back on the Dana the captain still had to find a way of serving them a celebration meal. Les Copains, a Michelin-starred restaurant in the town, agreed to provide bouillabaisse soup, bread, charcuterie, cheeses and salad. Bouillabaisse is a fish stew. Like a lot of peasant foods, it began as a simple dish but now the recipe is rigidly adhered to. The basic fish stew should be garnished with freshly cooked mussels, crab and garlic-rubbed bread, all added just before serving. This became important later to establish the sequence of the events. The restaurant wanted to leave a sous chef on board to serve the bouillabaisse properly but the captain said no. Leon Parker wanted the yacht to himself tonight. No sous chef would be permitted to stay. Leon wanted to be alone with his children.

Les Copains was so ashamed about their mis-service of the bouillabaisse that it took a week before they admitted that they left before the soup was served.

When the dinner was delivered from Les Copains, it was set up in the galley, the bouillabaisse in a thermal pot, ready to be served. The garnish was left on a separate plate. The cheese had been plated up, as had the charcuterie. The crew set the table in the formal dining room downstairs. Leon hadn't had a chance to use it yet and was keen to show it off. A magnum of champagne was put on ice, on deck, as per Leon's instructions and the crew awaited the family's return.

When they saw the Parkers walking down the dock towards the ship, the captain got the crew to line up and welcome them. Leon was last on board. He gave the captain a few hundred euros and ordered him to take the crew to a bar for a big football match, France vs Germany in a European Cup semi-final match. He told them not to come back before eleven.

The captain did what he was told. He led his men to a bar nearby and they watched the whole match. France won, knocking Germany out and gaining a place in the final. The French crew had a very good night. They went for pizza before getting to the dock at ten past eleven.

But the Dana was gone. None of the Parker family members were ever seen alive again.

There were no communications from on board but this is what was seen by diners at a nearby rooftop restaurant: sunset was around nine thirty. They saw one figure on deck, possibly Violetta, but it was dark. The Dana's engine started and the ship motored out into open waters.

As the top mast passed by the rooftop restaurant, just eighty yards away, onlookers gave her a round of applause. But the diners with sailing experience saw that something was wrong.

The navigation lights were off on the boat.

These lights should be on at all times

when a ship is in motion: a light on the main mast, one at the front and back, and coloured lights on the side — red on port, green on starboard, so that other boats know which direction the ship is going in.

Two diners were so troubled that they called the coastguard to warn them something was awry with the Dana. Someone had cast off without the lights on. It suggested an incompetent sailor with no training or awareness of the regulations. The coastguard tried to contact the yacht but the maritime radio was off.

The Dana motored straight out into the Atlantic, cutting across a major shipping lane. That's a dangerous thing to do without a radio because modern container ships are huge and sail blind. They rely on radio contact to warn smaller vessels to get out of the way.

Miraculously, the Dana crossed the shipping lane without incident but the coastguard was now reporting it as a safety hazard.

This drew the attention of other ships.

A nearby container ship stationed a crewman to watch the Dana until the coastguard got there. Much later, after Amila was sentenced for the murders, the crewman was interviewed for a documentary. He described what he saw.

There was a change of sound texture, better quality with the flat ambience of a studio. The man spoke perfect English with a thick Dutch accent.

'Yes, we radioed many times but no reply came back. I was asked to stand on the bridge and watch until the coastguard got there. It was a clear night, I had binoculars. I could see the outline, we were approaching, but no one on board. So, OK. That was a strange . . . um . . . situation. The lights were off, even the masthead, but the engine was still running. I could see fumes coming out and it was moving in a straight line. Maybe a power failure? I don't know. But as I watched, that yacht just dropped straight down into the sea.

'I watched it go straight down. It didn't list. It happened very quickly, sea folds over the deck, little puff of smoke as the engine went under, sea covered the top mast and then the water was calm again. It just went down and it was gone.

'It was weird. We all laughed. We didn't know there was a family on there. We thought someone had scuttled it for insurance, done it badly, that they would get found out. You have no idea how expensive these ships are, even sitting in dock. We thought that was what happened. Because, well, what else could have happened?'

What else indeed?

Amila Fabricase was charged and convicted of sinking the ship. The police found evidence that she had handled explosives and claimed that she set them in the engine room of the Dana before she got off. What the investigation never seemed to ask was this: who sailed the ship out to sea? It had to be someone on board.

Suppose Leon Parker had a bit to drink and decided to go sailing after dinner. Suppose he forgot to turn on the lights and the radio — even then, the rooftop diners would have seen him confidently casting off. But they didn't. One witness on the dock did see a lone figure but said they were staying low, being furtive, as if they were hiding. It was done surreptitiously.

Amila was traced, searched, interrogated and investigated.

The wealthy family was hardly looked at.

The police paid scant attention to Leon, who had invited the kids there and dismissed the crew after paying them in cash. Leon, who could both cast off and sail the ship. Leon, who ordered the captain to set out the dinner in the dining room, below deck, on a warm July night, when the most obvious place to eat would be on deck. No one asked if Leon Parker killed his family. The police focused exclusively on Amila.

Leon had recently married into a very powerful family. They are famously media-shy and connected. Is it possible that they asked the police not to look at Leon? Is it possible that it was strongly implied that the police's focus should be elsewhere?

16

I paused it. I knew it was my Leon. My friend Leon.

My heart was thumping in my throat. I picked up my phone and opened the podcast home page.

3

The background image was of the *Dana* hanging in a harness in dry dock. A fisheye lens distorted the image so the red-and-white bow loomed towards the viewer like a big friendly dog nuzzling up to the camera. The sky behind was crisp and blue, a Côte d'Azur winter sky, and the varnished wooden deck glinted in the sun.

Down the side of the image were files, each marked by the episode they related to. 'Ep1'. 'Ep2'. They were designed to look like stacks of documents that had been dropped on a desk and seen from above. But it wasn't a desk, it was a photo of a yacht.

I tapped 'Ep1' and a series of photos separated and slid across the screen.

There he was: Leon Parker.

Leon grinning, gap-toothed, older.

His arms were resting on the shoulders of two sleek kids, a gangly blond boy in an oversized T-shirt and a beautiful girl in a green-and-gold chevroned dress. She was smirking and wore a lumpy diamond necklace. She was touching it with her middle finger as if she was flipping the bird at the camera. They were all toasting the camera with champagne flutes.

Leon Parker was dead. God, that made me sad. I hadn't seen him for years but some people are just a loss to the world. Leon Parker was one of those people.

He hadn't aged much in a decade. He was tall, six feet, square, broad around the middle but still handsome for a man in his late fifties. His hair was a little more silvered, still longish and curly, salt-tousled from being at sea. White chest hair curled up at the wide neck of his open shirt, stark against weathered brown skin. He was grinning, missing a tooth behind his incisor. He looked happy.

My eye was drawn away from the blue-sky background, the kids and the diamond necklace, to the skinny cigarette burning between Leon's fingers. Leon rolled his own. I'd seen him do it with one hand.

In the picture he had his arms around the kids but held the cigarette away, keeping his cigarette to the side as if he didn't want the smoke to get near them. I could almost smell his cheap tobacco, warm as gravy, hear him chuckle at the end of a story he must have told a hundred times.

I didn't want to listen on but I needed to know what had happened to him. I pressed play.

Leon Parker was a character. No one could deny that. Whatever faults he had he certainly knew how to have a good time. Born to a working-class family in London's East End, he was a City trader, then a businessman. He took a lot of risks, made and lost fortunes.

After he died this little interview with him on London Tonight *was unearthed. It was made in the street, on Black Wednesday in 1992 when the London markets collapsed.*

The sound of buses rumbling on a busy London street. A plummy-voiced interviewer shouted over the noise:

'*Excuse me, sir, have you lost money today?*'

'*Everyfink.*' Leon's voice was hoarse and raw. '*I've lost the bleeding lot.*'

'*A very bad day for you then?*' The interviewer sounded sombre.

'*Yeah, well . . .* ' Leon's voice was suddenly lighter. '*Win some, lose some, don'tcha?*'

Then he cackled his fruity laugh, a gorgeous blend of despair and love-of-the-game. The interviewer haw-hawed along with him. I found myself smiling too.

Oh God, Leon's laugh. So dark and wild you could drown a bag of kittens in it.

It took me all the way back to a summer in the Scottish Highlands, way up the east coast, past Inverness, beyond the Black Isle, up to Dornach, where the hills are old and round and high, where the trains hardly go any more, where the weather is surprisingly mild and the land is pitted with abandoned farmsteads melting back into the land.

Back to Skibo Castle.

4

Skibo Castle is an exclusive members-only holiday resort near Dingwall.

The castle was dilapidated when it was bought in 1897 by Andrew Carnegie. He was Scottish, emigrated to America when he was ten and made his money there. He was the wealthiest man in the world at the time. Carnegie rebuilt Skibo as an Edwardian mansion to use as a summer home. Set on twenty-eight thousand acres of land it has every luxury: fly-fishing and deer-hunting, sailing and kayaking, horse riding, excellent kitchens and beautiful rooms. It has a spa, selling cures that don't work for things you don't have. Madonna had her wedding reception there.

Approached from the drive it looks quite big, but that is deceptive. It is built on a steep hill. It's enormous, with the functional rooms tucked away below ground. This leaves the main rooms unencumbered by utility, free to pretend to be a house with twenty bedrooms and no broom cupboard.

That part of the Highlands is polluted with castles. The owner of Harrods has one. Bob Dylan has one. The Queen Mother lived up there. The Dukes of Sutherland own Dunrobin Castle, which is open to the public.

It has a rather nice tea room and a museum that makes no mention of the clearances, when tenant farmers were chased off the land to make way for profitable sheep. They do have a Carrara marble bust of Garibaldi. The Duke only met him for a few days but Garibaldi was very famous at the time. It's the nineteenth century's equivalent of a signed Hendrix poster.

It's an odd out-of-the-way place for odd out-of-the-way people, often incomers pretending to be Scottish. The whole area is awash with fictions. I loved it there.

Leon Parker was visiting Skibo with his Dutch girlfriend. The club membership was hers but she didn't shoot or sail or swim or even horse ride. She wore heels that scarred the oak parquet and spent her time in the spa, sipping tea cures and finding fault with the service. She was small and dark and very beautiful.

Leon and I met one evening in the dark by a bin shed: I was on my smoke break, he was out for a walk. He asked me for a cigarette because he'd left his tobacco in his room. I couldn't tell him to piss off. I was already in trouble with the manager.

We stood and smoked in the quiet evening. I was wary of being alone with him. I made sure I could see into the kitchen window, kept an eye so that someone was always within calling distance. It wasn't because Leon was threatening, I just didn't really trust anyone back then.

We talked about the smoking ban and how much it had enhanced our smoking. He told me he once got so desperate on a long flight that he ate tobacco and felt sick for hours. We laughed at that.

He seemed kind of desperate for a laugh.

I can't remember how we got around to this but he told me a lovely story about a beggar he saw outside his hotel in Paris. The filthy man sat down on the pavement, took a clean tablecloth out of his pocket and laid it out in front of him. Then, from other pockets, he took out a knife, a fork, a spoon and napkin, set his place and propped up a sign that read 'Merci'. Then he tucked the napkin into his collar and waited. As Leon watched, the man was served a meal by a nearby restaurant. The next day the man arrived again, laid his place and was again served a meal, from a different restaurant this time. Leon was there for four days and the man never went without lunch.

'Paris!' he said at the end, as if that meant anything.

But I liked the story so I said, 'Yeah, Paris!' back.

Then we fell quiet and smoked and watched the sun go down. It was something to see. Sunsets that summer were shocking-pink skies battling navy-blue night. A lake below us glinted silver. The pool enclosure was a giant Edwardian dome and the panes of glass winked the pink passing of the sun behind the hills in the west.

The first night was a good laugh.

But on the second night Leon turned up at the bins again. I was worried that he had the wrong idea. We chatted stiffly about the day and he rolled cigarettes for me, payback for the night before. Blackcurrant-and-vanilla-flavoured tobacco.

Staff were not allowed to tell the guests to fuck off or hit them on the head with trays, as I had recently discovered to my cost. I had a bit of a temper back then.

I wanted that job. It was a good job, well paid, comfortable accommodation, safe and out of the way. I had a close friend there, Adam Ross. Club members came from all over the world and most were pretty nice. If they weren't, the manager, Albert, spoke to them and he could radiate shame in a five-mile radius. Service is a power game, Albert said, and formality is our only weapon. Always maintain a professional distance. But here was I, smoking cigarettes with a guest by the bins. It wasn't right.

Leon sensed my unease and addressed it straight on. Did I mind him coming out to smoke with me?

It felt like a trick question. If I said I didn't mind would he try to grab me? Best meet it with another question, so I said, 'Why are you coming out to the bins to smoke? I'd use the smoking lounge if we were allowed.'

'Well,' he smiled shyly, 'this lady I'm here with, my girlfriend, I really like her and all that, but she doesn't have much chat, d'you know what I mean?'

I thought she was a surly cow but I said, 'Yeah, I know people like that . . . '

'If I tell her a story, like that one about the Paris beggar, she looks confused and she's like: Why did he lay out a serving place? Where did he get cutlery if he was a beggar? She doesn't like stories.'

I said maybe she didn't come from a storytelling family.

'Yeah. Doesn't get it.' He looked worried and drew hard on his cigarette. 'She says, 'You're always telling stories, Le-on. Always a *little* story to go with everything.'' He was being disparaging, doing her accent, but he looked away, he wasn't trying to get me to join in, and then he muttered, 'Doesn't get it . . . ' He seemed a bit sad.

I said that one of the stories in the *Arabian Nights* is specifically about the urge to tell a story. It's primal, the need to tell. It's not about the listener but the storyteller. In some cultures, not telling your story is regarded as a sign of mental illness.

'*Arabian Nights*,' he smiled. 'Like *Ali Baba?* Like in panto?'

I was appalled. I went off on a rant about the *Arabian Nights*, the collective nature of it, how it created a whole world through accretive storytelling: layers of lives lived simultaneously, intersecting. And how it bounced from genre to genre, the stories were funny and brutal and romantic and tragic like life, I said, that's like real life. It was produced before stories could only be one thing, before the form was set. I said how stupid and narrow it was of Western culture to make everything about just one person. I sounded pompous. I sounded like my mum, she was a literature professor at SOAS. I was saying all this to impress him because he was very handsome and I think I wanted him to know that I wasn't just a chambermaid.

Leon nodded and listened and smiled and he said that was interesting. He knew a woman whose whole thing was *not* telling her story because her family history was so dark. Super-secretive, super-rich. Keeps out of the papers. When I think back, it was a clumsy conversational segue but I knew who he was talking about even before he said 'Nazis' because I was so hyper-vigilant back then.

'Her name is Gretchen Teigler,' he said. 'Is she a member here?'

'No.'

It was the first thing I checked when I got there. I wouldn't have been at Skibo if she was a member. She was the reason I was on the run. Gretchen Teigler had tried to have me killed.

Leon seemed surprised, tipped his head at me and said, 'How do you know?'

'I just know.'

'But how do you know her name?'

I realised my mistake.

'Oh Mr McKay keeps us up to speed with all of that.' It was a stupid thing to say, as if Albert would run the staff through a list of people who weren't members.

I saw Leon smile and look at my mouth. I was suddenly aware that my accent was slipping around. It was because he was a Londoner — I'd mimicked his vowels without meaning to. I was supposed to be a chambermaid from Aberdeen.

Scared, I mumbled something about not being supposed to talk to guests, anyway. Maybe he should just go inside.

Leon left a pause and then he said: 'Nah.' And dropped it.

He didn't pry about how I knew Gretchen

26

Teigler's name but maybe he already knew. I have a scar across my eye-brow that is pretty distinctive. I'm recognisable if you know what to look for and Leon was from London. He would have heard about the scandal. It was pretty hard to miss.

Anyway, Leon rolled his eyes and moved on to talking about smoking again. I thought he was just in this moment with me, his new friend, smoking and telling stories. Then he came back to it and said, 'Bollocks to Nazis, anyway.'

We both laughed at that. Then we laughed because we were both laughing, apparently at nothing, but we understood each other quite deeply, and it was fleeting and laughing was a way to keep it alive. But then it was over. We wiped our eyes and he sighed and I said, 'Hey, Leon, did I tell you about the boys swimming in a salt lake with their mule?'

And he looked greedy-eyed, and growled 'AHHHH!', telling me to give him the story. I did. It was a good one. Then he gave me one back. It was a peach. I can't remember what happened in his story, just that it was small and round and the tail tucked neatly into its mouth.

Our stories weren't disguised curriculum vitae. We didn't tell them as a way of boasting or declaring our relative place in the social order. There was none of that crap. These were stories to entertain, told for the shape of them, for the sake of them, for the love of a tale. It was all about the stories and the shapes of the stories. Round ones, spirals, perfect arcs, a ninety-degree take-off with a four-bump landing, and one of his, I remember vividly, was an absurdist finger trap. Whatever happened afterwards, whoever he turned out to be really, at that point it was pure with me and Leon.

I trusted him a little. When no one came to kill me the next day, I trusted him a little more. During the day I saw the manager, Mr McKay, and he made no mention of Gretchen Teigler so I knew Leon hadn't mentioned my slip-up. Maybe it meant nothing to him.

The next night by the bins he told me about his daughter. When men talk about a daughter it's often a coded way of saying they are not planning to attack you. Mothers are a different code. Mother stories can go either way. Leon had divorced the girl's mother and abandoned his daughter. The girl grew up in terrible circumstances, her mother was a drug addict and the girl's upbringing was wild. He only found out later. It was a bitter break-up and he was so wrapped up in himself he hadn't even thought to find out how she was. He was in his late thirties when she was born, he didn't know what it was to be a father. He was supporting them now but his daughter was very angry with him. He thought she was right to be.

It was honest, clearly true and he felt awful about it. I felt he was making himself vulnerable. He asked me if I had family and, for some reason, I told him the truth. My mother died of breast cancer when I was seventeen. She was everything to me. My father had killed himself when I was young. I didn't remember him. Leon tutted and said that was dreadful. He wasn't being judgemental, just, it was a terrible thing to deal with. He said my father should have waited, that it would have passed, usually does. Then he took a deep draw on his cigarette, burning a half-inch stub of ash. It felt as if he had considered suicide and talked himself out of it. I liked him even more for that. I never forgave my father for what he did. Suicide is virulent. It can rip through families the way TB used to scythe down whole streets. He brought the pathogen into our home. Especially towards the end, when she was terribly ill, my mum struggled because of what he did. Some days, my own staying alive felt like an act of defiance, like a big fuck you to my dad.

Then Leon went back inside.

He was there for a week. He came out each night and we smoked and told stories but he wasn't afraid of being quiet and he always left me time for a smoke alone.

On his last night he came to the bins with two glasses of fifteen-year-old Springbank. He said it was the best malt ever made.

I thanked him and we drank and watched the hot-pink sunset lose the good fight over the bin shed. It was nice malt.

Leon said chumps go for the expensive whisky but this was the best. He told a long story about a millionaire who paid eight grand for a single measure of a hundred-year-old malt and posted a picture of the bottle. Experts replied and told him that the distillery didn't even exist until thirty years ago. They tested it and the whisky was a cheap blend, the bottle was a fake. Leon liked that story a lot. I don't really know why he enjoyed telling it so much. At the end he laughed with surprise and his laugh was full and deep. It came from his belly and he opened his mouth wide to let it out in gusty barks. And then he said, 'I'd have paid that at one time. You can't buy special, though. Cost me a lot of dough to find that out.'

I wanted to ask him what the fuck he was doing at Skibo Castle then, but he might not have found it funny, and I liked him, so I didn't. Did he have money of his own or just a rich girlfriend? It was never clear, really. And then my break was over and the malt was gone and we had smoked our cigarettes down.

He turned to me, which felt weird, because we were usually looking out at the view, but he turned and looked at me and said, 'You're too good for this job, Anna. Promise me you'll get out of here.'

I was already working my notice. I had been asked to leave because of the tray incident and several other things which, in hindsight, I'm astonished they tolerated at all. But Leon didn't know that and I liked him so I let him have the win.

'OK, I promise,' I said. 'And you should get away from that miserable Dutch woman. Find someone who likes you.'

He grinned and I noticed the gap behind his incisor. 'Doesn't she like me?'

'She doesn't like anything.'

He laughed again and told me to take care and he left.

When I came on shift next morning Leon was gone. He had driven away in the middle of the night without the Dutch girlfriend. She was in reception, very angry, giving the staff a hard time about the spa bill and demanding a limo to take her to the airport. I was sent upstairs to pack for her. I'm ashamed to say that I spat in her Creme de la Mer. I really was a poisonous little dart back then.

Sitting in my gleaming German kitchen, with my girls and Hamish asleep upstairs and the mug of coffee going cold in my hand, I looked at the photo of my friend Leon and wept. I was very upset that he was dead.

Grief is a scar. The tissue is tough and when it's cut again, it heals poorly.

I thought that I needed to talk to my best friend, Estelle, that if I could describe Leon to her, tell her what a good bloke he was, what he meant to me, my sadness would be lessened. It would put it in the past. She was due to come by and pick me up for our Bikram class at nine thirty, but it was still early. I glanced at the clock and realised with a start that it was after seven o'clock. I had to wake up my family and begin my mundane suburban Monday.

I should have stayed under the sea with the ghosts.

5

I first heard the knocking on the front door as I was packing the girls' lunches. I glanced at the clock. Five to eight. I assumed it was a lost taxi driver or a parcel with the wrong address.

Everyone else was upstairs, getting ready. I had lists and sports timetables running through my head: Jessica had swimming today and Lizzie had gym. Jess needed her costume and shampoo because chlorine made her scalp itchy.

I heard the knocking again but I was ticking through lists in my mind and didn't want to break my chain of thought. I ignored it.

I took the school bags and put them in the hall, called up to the girls that they had ten minutes, come on now, went to the airing cupboard and took out a swimming costume and a fresh towel, rolled one inside the other and came back out.

As I walked down the hallway, I blinked and saw Leon laughing against a pink sky. The memory was so vivid that it winded me. I slumped against the wall to catch my breath. Fuck.

I hadn't mentioned the podcast over breakfast. Hamish didn't know I'd worked at Skibo so there would be no straightforward way of telling a story about Leon, and anyway, we were barely talking.

I was in the hall, thinking about Leon, when I

heard Hamish's mobile ring out in our bedroom above.

A scuffle of feet as he hurried across the room to pick it up.

I was angry. When I rang Hamish he just let it go to answerphone. Sometimes he called me back later. Sometimes he didn't and just said he hadn't noticed his phone ringing. But when his office called he always answered immediately. Now he was scampering across the bedroom to answer a call at eight in the morning. Funny business, corporate law. The calls were day and night.

I could hear him murmuring urgently, his voice snaking down the stairwell. Then I heard him shut the bedroom door for privacy.

That made me furious and I couldn't justify it.

I shoved the swimming kit into the bag.

The front door was knocked again, quite deliberately this time. Three knocks, equally spaced. Knock. Knock. Knock.

I walked over to the door and reached for the snib but darkness fell in the hall.

I looked back. Hamish was standing on the landing, blocking the light from the window. His outline was wrong. He wasn't wearing a suit and tie but some sort of T-shirt with a horrible collar and disgusting beige trousers with pleats. I didn't even know he had clothes like that.

'What on earth are you wearing?'

He didn't answer. His face was backlit, I couldn't see his expression, but then I saw the suitcase sitting at his heel; a yellow roll-on cabin bag. I had put it away in the cellar when he came

33

back from his law conference in St Lucia just a month ago.

Knock. Knock. Knock.

I knew. Just outside that door was the answer to his moods over the last year, to my paranoia, to everything. I reached over and opened it.

I didn't expect it to be her.

My best friend Estelle, wearing a brand-new dress and quite a lot of make up for a Monday-morning Bikram class. And she had a little suitcase with her.

No.

Wrong.

I was in the wrong story.

I was in a family saga about a May-to-December couple and their two eccentric daughters. Our troubles were minor, our conundrums comedic. Only I wasn't in that story at all. I was in a love story and I wasn't even a central character. I was the 'all' their love would overcome.

'Mummy?' Jess galloped downstairs past her dad. 'Can I have a smoothie in my lunch box?'

I wanted to scream a warning, bellow her out of this moment and back into the before, but I felt as if it was raining glass in the hall and I didn't dare open my mouth to speak.

6

I'm not proud of how I handled it.

There's no way of describing it without me sounding mad and awful. It's humiliating. I'd rather skip over all of it, but what comes next — running back to Skibo Castle, Demy and the thing in Paris and all of that — it only makes sense if I explain how brutal the morning was and how close I was to the rope.

I'll tell it in vignettes. I'll edit, not judiciously but self-servingly. This isn't to trick anyone but some things are hard to admit about yourself. It was a death. Death needs padding because it is unbearable.

So: these are bits I can stand to tell, edited.

The girls were sitting at the table wearing their school uniforms. Seven and eight. Funny little scraps of nonsense. Hamish was telling them he had a new relationship with Estelle, Estelle was moving in and I was moving out to a shitty little flat he had bought me nearby. *Mummy has got all this money to do it up.* He held up the brick of notes. Estelle was not sitting at the table, she didn't have a seat, yet. She was standing nearby, waiting for me to vacate mine. She smiled uncertainly, trying to seem friendly to the girls while avoiding my gorgon gaze.

Hamish outlined his plan: the girls were going to miss a week of school and go to Portugal with them to meet Estelle's family and 'get used to the new arrangement'. The girls were wary of Hamish. I saw that. He is emotionally distant and high-handed but they've always liked Estelle.

Hamish said that he wouldn't make them go. It was their choice. Perhaps they would choose to stay here with me. Everyone looked at my shocked, red eyes and bloody, swollen right hand (I had punched a wall. I left that out because it sounds so bad). Or perhaps they would choose to go on a breezy November holiday with the sunshine couple. The choice was theirs. They were only seven and eight. They couldn't choose socks on their own and they'd remember this, replay this scene in their minds for the rest of their lives.

I had the sudden feeling of being in an anecdote told by the girls in the future. *He made us choose between them and we were very young, it was awful. And Mum, remember Mum? Mum just sat there while Dad made us choose and she just did nothing. And poor Mum, d'you remember Mum?*

I wasn't going to be that Mum. I mean, I can do passive as a party trick but I will not raise girls to it.

★ ★ ★

Cut to: Estelle crying and shaking sugar out of her hair and eyes. The bowl had hit her so hard that she had a red crescent throbbing on her forehead. Granules of sugar were stuck in her lipstick, twinkling like glitter. In the ensuing silence Lizzie giggled nervously and Jess hissed 'don't' at her.

Subsequently, things were said, largely about Estelle, things that could not be unsaid or unheard. In the final accounting that's what I'm most ashamed of because all of those things were said by me. And I shouldn't have because my kids will know her for the rest of their lives. And also, whatever she did, I've done worse. Hamish was married to someone else when I got pregnant.

Lizzie loved the sugar throwing and the shouting. She sat up tall, eyes wide with excitement. Jess is older and was less pleased. She still liked it though, or am I reading that into the memory to make myself feel better? Probably.

Then Hamish was leading Estelle out of the room. I reached for his arm and she swung around, spraying sugar from her hair. 'Don't you hit him!'

I reeled. I have never hit Hamish. I am angry, possibly a bit scary, but I have never hit him. He looked ashamed. I don't know what he had told her.

I looked back and saw my girls sitting at the table, patiently waiting for someone to sort this mess out. They were looking to me.

Hamish did not know who I was. He didn't know that I was using a stolen ID and wouldn't go to court for custody of the girls. That would expose me and, more than anything in the world, I did not want the girls to know who I really was. Ever. I wanted to shield them and to do that, whatever Hamish did, I would make peace.

This is who I was for my children: I told them to go. I told them to leave me. I said their dad had gone a wee bit mad but he had decided to do this and there was no going back. Jess shrank in her chair. I squeezed her hand. Come on. It'll be fine. Don't be scared. It's just change. We're strong women, aren't we? I looked at them. They looked blankly back. They weren't women. They were tiny little girls. But I made them say that we were strong women. And I told them that I didn't want this. I didn't want to be away from them for a second but sometimes you have to fit into life, or waste a lot of time and energy wishing it would fit in with you.

Calmly, I told them to go with Daddy and try to have a nice time. Seven sleeps, that was all. And if it got too much I would always have my phone with me, Jess could take my old one and she could call and I would come and get them. I could be there within hours. Just keep it charged and call me. I gave them the phone, a charger and a power bank. They were thrilled because I'd forbidden them to have phones.

Jess said, 'But you don't like travelling abroad.'

And I said, 'Well, I will suffer it for you.' With no idea how I could travel on the passport of a woman who was missing, presumed dead.

★ ★ ★

Cut to: Hamish and I alone in the kitchen. Hamish shocked and staring at my mouth, waiting for more words. I hadn't rehearsed it, these were not things I was running over in my mind the whole time, but my mouth opened and they just fell out. Cold things: I'm going to shit in all your shoes when you leave. Rude things: you add nothing to the world, your intellectual growth ended at Cambridge, you have no eye for art.

That last one made him very angry.

Then he said his piece: you're a fantasist, you're a threatening presence in the house, you are deeply damaged. I mean yes, he did make some good points. But then he brought up specific instances of my rudeness, my selfishness, my shutting down. Like that time he was opening up about his feelings of inadequacy and spotted a book on my lap and realised I was reading it under the table. He said I was a cold bitch.

I stopped listening to the words and just watched him. His eyes narrowed, his cheeks flushed. I watched his mouth flap, saliva flecking. I remembered waking up next to him in the bed, knowing he hated me. Getting out of the bath and pulling clothes on over damp skin so that he didn't see me naked because I felt so harshly judged. Him glancing at me as I ate and knowing he found me disgusting.

Suddenly I couldn't wait to get away from him. 'I need a piss,' I said.

'You're doing it now! You're shutting down, Anna.'

He followed me to the loo and accused me of 'fucking off to read or something', as if that was the worst thing you can do in the middle of a fight.

I saw a chair in the hall and thought about picking it up and smashing it over his head but I'm a lady. And anyway, I wouldn't give Estelle the satisfaction.

7

I locked the bathroom door behind me. I felt so hopeless, overwhelmed, I needed to make the noise in my head stop. I remembered the washing-line rope in the cellar. I cursed my father and thought of the rope again. I vowed not to try anything while the girls were still in the house. It was already too much for them. I told myself: get through the next hour, that's all, and then you can think about it. But just for a moment, I needed to get out of here. I sat on the side of the bath and fumbled my earbuds in and pressed play.

Could Leon Parker have killed his family and himself? Why would he? French police never asked these questions. But the Dana murders have the extreme and often unique signature of a family annihilation.

There is a warmth and a comfort in hearing about people in worse situations than your own. Pity is a hollow virtue. I like it. It's a form of self-aggrandisement really, bigging yourself up by defining someone as below you. True crime podcasts are usually great for that but sometimes you have to look really hard to find anyone down there. I had not murdered my family and killed myself. I hung onto that.

Family annihilation is a peculiar crime. This is when a man, and it is almost always a man, murders his immediate family and then kills himself.

The term 'annihilation' is apt because what these events always have in common is the thoroughness of the murders. It is literally overkill: stabbing and then burning. Shooting then drowning. The annihilator is in a state of high emotion and overcommits the murders. Often they kill everyone and then burn the family home down around the dead.

To me, the Dana murders have that passionate, overwhelming signature of annihilation. They do not feel like the action of a disgruntled employee with no motive other than a tenuous link to radical politics, as the French police came to believe.

Family annihilations can be divided into four types.

The first is the disappointed family member. They are often hyper-competitive people whose identity is drawn solely from their achievements. They feel let down by their family's performance: a wife gets fat, a kid drops out of university or fails in a competitive sport. And because the family members have not fulfilled the role assigned to them by the annihilator, they are murdered as a punishment.

This doesn't seem like Leon. He was an adventurer. He celebrated chance-taking, not achievements. Neither of his kids was involved in sport and there were no recent failures or dropping out of anything. We can rule that one out.

The next motive is spite. This scenario is very often a parent who kills the children of an estranged partner, a controlling family member, usually reacting after a victim has made a bid for freedom. The killer communicates their fury through escalating threats to the escapee leading up to the deaths. They issue ultimatums and believe that, having not met the demands, the person they want to hurt is responsible for the deaths.

Again, none of this applies to Leon. He had two kids with two different women. He was not especially controlling, was on fairly good terms with both of them and had recently married someone else.

The third type of family annihilation is the paranoiac, where the killer is deluded and thinks that they are saving the family from a fate worse than death. The delusions are usually religious or psychotic in nature. Everyone agrees that Leon was in his right mind during this voyage. He was not deluded or religious, he had no especially strange ideas or sense of the world coming to an end. There are no reports of him ever having a psychotic episode.

Most likely to be relevant here is the annihilation where the person has suffered a perceived loss of social status, for example if they are bankrupt or expelled from their community for some social contravention. Here, the killer sees his family as part of his own social identity and when he loses status — I'm using gendered language advisedly here — with no means of restoring it, he kills them and then himself. He values nothing else about himself but his status and failure is experienced as a personal annihilation. The family are his chattels, they are nothing more significant than his limbs or his car. If he ceases to exist there is no point in them continuing to do so.

I was sitting on the edge of the bath, thinking that the last one did sound a bit like Leon. Being successful meant an awful lot to him, more than it would to most people. He liked Skibo and fast cars and rich, beautiful women, even if they were obnoxious.

Yet just six months before the sinking Leon had married into one of the richest families in the world.

Was he even capable of a family annihilation? Usually perpetrators will have a history of mental illness or suicide attempts, of controlling behaviour with previous partners or records of domestic violence. There was little in his past life that would support this. Leon had no history of suicide attempts.

Well, I wasn't sure about that. I had the impression that he had at least contemplated it.

Leon wasn't controlling but did have one allegation of domestic violence against him.

In his late thirties he married Julia, Violetta's mother. Julia was an Italian supermodel, very famous in her time. Towards the end of their marriage she gave a bizarre and rambling interview to an Italian magazine. She showed the interviewer bruises on her back and arms and claimed that Leon had beaten her. They divorced shortly afterwards.

Leon never spoke about these allegations or his relationship with Julia. None of his subsequent partners made domestic violence claims against him.

Julia later recovered from an addiction and wrote a tell-all, cash-in autobiography, full of anatomical details about the famous men she had slept with. But she did not repeat the domestic violence allegations against Leon. She said Leon was the love of her life and her cocaine addiction drove him away.

Maybe he didn't hit her, or maybe she hit him and he defended himself. If you've lived with a drug addict you can probably fill in the spaces in that story.

I liked the way Trina Keany told that. No drama. No personal share. Just a coded call to those who knew that chaos.

Poor Leon. I tried to remember how he had spoken about his daughter back at Skibo, but that was years ago and Hamish was banging on the bathroom door. I pressed pause and heard his muffled voice.

'Anna. Please come out. I need to tell you something.'

I was straddling worlds: from a cocaine-addicted Italian supermodel's autobiography to a cold bathroom in Glasgow.

Then I wasn't.

I was just sitting on the side of the bath, wishing I was dead. Hamish was leaving me. He was taking my girls. My friend had betrayed me. There were no mysteries here, just banal miseries.

'Anna? Please?'

8

I shoved my phone and earbuds into my pocket and went back out, hanging on to thoughts of Leon's glamorous life because what was outside the bathroom door was so tawdry and real.

Hamish was waiting for me. He turned away and I saw something — was it just a movement of his hand? He had such graceful fingers — some detail that sparked the deep furnace of love I had for him and suddenly I wasn't angry. I loved him. I loved our little girls and our family. I knew it wasn't working but I loved him. I loved our counsellor and our fights. I loved my girls and early mornings and quiet Sundays. I knew it was over but I wasn't ready. I was drowning in loss.

I covered my face and sobbed. 'Please, Hamish, don't leave me. Please. I'm sorry for how I am. I love you.'

Hamish turned back and he was crying too. He put his arms around me and I sobbed into his chest and I kept saying over and over 'be kind to me' — where did that come from? I don't know but we both knew it was over. I was desolate.

I begged him not to take the girls. 'I can't stand to be away from them. A week is too long. I'll die. Stay, please. I'll leave the house. But stay. Stay-stay-stay.'

He mumbled, 'Anna, listen, I have to say

something — ' but then Estelle shouted from downstairs that the taxi was outside and Hamish pulled away.

And then we were all downstairs and I was scattering the brick of 'resettlement' cash all over the hall. Hamish's suitcase was all smashed up and I had cut my leg and blood was running down my shin. Estelle was furious because I scooped up some of the blood and flicked it on her new dress.

I was completely baffled by Estelle. Estelle was feisty and funny and intolerant. She once laughed so hard at someone farting in our yoga class that she fell over and broke her wrist. She was no fool. Had Hamish told her I was abusive? *Was* I abusive?

But she knew that he had done all of this before. I'd told her about it.

I was five months pregnant with Jess when Hamish invited me to his house for the first time. Come to the house at eight in the morning, he said. We'll be grown up about it. We'll tell Helen together. I knew then that he was a coward.

Estelle knew that I got to Hillhead Underground Station and, instead of getting off and walking up here and telling Hamish's wife that she was being usurped by a younger model, I stayed on the train. I turned my phone off and went all the way around the circuit then I got off in town and jumped a train to Manchester. I stayed with a friend for a while. When I came back Helen was gone.

Helen wrote to me for a number of years.

Unfriendly, let's say. I made myself read them. They were nasty but I didn't tell Hamish about them. He might have cut her allowance. She wasn't working and the letters had the sour tangy odour of vodka about them.

Estelle knew all of this and she still came to the door as ordered. Following orders isn't for everyone. It's not for me.

I watched them drive off in the airport cab. I was on the top step outside the front door, weeping with fury and impotence when I saw our bitchy neighbour, Pretcha, coming back from walking her fat dog, Stanley.

I couldn't deal with her; I was watching the cab leave with everything I loved in it.

I wanted to run after it barking like a dog, rescue the girls from their nice holiday, save Estelle from her new relationship, drag Hamish back to our mutual misery.

Pretcha sauntered up slowly, hypnotised by her phone as usual. She is fifty to sixtyish and has never liked me. She calls me 'the au pair' behind my back. She took in the drama through her tight, botoxed face. We all had to pretend she hadn't had a metric fuckton of bad surgery. *Be nice to them*, Hamish always said, *he basically runs German banking. He's incredibly rich.*

'Hello, darling?' she said.

Just when you think something can't get any worse someone who dislikes you comes to watch.

I'm making this sound eventful. I'm making it ridiculous and action-packed. It wasn't like that. It was just humiliating and sad.

Standing on the steps in spiteful rain, watched

49

by an unkind neighbour, the cab pulled away with my life in it and I felt something snap in my chest. I wanted to sink to my knees and howl, rent my clothing, cover my hair in dust and curse God. But this is Glasgow and I'm Anna McDonald, so I just turned and went inside and hid.

That was a mistake.

I very nearly didn't get out of there alive.

9

I was on the floor in the hall. Mood very low. Paralysed with shock. I think I was there for a long while, hours anyway, but it was hard to gauge time, it was sliding around like a puppy on a greasy floor.

I had settled on hanging myself, in the bedroom, but was worried about who would find me. I saw the girls coming home from Portugal, rushing upstairs and finding my body, one week old, bloated and rotting. I was disgusted by my weakness. I couldn't save them from what my father had passed on to me but maybe I could save them from finding me.

The attic. The girls couldn't get up there without a ladder. The smell would alert Hamish and he'd come up and find me. The washing-line rope was in the cellar, curled on a shelf, coiled and waiting for me.

In a minute. I couldn't get up. I was there for an hour or two.

At one point I found my phone in my pocket. I had to do something. I couldn't speak to anyone. I couldn't have coped with listening to music, a stray minor key might have finished me off. I'm not on social media, for obvious reasons. All I do on the phone is listen to books and podcasts.

Podcasts.

I didn't know if I could face listening to that

podcast. True crime only works if it's about people you don't know, scenarios you're not in, but I didn't know what else to do.

I opened the phone and found myself on the *Death and the Dana* website. That was when I spotted the video file at the bottom of the home page.

It was seven minutes long, not much of a commitment. 'Dive A241–7'. It was hanging alone and didn't seem to relate to any of the episodes. I tapped play.

The screen blacked out. The narrator, Trina, delivered a trigger warning: basically, don't watch this. Don't watch if you're too young or old or nervous or squeamish. Does anyone ever think those warning are addressed to them? I didn't, and nothing could make me feel worse.

Angry green sea filled the frame. It was silent, filmed underwater.

A diver was alone in the depths, working his descent hand-over-hand down a drop line, filming from a GoCam on his chest. A beam of light swept back and forth from his head torch, criss-crossing the rope. Deep waves buffeted him. His muscled arms were tense, slick as sealskin in his wetsuit.

The camera struggled to focus in the murk, fixing on specks of flotsam just before they were blown out of frame.

An ugly industrial yellow font came up over the swirling green — **Narrated by O. Tasksson — diving instructor** — then faded away.

'He feels his way down the drop line,' said Tasksson. 'His hands do not leave the rope.' His voice was flat and colourless, his accent mildly Germanic. He sounded bored, describing the scene with the muted emotions of a man who has seen a lot of life.

'Visibility is poor. The sea is violent. Many dangers. This is the life of a professional diver. Very hard. Not a leisure sport. You will have many bruises from a descent like this.'

A rope attached to the main line snaked away to a metal cylinder in the foggy green distance.

'The decompression tank is attached so that he can find it when he comes back up. He will not come back up.'

I thought I had misheard. Tasksson's voice was so dreary that it was quite hard to listen to. I watched as the diver descended further, passing a bushel of oxygen tanks attached to the rope.

'A dangerous moment in a heavy sea,' droned Tasksson. 'Spare tanks might swing around and knock him out. We can look at his oxygen and pressure readings here. They are good. At this point he is well saturated with oxygen and is thinking clearly. He is in charge.'

Nothing but hands feeling down the rope for minutes, it became quite tedious to watch, but visibility gradually improved. Every so often Tasksson commented on the pressure or the diver's oxygen readings. Down and down the diver went, buffeted around the drop line by deep-water waves.

'Now we see the *Dana* for the first time.'

The GoCam pointed down. In the grainy distance, like a dream remembered, the massive yacht was sitting on the seabed, banked precariously against a sheer rock cliff, upright but tilted. The mainmast had snapped and lay across the deck. He moved closer.

There was a hole in the hull, small and round, the wood rotting outwards so that the splinters looked like soft, rotting teeth falling out of an open mouth. It was sickening.

'There is a hole in the hull. Caused by something inside. Now we have the answer to the question of what has caused the sinking. Something has exploded in the engine room and caused this breach. The ship would sink very quickly from this. Discovering this is the purpose of this dive.'

The diver lowered himself, moving slowly, pointing the camera on his chest at the damaged hull to get good crisp film of it. Then he carried on moving down the line.

'This is his first mistake. He has secured the site and identified the cause of the sinking. According to the dive plan he is supposed to return now to the decompression chamber.'

The diver moved on down, letting go of the rope once his fingers reached the buckled handrail on the deck. He moved along the ship towards the back.

'He is making his way without a line. He is alone. He should not do this. He is in danger. His oxygen level is good, but now begins the countdown to his tank change. He has two minutes and fifty-five seconds of oxygen left.'

The diver pulled himself along the rail around the deck.

'He is alone. I would not do this. This is a bad

choice. A dangerous choice.' Even in a monotone, Tasksson's exasperation was clear.

The diver got round to the back of the ship and turned to face two small doors like a kitchen cupboard.

'He should *not* go in.'

The diver tried to pull the doors open but they were jammed.

'The wood has swollen. Also: differential pressure is holding these doors closed. Inside and outside are different, like the vacuum in a jar of pickles. This tells us that the cabin has been sealed since it was on the surface. No one has been in. No one has come out.'

The diver lifted a foot to the surround and pulled hard. The doors opened and all around him water was sucked into the cabin. A rotting white ribbon on the handrail flapped in, then out as stale water rushed out of the cabin carrying a cloud of papery grey flecks. The diver stood still until the water cleared, the grey washed away on an updraught.

'Two minutes. This is another mistake. Performing acts of physical exertion while low on oxygen puts him in danger. It is this series of bad decisions that kills this man.'

Kills the diver? I straightened at that. I didn't want to watch someone die. My finger hovered over the pause. Maybe it was a joke? But I knew it wasn't. I lied to myself because I wanted to see what happened. I ignored the second warning.

I watched on.

10

The diver took hold of both sides of the door frame and pulled himself down into a narrow corridor filled with the dirty water. Papery fragments covered the lens. When it cleared I could see that it wasn't paper, it was rotting varnish from the wooden walls and had settled in a thin silt on the floor. Every step the diver took sent a gritty grey squall curling slowly up to his knees.

He stood still. The darkness inside was profound.

Abruptly, the world jolted sideways. The diver's hands shot out to the walls, steadying himself as the *Dana* listed left. She shifted on the seabed, dropping half a foot.

'This is a danger sign. This means the internal pressure has been strong enough to play a factor in stabilising the wreck. He has altered that. He knows this. His heart rate is up. The whole cabin could collapse in on him. Why is he in there? This is crazy. He should leave.'

But he didn't.

The beam of his head torch stroked the peeling walls. Ragged grey fragments of varnish floated slowly up from the floor, hovering in front of him, a chorus of tiny ghosts gathering to watch.

Feeling his way with both hands, he made his way deeper into the ship down the narrow corridor. He seemed to know exactly where he was going. He came to the biggest door at the very end, turned the handle, heaved. It was stuck.

'He is too far in. He has fifty-five seconds. He should turn back. His calculations do not allow for physical exertions. His oxygen is running down.'

Again, the diver used a foot against the wall and pulled with all of his strength. It wouldn't open. He tried again.

'Forty-five seconds. He should be leaving right now. He thinks the diamond necklace is in there. He is making bad decisions.'

One last hard yank and the door opened violently, knocking the diver off his feet.

It took a moment for the camera lens to focus.

It was a wood-panelled dining room. The grey muck was an inch thick on the floor. Three people were at the table, slumped in their chairs.

'They have been in there for a month.'

They had been there for four weeks, in the salt water and the dark, the colour sucked from the meat of them. The soft tissue on their eyes and noses and fingers had rotted away to sockets and bone.

Fresh track marks through the grey silt showed that the chairs had moved when the ship shifted but it looked as if the corpses had pushed their seats back to get up and greet the new arrival.

'The ship has moved. Their thighs have been pinned under the table but now they have been moved. These bodies are untethered.'

Leon was in shadow, facing the door. I saw his silver hair hanging over what was left of his face.

He was looking down at the table, head at an alarming, acute angle to his neck. He was in shadow because the diver's torch was on the girl in a rotting striped dress in front of him. I could hardly look at her. The image, what had happened to her face, that was hard to see. There was another body there. The T-shirt boy, slumped face down over the table.

'Thirty seconds.'

But the diver had frozen in the doorway. His torch beam and camera were locked on something in the shadows at the very back of the room.

It was a boy, seven or eight, same age as Jess, looking straight back at the diver. This face was not decayed. It was wholly intact and his skin was piercing white. He was crouching in the dark, hiding in the far corner, glaring out with angry, black eyes. Suddenly, a long strip of white light flashed from his mouth.

This all happened in a few startling seconds, while water rushed in from the corridor and filled the chest of Leon's shirt. His head began to rise. Everything in the room began to lift.

'It is the change in cabin pressure that makes this happen.'

The bodies rose from the table, standing up, coming apart, heads tumbling from necks, arms dislocating and rising at the same time.

The diver panicked. The camera lurched up to the ceiling, smearing trails of light. Desperate, he backed out, his gloved hands swiped through a swirl of murk as he got to the corridor, tumbling into black space.

The camera snapped focus on peeling walls, on rotting ceiling, on his own frantic hands flailing and slapping at the walls. The hands slowed, their actions becoming soft and vague. Then they stopped. A final gloved hand floated across the frame, bidding the world adieu.

The screen froze.

'He has run out of oxygen. He has died.'

I dropped the phone in shock and it skittered across the hall floor, rat-like on its thick rubber cover. I stared at it. The light from the screen shone upward in the dim hall like the dead diver's torch.

I had forgotten all about Hamish and Estelle for a moment. I wasn't thinking about my girls. I wasn't mapping the journey from the cellar, rope in hand, to the attic. For those seven minutes I was thinking about silt, about the diver, about a boy hiding under the sea, about matter out of place.

I pressed play on the second episode.

11

By the time Estelle's husband came to the door I was half mad. The rest of the day was sore. I had ambitions at one point to get up and put the lights on but somehow it never happened.

I spent a long time sitting by the front door, not listening to the podcast. I sat between the ottoman and the cold marble pillar at first. Then I moved on to the ottoman. I was in shock, I think. I was there for a very long time, afraid to stand in case my feet took me to the cellar, tricking myself into living through the next moment by waiting for answers: who was the boy? How did he get there? Who steered the ship? Where was Amila running to? Mostly though, I was wondered what Amila was running away from. Any story about women bolting catches my attention. Had Amila been attacked by a member of the crew? If so, did Leon know about it? Was he killed because he knew?

Hours into the day, when my mind ran out of circles and it was starting to get dark outside, I pressed play on episode 2 and put the phone in the cup of my bra, speakers towards my face, forming a sound barrier between me and the door to the cellar.

Episode 2: 7 July

In this episode we will look more closely at what actually happened that night. We will profile the people who died on board the Dana: Leon, Violetta and Mark.

To celebrate Violetta's coming of age Leon had bought her an extravagant gift, an antique diamond necklace. It cost almost three-quarters of a million euros and had a great provenance. Leon bought it at a charity auction in Malaga from Princess Elana of Sweden. But the necklace was ugly, an old-fashioned rope of daisy flowers made from diamonds clustered around bigger diamonds.

Violetta made it clear that she didn't want the necklace.

She emailed her father, saying that money or help with an apartment would be more useful. But Leon had a grand-gesture style of parenting. It didn't really encompass financial support or help finding a flat. It was more suited to buying the most expensive item in a public auction in front of an international audience.

Violetta texted her father. Please forgive the bad language here, but it's important to give a flavour of their relationship:

V: I don't want jewellery. You shouldn't buy over-priced crap like that.

Again, later on the same day:

V: Because I have to insure it & store it & I can't fucking wear it anywhere. It'll COST me money.

Gaudy jewellery was not Violetta's style. She liked plain designs. She was elegant and Leon couldn't have picked a more inappropriate gift. He didn't seem to know her very well.

According to the phone company, Leon was out of range for a while but when he docked in Balboa he replied to both texts.

L: Fine, V. If you don't want it I'll give it to someone else.

V: Fine.

L: It's the nicest thing I've ever given you.

V: It's the only thing.

Again, long pause.

L: Are you even fucking coming to St Martin?

V: Of course, you crazy old bastard.

Then a flurry of texts from Leon:

L: You ungrateful little shit.

L: I'm trying to give you a fucking necklace worth [euro] 750k RETAIL.

L: FFS

Violetta replied:

V: Leon! NEVER PAY RETAIL.

L: Hahahaha! I love you.

L: Come and see me.

L: Sell the fucking thing, I don't care.

And then, three hours later:

L: Hahahaha still laughing at that!

Those texts give you a flavour of their relationship. Violetta and Leon were informal with each other. She wasn't intimidated by her father or afraid to complain about his inconsistent parenting. Leon had not been a good father to Violetta. As a very small child he left her in the care of an addict and walked away. When she was nine Violetta was hospitalised for malnutrition. In recent years Leon had been trying to compensate for that and, although she was still angry, they seemed to be getting on.

Mark was the younger child. His mother, Daniela, worked in local government in Southampton. Daniela and Leon didn't marry. They met in a local pub and lived together in Leon's house in Sandbanks for nearly a decade. Sandbanks is a small spit of land on the south coast and is home to the most expensive property in the whole of England. After he died Leon's house was sold for twenty-one million pounds.

Of the two children, Mark seems to have fared best in his relationship with his father. He got to six before Leon and Daniela split up but saw his dad regularly. Leon attended school concerts and paid child support for Mark. No one said how Violetta felt about Mark but he was clearly the favoured child. He was just sixteen when he died.

Daniela, for me, is the best argument against Leon committing a family annihilation because an obsession with status is a major predictor of that style of murder. But Daniela plays fiddle in a folk band. She is a social worker. When Mark was a toddler, she worked part-time and studied for a Master's. Their relationship was not about status. This was love ad hominem. They liked each other, were together for a long time and when they split up it wasn't acrimonious.

Leon had recently married for the second time, to an heiress. He boasted that they spent longer signing the prenup on their wedding day than making vows which doesn't seem like a man keen to make people to think he has money and power.

Leon picked Saint-Martin as the rendez-vous point because it was reachable from both of his kids' starting points.

Violetta arrived on a private jet from Venice, was met by a car service in La Rochelle, and checked into Saint-Martin's only five-star hotel. She went shopping and spent over a thousand euros on a Missoni dress. She went back to the hotel, had coffee in her suite of rooms, put her new dress on and went to meet her younger brother.

Mark Parker flew Easyjet from Southampton. He arrived a day early because the cut-price airline only flew every second day. He stayed in an Airbnb. In the listings it looks like a camp bed in a shed. While Violetta was booked into the hotel for two nights, Mark was planning to sleep on board the Dana once his dad arrived, presumably to save money, and had his luggage with him: a boogie board bag. He had probably spent the day at the beach.

These kids came from different back-grounds and very different income levels.

That puzzles me. Leon was rich. Why was Mark staying in a shed while Violetta had a private plane? Julia might have remarried or made a fortune. She's hard to track. Also, expenditure doesn't always speak to income: Daniela may just have been careful whereas Julia was flamboyant. Perhaps Mark was being taught to travel on a budget.

That's just speculation. Let's go back to what is provable, what we know about the movements on board that night.

The kids walked down to meet Leon. He got off the ship and they went for a walk and a drink. The trio got back to the boat at around 7 p.m. The crew left. The Parkers gathered on deck and had a drink. Leon presented Violetta with the necklace she didn't want and made her put it on for a photo. Mark instagrammed it and texted it to his mum. It was to be the last time anyone ever heard from any of them.

Then the deck was empty. We can assume they had gone downstairs to the dining room because this is where they were found. Whether they were in there when the Dana motored from the harbour or elsewhere on the ship, we may never know.

It was Leon who insisted the family would be alone on the Dana. Is it possible that Leon asked Amila to leave the boat? She has not spoken about him. Did he plan to kill the kids, or was there a more benign reason for him ensuring they were alone?

The crew thought it was because of the

65

necklace: Violetta was travelling alone, going home the next day, and the diamond necklace was a high-priced item for a young girl to carry home. The crew weren't supposed to know about the necklace. Crew aren't supposed to know a lot of things but they see it all.

The bodies were found in the dining room with the door shut. From forensic video analysis of the remains on the table, the mussels garnishing the soup were still all in complete shells, not yet shucked apart. This means they hadn't been eaten, which means the Parkers were yet to begin their soup when the yacht went down. Were they already dead when the ship left the dock? Were they drugged?

Leon wanted to show off the dining room but it was a hot night. The natural thing would be to leave the door open for the breeze, especially if they were eating hot soup. But the door to the dining room was firmly shut. Wiry would they shut the door on an empty boat?

What if Leon poisoned the kids before they started eating: both kids die, Leon doesn't. With his dead children in the dining room, Leon casts off in such a state of high emotion that he forgets the navigation lights and the radio, and then returns to the dining room, shutting the door and sealing himself in with the two kids he has murdered, knowing they will sink when the explosion goes off in the engine room.

This seems unlikely. In family annihilation the killer usually covers or hides the bodies. They are not product killers' — that is people who murder so that they have a body to play with. They are not process killers', who kill because they enjoy the act of murder. They are 'outcome killers'. They kill so that people are dead. They are repulsed by the sight of dead bodies. They cover them with sheets, cover their faces, turn away from the bodies.

This bothers me. The door being shut makes sense if the killer is outside the room and does not want to see the bodies which raises the possibility of a fourth person on board but there is scant evidence of that. The Dana was being watched by all the rooftop diners and someone would have spotted an extra person on deck. No one that night saw anyone other than the two kids and the dad.

These are all questions the police didn't seem to ask. Leon was barely glanced at by the investigation. Was it his new rich wife, Gretchen Teigler, who ensured that was the case?

Do you like to cook at home but find it hard to make the time? At Fast'n'Fresh, our service provides —

I stopped it there. I rewound. I heard the name again. Gretchen Teigler.

I rewound. I replayed and I heard it again. Gretchen Fucking Teigler. I had vacillated about whether or not it was my Leon Parker, but I didn't doubt this was my Gretchen.

Leon married Gretchen Teigler. I could not believe he'd done that. With no good reason I felt personally betrayed.

But now I knew what had happened to the *Dana* investigation. Gretchen Teigler had done it again. She chose a lie that suited her and used all of her power and money to make it the official version.

I hadn't thought about Gretchen for years. When I stumbled across news stories that tangentially referred to her I always turned away. I'd done a deal with myself: I could let the past go because I had my girls, Hamish, my new life. Only now I didn't have those things.

I looked up at the hall and hardly knew how I came to be here all these years later. I stood up, my knees stiff, pins and needles in my feet, and found myself turning, almost against my will, to face the cellar door.

That was when I heard someone outside the front door. For just a moment I thought I had conjured Gretchen Teigler.

12

'Hello?' It was a male voice, muffled by the heavy door. 'Is that you, Anna? I can hear a radio.'

By this stage I found it hard to even speak. I felt I was going blind. *What's the point?* I kept thinking, over and over. *What's the point of this?* It's often the case, when I'm down, that everything dark that has happened comes back and swamps me. That thin voice outside was a pinprick of light. When I was small I believed stars were pinholes and their light was the brightness of heaven shining through. This is what his voice felt like. A glimpse of an unreachable dimension of light beyond my catastrophe and Leon's death.

'Anna? It's Estelle's husband, Fin. Could you open the door? It's rather cold out here.'

Fin Cohen opened the letter box. He looked in at me. I turned my head and caught his eye. He must have been kneeling down.

'Anna? You don't look too good. D'you want to open the door?'

I couldn't speak.

His fingertips withdrew. The dry metal spring shrieked as the letter box guillotined shut. The sharp echo rattled around the hall, up the stairs, humming off the stone floor, until I didn't know if I was hearing or remembering the sound.

For a terrible moment I thought that Fin had

gone. If he left me here I knew where my feet would take me.

But he didn't leave. He opened the letter box again and looked at me. He wasn't asking for anything. He wasn't giving anything either. He was just there.

Gretchen Teigler, again. Married to Leon. How could it happen again? How often had she done this? Looking at those eyes peering in through the letter box, I saw a thousand other pairs of eyes, all the human detritus left in Gretchen's wake. And behind them all the gatekeepers who helped her, the lawyers who drew up the non-disclosures, the journalists who didn't ask questions, the cops who took hints.

I took the phone out of my bra and pressed pause. I looked back and Fin was still there, still looking at me.

'PLEASE DON'T LEAVE.'

He blinked. 'I won't leave.'

'I'M COMING OUT.'

' . . . There's no need to shout.'

' . . . OK.'

The letter box screamed shut. I swung my body away from the cellar door and staggered upstairs on stiff legs.

13

Pants, passport, cash.

I changed out of my blood-stiff pyjamas into a shirt and trousers, grabbed an expensive leather coat I had been saving for the right weather and took the keys to Hamish's car.

Hamish thinks I can't drive, that I am too afraid to learn, it's one of my many random fears. Of course I can drive, I just couldn't use my licence because it's under the name of someone who is presumed dead, possibly murdered, but that's another story.

I kept my eyes down, walked back downstairs in the dark and scooped up the resettlement money scattered around the hall, shoving it into my pockets. I had a sudden, strong urge to swing around and go down to the cellar and I hurried away from it, almost running by the time I got to the front door. I threw it open, startling not just Fin but also Pretcha.

It was an odd scene. They were standing together on the top step. Fin Cohen was tall, blond and far, far too thin. His nose was long, his skin creamy. His beard was neat and pointed but his blond hair was thick and messy. He was dressed in a tailored green tweed suit jacket, jeans with turn-ups over brown brogues and a tight grey shirt on his very slim frame. The top button was done up but he wore no tie. He looked like a dapper, starving Viking. His look was stiff and formal, his shirt could have been cut out of cardboard. He was always groomed to the nth degree, which annoyed me.

Pretcha was clutching her phone to her chest as her forgotten dog Fat Stanley lumbered up the stairs behind her. She was simpering up at Fin. I had never seen her do that. She was smiling and doing a strange little dip with her knee, as if she was trying to make herself smaller.

'Oh, hi, darling.' She tried to smile wider but the top half of her face was frozen. She may have been trying to express empathy. Or sarcasm. Who the fuck knows.

Fin and Pretcha looked past me into the hall.

'Oh!' she exclaimed, her eyes widening at the scene. 'My gosh!'

'Good God,' whispered Fin.

I looked back. Breakfast plates were smashed on the floor. A bloody hand print was smeared on the wall. The contents of Hamish's yellow suitcase lay scattered, the toiletries stamped on. Flecks of light from the street were twinkled randomly everywhere in the dark. Sugar.

I shut the door behind me and locked it. I took a deep-down breath.

Pretcha was the first to snap back to the script.

'Ooh, Anna! I didn't know you knew *the* Fin Cohen.'

I didn't want Pretcha thrilling at the sight of Cohen or weaselling details about this morning out of me to pass around to the neighbours in little hors d'oeuvres of spite-laden gossip.

I sound as if I'm being unfair to Pretcha, who never really did anything worse than wear a gilet and dislike me for being scary, but wait for it. I'm not wrong on this. She very nearly killed me.

'I don't know him,' I said and showed him the car keys. 'I'll drive you home. Come on.'

Fin Cohen followed me down the steps.

It was rush hour. Beyond a row of bushes the Great Western Road was in full gridlocked swing. Headlights flashed, indicators blinked and engines growled. It was noisy and distracting. That's why I didn't notice Pretcha's flash going off as she took the picture.

14

It was a nice car. I have to give Hamish that. His intellectual life might have ended at Cambridge but he does have an eye for a nice car. The engine was quiet and smooth, the seats deep and comfortable.

Fin was shivering in the bucket of the passenger seat. Not in his extremities, not a tremble, but from so deep down in his middle it looked like tiny convulsions. He was embarrassed about it and didn't want me to ask so I didn't. I just turned the heating up and pulled out of the parking space.

Great Western Terrace has a sharp drive down to the Great Western Road. It was jammed with cars and buses and it was a long time since I had driven. I kangarooed violently down the steep slip road, straight into the stream of rush-hour traffic almost hitting a car side-on. The driver was angry and gestured at me eloquently. I pretended I hadn't noticed, though he was only five feet away from me.

'Where are we going?' asked Fin, his voice faint.

'Well, I'm going to Fort William. Where do you want me to drop you? Are you going home?'

Fin didn't answer me but there was a lot going on in the road, I hadn't driven for a really long time, so I didn't notice. The lights changed and the driver I'd almost rammed gave me an ardent finger as he moved away. I gave an apologetic wave. A few cars further down a man let me edge clumsily into the stream of traffic ahead of him. I could tell from his expression in the rear-view mirror that he was shocked at my driving. He left quite a big space behind me.

'Fin. Where do you want dropped off?'

'No,' he muttered, 'I'm just, around . . . '

I stalled and had to restart the car. A lot of drivers were watching me now and it's an understatement to say that they were unimpressed. I didn't care. Up ahead a bus edged into a yellow box and a chorus of car horns sounded around the junction.

I was elated at escaping from the hall; I had got away from the cellar. God alone knew where reminders of Gretchen Teigler would have taken me if I hadn't. I was grateful to Fin for that but I wondered why he had come to the door. Did he come to tell me something? We didn't know each other. He may have been my best friend's husband but he'd always been cold towards me.

'Why did you come to the house? Did Hamish send you to check on me?'

'Send me? *Hamish?*' His voice was very faint. 'He's . . . they've run off together. D'you know that?'

'I — yeah. I know. To Porto. They took my kids.'

For some reason I had assumed Fin was in on it, that he was OK with, or even the cause of it. I thought he would have been having affairs with other women and, you know, maybe, you couldn't blame Estelle. I didn't think it would be the same for him as it was for as me. But that's part of being down. Empathy loss. I can't imagine anything might be worse for anyone else, not really.

He sounded indignant. 'I'm not friends with Hamish.'

The bus moved and we got across the junction to the next set of lights. It felt like another tiny triumph.

'Why did you come to the house?'

'I dunno. I was a bit, you know . . . ' Fin's voice was soft, his breath stuttering. ' . . . I thought of. You and just. I wondered . . . '

I glanced at the passenger seat. Tears were dripping from his beard as he stared straight ahead at the road. He looked glazed and grey and his jacket was buttoned up over his concave belly.

'Fin?'

He didn't answer.

'Fin?'

Nothing.

I couldn't stop the car and put him out, not in two lanes of heavy, bad-tempered traffic. He didn't seem capable of finding his way to the pavement. I wanted rid of him now though, now we were away from Pretcha and I had spoiled her fun. I wanted him out of the car and I never, ever wanted to see him again.

Because I didn't like Fin at all.

It wasn't personal, though I did think his band were whimsical and a bit crap. I didn't like him because he had snubbed me the few times we had met and, I suppose, because Estelle

76

bad-mouthed him a lot. Also, he scared me. I hate famous men.

I don't remember him becoming well known. I didn't know Estelle at the time. It seemed to happen very quickly, while I was having babies and being a happy bit of furniture. His band were young, just in their late teens. They had only played small gigs in the living rooms of fans who won competitions. Without releasing more than a couple of demos they were suddenly everywhere. I can't remember how that happened. It was Fin Cohen people were interested in, really. He was tall, groomed and very good-looking. He was vegan, anti-capitalist, all the buzzwords. Hailed as the leader of a new subculture, he was interviewed on every topic from summer colours to climate change. He was everywhere, worldwide fame, huge in South America and Asia. It took less than two years for capitalism to eat him.

Cohen lost a lot of weight. The press followed him around, taking pictures, charting his decline. He became terrifyingly thin and wore very tight clothes. His face hollowed out. Suddenly he was forced into rehab for opiate addiction. So far so on trend.

The band were self-managed, which Estelle said was like trying to run a train company from a smartphone. A massive unexpected tax bill came in. All of their stage equipment was stolen in Germany and they had taken out the wrong insurance.

Then came the famous interview. The drummer got wasted and gave an interview to a nasty vlogger. I haven't watched it but apparently the vlogger prises everyone's secrets out of the very drunk twenty-year-old. Their bass player was sexually predating on their young fans. This was true, he later went to jail for it. The guitarist painted miniature dragon statues as a hobby and lived with his mum. Their frontman, Cohen, wasn't an addict, that was a lie. Fin was anorexic. Addiction was cool but an eating disorder wasn't, apparently.

The band imploded, gone as quickly as they arrived, a footnote in music history. But celebrity sticks in a small town and Glasgow is small.

Estelle was Portuguese. She married him at the height of his fame, big diamond ring, rush-wedding in Vegas. This was before the weight loss began. She was there for the car crash and she stayed, but it was hard. They were broke. His eating ruled their lives. He was in and out of hospital. I still saw blurry pictures of him on the cover of the schadenfreude magazines, speculating about his weight and mental health.

I looked at him sitting in the passenger seat, his thighs hardly touching, so thin that the safety belt might as well have been done up over an empty chair. He looked as if he was dying.

'Fin? Have you eaten today?'

He didn't answer.

'Drunk water?'

'Huh.'

'Do you want me to drop you somewhere?'

He didn't answer.

Mothering is a comfort. Even through a smog of suicidal self-pity I found the voice I used for the girls:

'OK, Fin. You want to come and meet my pal Adam? Have a wee road trip up and down to Fort William?' I think he nodded. It was hard to tell. 'Yeah. We'll go on a drive and see some sights. Shall we?' He didn't answer. I should have listened. 'Come on, then.'

I was driving, my life was in pieces, I had someone to look after, my leg hurt, it was all good, except that one small part of my mind was still unoccupied. I remembered Hamish and the old dark feelings began to rise again.

I couldn't stand to be alone with those thoughts.

When we stopped at the lights I got out my phone and I pressed play.

15

Episode 3: The Haunting

In this episode I am going to give a brief biography of the Dana to explain where the ghost story came from.

Seafarers are superstitious. They are always looking to divine the future by looking at signs and patterns in the past. It's understandable; the sea is dangerous and unpredictable. Superstitions give people a sense of control. From her very beginnings the Dana had a reputation for bad luck.

In researching this podcast, we began to wonder if this was true. None of us knows the history of any other private yachts and maybe these are common events in the lives of extraordinary people. So we looked into it and, compared to other yachts of the same age and size, the Dana had belonged to an unusually high number of people who met terrible ends. Was she cursed? Or was she simply a luxury yacht that was often the subject of a disputed title and therefore bought by people likely to take other risks?

The Dana was commissioned in 1929 by Harold J. Webb of New York City.

Webb had learned to sail as a boy, off the coast of Mayo in Ireland. He arrived in New

York a penniless fourteen-year-old, threw in with Owney Moody, made a fortune from prohibition and set about gathering the totems of wealth. He bought a mansion, got a good Catholic wife from an old Boston family, bought cars and horses and he suits and he commissioned a yacht.

The Dana was considered a masterpiece of her time. She had two generators, central heating and electric refrigeration. But Webb didn't live to take possession of her. He lost his fortune over the course of three days of tumbling stocks in the Wall Street Crash. On day four he rented the presidential suite at the Biltmore Hotel. There, he sat down at the desk, three arched windows at his back, wrote a short note and then shot himself in the temple.

But his hand slipped.

He was using an antique .32 Derringer, a small pistol with a kidney-shaped handle. He lived on for another eight months with no jaw, mute and bedridden, in excruciating pain, nursed by his estranged wife.

There is a taped interview with Dana Webb, done in the 1950s, but the quality is very poor. I'll play a little bit in a moment but she says she kept her husband alive by hand-feeding him with a glass pipette. She kept him going for as long as possible. She made it her 'mission'. They were both Catholic and suicide is a mortal sin. It was the least she could do for another human being, even if he wasn't a terribly nice

81

human being. Here is some of the tape. Forgive the quality.

The sound was crackled and muffled and scratchy and Dana Webb's ageing voice high and breathless. Her Boston accent sounded like a Kennedy parody.

'No!' she said, answering a mumbled, off-mic question. 'No! Mr Webb was NOT a nice man. He was an all-round louse — God forgive me for speaking ill of the dead. May God. Rest. His. SOUL.' She sounded as if the benevolent prayer was being punched out of her.

Eventually, a bank took possession of the yacht in lieu of loan payments. Then the bank went bust. The Dana's title was contestable, everyone knew that, so the beautiful ship languished in a shipyard, waiting for some-one to take a chance on her.

The Dana had a series of owners, seven over a six-year period, all of whom tried and failed to use her for profit. Then she was bought by a Parisian family who used her for a happy few years of family holidays and pleasure sailing. In 1939 she sailed to Bermuda to overwinter. No one ever came back for her. The French family had evaporated during the liberation of Paris. By 1947 the Dana was impounded for mooring fees. Then the Danish government owned her, using long sea journeys as a form of drug rehab, but the ship was too expensive to maintain.

Eventually, the Polish millionaire and playboy Andris Larkos bought her and so began the darkest episode in the yacht's history.

Larkos spent a fortune renovating her and then hosted lavish parties on board, hung priceless artworks in the dining room, served cocaine from a punchbowl. But that was when he was alone with his friends. The ship was stripped back when his five children and wife boarded for their annual holiday.

The events that would make her famous happened on 7 July 1976, coincidentally, the same day and month in which she sank with the Parkers on board forty years later. The Dana was docked in Crete during a stultifying heatwave. The cabins were unbearably hot and airless so cots had been set up on deck. Larkos's five sons were asleep next to their nannies. The deck was a lake of white sheets.

At quarter past three that night one of the nannies was awoken by a deep, sonorous vibration through the hull. It was rhythmic. Thunk. Thunk. Thunk. Thunk.

Something was banging against the side of the boat. She pulled back her sheet and padded over to the side. One of the Larkos boys was face down in the water. His head was being washed against the side of the boat by the lapping waves. Thunk. Thunk.

The boy was seven. It was a terrible accident. His mother, Angelika Larkos, had

83

never had good mental health but she broke down completely afterwards. She tried to cut her own throat and was admitted to a sanatorium. Diagnosed with a schizotypal disorder, she stayed there for the rest of her life.

Andris Larkos put the Dana up for sale but unsurprisingly no one wanted it. While he waited for a buyer his other sons began to die. The press called it 'The Larkos Curse'. Hauntings, curses and alien myths were fashionable in the 1970s. Human beings are programmed to find patterns, to make sense of random events, and, back then, curses were a favoured explanation. The modern equivalent might be conspiracy theories.

Looked at objectively there was no mysterious supernatural force causing the deaths of the Larkos boys because this was far from risk-free parenting. Andris did his best but he took the boys to places where no child should be. They visited refugee camps, they were in the Sudan during a cholera outbreak. They were taken on a crazy three-week free-camping safari in Tanzania.

One boy died when he fell from an open-sided helicopter in Miami and broke his back. Another died from an overdose of barbiturates prescribed to the housekeeper. A third boy simply got lost on the slopes of Kilimanjaro. No trace of him was ever found.

With only one son surviving, Andris sold

the Dana *dirt cheap to a Mr and Mrs Clarke. This was when the public myth of the Dana really began.*

The Clarkes were publicity hounds. Soon they were all over the papers claiming that the Dana was haunted. The ghost sightings were always the same: in the middle of the night a small boy would be seen standing on the edge of the prow, his hair and clothes dripping wet.

I was really only listening for more mentions of Gretchen Teigler and was slow to realise that the boy with the angry black eyes in the diver's film was somehow related to this part of the story.

One man who saw the ghost was a crewman from Malta. He told the story to a journalist from RTE.

It cut to a radio interview. The man's accent was a cross between Blitz-era London and southern Italy, his voice was soft.

'*The middle of the night. We were, maybe, two hundred feet from dock. I was on deck alone and I see a boy standing on the prow, a small boy. He is silhouetted by moonlight reflected from the sea.*

'*I stop. I stare at the boy. I blink but the boy is still there. A boy? What? I approached him and I said 'Hello?' But the boy didn't answer me. I asked the boy: 'Is your father on board?' The boy looked up.*

85

He didn't look at me, just, sort of, up. Then the boy speaks. His voice is clear but his lips don't move, he says, 'Loto Vady.' But . . . that boy didn't look like a ghost in a film, he isn't see-through or floating around or anything. Haha! No! Is just a sad wet boy, lost in the night.

'So, I am wondering, how does a boy get on a boat in the night? Well, he could not have come here tonight, he must have been here all along. Maybe a member of the crew has smuggled their child on board with them? Many of us, we're unemployed fishermen. Paid only on the end of the voyage, no upfront payment, no banks, so can't send money home. What do you do with the children? So: maybe someone has no family to leave their child with and they bring him and hide him on board, maybe? I don't know.

'Anyway, I can see he is close to the edge, he is upset and I know I should get him away from there.

'I hold my hand out. This boy doesn't move or look up.

''Loto,' I say.' He was singing in a gentle, coaxing voice. ''Loto, my dear, take my hand, please?' And I stepped towards the boy.

'We are close to the edge. I glance down for a split second to check my steps. I glance back up and — WHAT? That boy is gone!

'I run to the edge and look over. Nothing!

'I am in a panic. Very frighten. Where is

this boy? *I was a young man and didn't know what to do, so I wake the rest of the crew and ask: who brought this little kid on board? A boy called Loto Vady? I describe him.*

'The crew, they laughed at me. I am seeing things. Maybe there is a gas leak next to my bunk. The captain comes down and hears what happened.

'I am Maltese. I speak Maltese, English and Italian. Little Spanish, some Turkish. But I didn't speak Polish. The captain speaks Polish. He say: 'loto wady' is Polish. It is not a boy's name. It means 'icy cold'.'

There was a pause before Trina Keany came back on to speak:

This story became an urban myth. It was told in occultist magazines and around campfires. A journalist with an eye for a moneymaker contacted the Clarkes and convinced them that he could write a book about it.

They agreed, a contract was drawn up, they got a publishing deal but there wasn't enough to fill a book. Someone thought they saw a boy, a boy had died, there were odd sounds and strange smells. Sinister, but it made no narrative sense. So one night the Clarkes and the journalist met in a London hotel room, got drunk and hashed out a proper story.

In this new version, Angelika Larkos was

the mother of seven boys, not five. She is still alive, remember, when this book comes out. No one fact-checked anything at the time. The night before her marriage to Andris, she had held a seance with her sisters — this was all totally made up by the Clarkes and their co-author. In the fictional seance Angelika became possessed by an ancient Polish demon called a 'bies', the same demon that had possessed her recently deceased grandmother.

In Polish folklore 'bies' are demons who bring terror and dread to those around them. They rob the free will from those they possess, use them as slaves until the person's mind cannot take any more and they break down, never to recover. Bies suck the life force from people around them, take their warmth, hence they are always accompanied by an abrupt drop in temperature. It's the sort of cold that starts inside and worms its way to the skin. Bies possess a person by degrees, so the person can appear normal for long periods of time until suddenly, without warning, they push you off a bridge, burn your house down, attack a stranger. Perhaps the most brutal aspect of a bies possession is those periods when the person is aware of the terrible things they have done.

Like a lot of folklore, this has some basis in fact. Angelika's family have a history of schizophrenia. Bies possession may have been a useful explanation at a time when schizophrenia was little understood.

In the Clarkes' story, Angelika's possession was intermittent over the first few years of her marriage. The demon was waiting for the birth of her seventh child.

As an aside: the numbers three and seven feature prominently in all world religions and many myths and legends. The significance of the seventh child was supposed to be that the power of the bies would be stronger or transferable to a seventh child. But, honestly, the theology of The Haunting of the Dana hasn't been thought out terribly well. They were drinking and in a hurry to meet their publishing deadline.

According to the new version of the story, Angelika knew what was happening and tried to warn her husband, her mother, her other sons, but she wasn't believed. She was sent to a sanatorium and couldn't protect her seventh son. So her seventh son, in his seventh year, became possessed and was lured to the side of the Dana and drowned. Ever since then malevolent bies have lingered on the Dana, using the ghost boy as bait for souls to feed on.

The book had a creepy cover design of a small boy silhouetted on the prow of the Dana, seen from the deck. It was so famous at the time that it was parodied by Saturday Night Live.

The book sold millions worldwide. Amid much fanfare, a movie company bought the film rights and the Dana itself which they used as a promotional device.

The movie was very successful. The Exorcist, The Omen and The Amityville Horror had been smash hits and The Haunting of the Dana seemed to ride the tail of the occult movie craze. A sequel followed. The Dana II. Then, a decade later, a low-budget reboot, Dana: the Revenge, but interest had faded.

The yacht was put up for sale. Anyone who could afford a private yacht wanted one that wasn't famous for being in crappy horror movies and the Dana attracted ghoulish attention wherever it docked, which defeats the purpose of having a private yacht.

This was why Leon Parker managed to buy it so cheap and in perfect condition. The reputation of the Dana coloured all of the subsequent coverage when it sank.

In the next episode we will look at the chronology of the story breaking and how it became an international obsession.

Are you keen to cook fresh, nutritious meals that will invigorate you? Find yourself too busy? Why not try Fast'n'Fresh —

We were on the outskirts of Glasgow, approaching the high dark hills framing Loch Lomond. We still had a long way to go. I wanted to see my friend Adam Ross again. I wanted to ask him about working as crew on a private yacht. Mostly I just wanted to see someone I didn't have to lie to.

I thought Fin had fallen asleep. I was still nervous about driving and didn't dare glance away from the road. His breathing was shallow. He wasn't moving. I picked up my phone, found the next episode and pressed play.

16

Episode 4: How the Story Broke

Initially the sinking of the Dana attracted little attention. A footnote in Le Figaro. A small obit in the Daily Echo, Leon's local paper in Southampton. It was just a boating accident, a misadventure. The circumstances were strange but no one suspected foul play. In Mark Parker's instagrammed post, they were all holding glasses of champagne. They were drinking. Drunk kids, big boat, indulgent father. Sailing is dangerous.

It was the order of events, the way it unfolded, that made the story what it became.

The insurance company, expecting a big claim from Leon's widow, initiated a sonar investigation of the seabed. They found the wreck of the Dana forty yards underwater, jammed upright against a rock. In fact, the insurance claim was never made. Gretchen Teigler never did submit a claim. That seems strange. She has a staff. It was a debt. It would be usual to ask for payment as a matter of course.

Anyway, towards the end of the summer while the sea was still diveable, the company sent a team down to film the wreck, hoping to find the cause of the accident, but something went very wrong. The diver adopted a course of action no seasoned professional would. He deviated from the dive plan, went inside, ran out of oxygen and died down there.

The film he live-streamed to the surface vessel was reviewed by investigators. It was very disturbing. What they saw made no logical sense.

I recalled the sensation of watching the film in the dark hall, my mood low, my blood syrupy, the mounting tension of the film and its shock ending defibrillating me back into the world.

Trina Keany continued:

In the insurance film, the diver dies after finding what is left of the Parker family sitting in the dining room at the table. The change in atmospheric pressure when the diver opens the door makes it look as if the dead bodies are trying to stand up from the table.

The diamond necklace is gone from Violetta's body. She is no longer wearing it, though the box is discernable in the ·shadows, sitting on the table, open and empty. There is a general agreement that the antique necklace fastening might have rotted in the salt water and the necklace could have fallen off and been buried in detritus on the floor.

But the final image on the diver's film shows a boy's face. It seems to materialise out of the darkness and flashes a light at him. The face looks like the boy from the film The Haunting of the Dana. It's all very weird and creepy.

Someone leaked the film online and it went viral. If you haven't already watched it I would suggest you don't. It's upsetting. It features dead bodies in a state of decay and you don't need to see it for this podcast to make sense.

I have friends and family in the States. Talking to them after 9/11, it was clear that they did not see the footage of people leaping from the Twin Towers that we in the UK did. They didn't see people at windows, their faceless courage, the shirts flapping. This is because broadcasters conspired not to show it and they did that on compassionate grounds. That decision could not be made now, there are too many outlets, but it did happen back then and they were right to do it. There are things that should not be seen. For me, this film is one of them.

But how did a boy get into the film? I think the image has been altered for hits. Someone pasted the picture into the movie. The question is why would anyone do that? Why would someone go to the trouble of elaborately doctoring an insurance film to make it more frightening?

Not for money: there was no paywall on the film when it was leaked.

Not for fame either because the source of the leak never came forward.

This is a sub-thread mystery: why didn't they come forward? Did they do it as a joke for a friend in the office and they leaked it? If so I think they must have realised they would get into a lot of trouble for it. It showed actual dead people in an inappropriate way, they'd disrespectfully edited a film of dead people, and they might never work in the insurance industry again if their identities were known. It damaged the insurance company's reputation for professional confidentiality and they could have sued and ruined whoever was responsible.

Other people say the image of the boy couldn't have been pasted in. Bits of paper and silt can be seen moving in front of the image. Also, the diver seems to react to the boy's face being there. It's the boy that makes him panic and scramble for the exit.

This is the problem with speculation: it's unsatisfying. We want clean answers and better stories than 'maybe this', 'possibly that'. Real life often makes no sense.

So, a cleaner, more definitive story took hold in the popular imagination: the vengeful spirit of the Polish boy who haunted the Dana had killed the Parker family and lured the diver to his death. 'Beis believers' argue that the diver was hypnotised by the ghost when he approached the ship, was tricked into entering the cabin and fed the beis demon with his fear and his death. This was a film of an actual ghost and anyone who denied it was conspiring to

95

suppress that. Deniers were actually working for the beis.

Isn't that better than 'I think someone may have pasted this in for a joke'?

All the different theories found their congregations.

Facebook groups and Reddit threads formed. They split into cliques. Armed with nothing but their conviction, some formed posses and took direct action, gathering in Saint-Martin to look for clues. Illegal dive expeditions were broken up by the coastguard. Ghost tours were running out to the wreck site, incredibly dangerous given its proximity to a major shipping lane. Locals hated it. Remember, this is a very exclusive holiday resort.

The town of Saint-Martin was full of bungling citizen detectives and news crews, each trying to prove what they already believed. Restaurants and cafes in the town put signs in their windows saying they would not answer questions about the Parkers: please refer all inquiries to the police. Violetta's hotel posted a notice saying that they had returned all of her belongings to her mother because 'Dana tourists' were trying to bribe staff for mementos.

If you go to Saint-Martin, as I have, you'll find that the locals won't talk about it any more. As soon as you say 'Dana' they ask you to leave.

The French police investigation was a mess. Driven by headlines and hysteria, the investigation took routes that seem bizarre in the cold light of day. One police press conference centred on a discussion of whether or not ghosts really existed.

In fact, there are rational explanations for everything. The diver was not hypnotised by a ghost but he might have been offered a bonus if he retrieved the diamond necklace. That could be why he went in there. Even if he wasn't offered a bonus, he may have seen the instagrammed picture, assumed that if he found Violetta's body he would find a necklace worth three-quarters of a million euros. Unofficial salvaging is not that unusual and professional divers with a lot of experience sometimes take risks no one else would. They trust their experience to assess difficult situations. The story doesn't need the supernatural to make sense.

To defuse all of the hysteria over the film, the insurance company hired Olaff Tasksson, the famous diving expert, to do a commentary and explain to audiences what they were actually seeing. Not corpses standing up to greet the damned, but a change in cabin pressure. Not a diver possessed by a beis demon but an overconfident professional taking too many chances.

The second version of the film with Tasksson's commentary was released only three weeks later but got a fraction of the views for the first one. The world had already decided which version of the story they liked best.

Tasksson's version is the one we have on our website. Personally, I would not urge you to watch that either.

Do you always mean to cook fresh meals from scratch —

I switched it off. 'Have you seen that film?'

Fin said nothing but made an odd snuffling sound through his nose.

I wanted to glance at him but we were on a dark, fast road, skirting the side of Loch Lomond. Giant hills loomed over the still black water. I was unsure of my driving and the car behind me was too close for me to slow down. Their head-lights were reflected in my rear-view mirror, blinding me to distance. I slowed and they slowed. They wouldn't overtake but just stayed too close.

'Fin, I need you to answer me so I know you're OK.'

I heard his dry mouth make a 'shlack' sound as it opened and he said, ' 'M OK.' He sounded groggy.

'Fin, have you taken something?'

'Nah.' His voice was faint. 'I'm not well . . . '

I don't know anything about anorexia except that it's dangerous. A famous man needing resuscitation in a car I was driving with a stolen ID was a complication too far today. Without the skills to drive well, I took a turn at a sign for a restaurant too quickly, flattening Fin to the window.

I knew he wasn't dying because his hands flew up in alarm.

17

The restaurant was a big corrugated-iron shed, painted black. The car park was empty but the lights were on inside, the place was open.

I parked near the door.

'Look, Fin, you're not well enough to travel. I'm going to drop you here and you can get a taxi home.'

He looked despairingly at the rain pattering softly on the windscreen and raised a weak hand.

'You're too fragile, Fin. It's another hundred miles to Fort William.'

'I'm OK.'

'You haven't spoken for forty minutes.'

He looked at me with cold-eyed fury. 'It hasn't been the best day.'

'Oh, really? Well, I've had a lovely day. I'm glad you came to my home to saddle me with looking after you because my day has been a non-stop fucking fiesta.' This was said with a lack of warmth and excessive volume.

I got out of the car and slammed the door. I was shaking.

He got out of the car.

We stood in the rain on either side of the car. I half thought that he'd come round and we'd have a punch-up. Or was I hoping for a punch-up? Those two things often feel the same. But that isn't what happened. He walked round the bonnet, heading into the restaurant. I locked the car and followed him.

Inside, it was an assault on all the senses. The room smelled of Christmas cake and floor cleaner. The carpet was tartan and the walls were covered in stag heads, whisky posters and swords. Fiddle music jangled around the metal room with manic cheer. The staff were all dressed in kilts and Aran jumpers but they were young and you could still see who they really were underneath, the tattoos and piercings, shaved undercuts and pink and blue hair.

We were the only customers but they were expecting a coachload: two long tables were set and ten members of staff were idling by the bar.

The waiter showed us to a table up on a wooden platform. A shield and claymore sword decoration loomed on the wall above us. The menus were laminated.

Haggis. That was the menu. Haggis burger, haggis stew, haggis pakora, tempura, even soup. Let me say: no one in Scotland eats haggis without a sense of irony. It's one of the things I like about the place. Anyone eating the national dish will tell you, 'I'm eating haggis!' French people do the same with frogs' legs. People claim to love haggis, or the veggie version which is a nut roast and nothing at all to do with haggis, but it's not a staple. It's tourist food for special occasions.

The waiter shrugged at the menu. 'We do have proper food, like chicken and that.'

I looked at Fin. He was frowning intently at the menu. I ordered two chicken things and water to drink.

The waiter stared at Fin. 'You're him, aren't you?'

It took Fin a minute to look up. 'What?'

'Oh, I just saw you trending on Twitter there, so I knew it was you.' He nodded at the rest of the staff sitting in a huddle around the bar. 'Can I get a selfie?' Fin obliged, smiling warmly, but his smile dropped as soon as the flash was done.

'We'll leave you alone,' said the waiter. 'Don't worry.' He took the menus and walked away.

Fin had left his phone in the car and asked to borrow mine. I gave it to him. He googled himself. His expression, uplit in the dark restaurant, shifted swiftly from furious to calm. He scrolled down and a confused smile warmed his face. His eyebrows rose slowly. He was sucked into the face of the phone and lost to me.

I looked around for a bit but there wasn't much to look at. Tourist tat and teenagers whispering about Fin at the side of the bar. I picked up some brochures from the menu stand and read one about boat trips and another about an aquarium.

Fin was still scrolling, his face very animated, having more of an interaction with the comments about himself than he had with me in nearly an hour of driving. He looked worried.

'What is it?' I asked finally.

'Your neighbour tweeted a picture of me on the steps outside your house and the pro-anas are saying I look great, which is worrying. I should eat something.'

'What's pro-anas?'

'Pro-anorexia.' He looked ashamed. 'It's — I

101

have anorexia. I struggle. Hm. The pro mob encourage it. They're kind of poisonous. I feel I'm endorsing them if I don't stay well. It's too much pressure. I've been on hiatus from social media recently.'

He seemed pleased though, revived, as if the world talking about him had breathed new life into him.

The food arrived. The 'chicken thing' was unexpectedly fantastic. It was slow-roasted and served with a creamy smoked garlic sauce on buttery celeriac mash. I hadn't eaten all day and got lost in the interplay of flavours, sharp and soft, pleasing textures and a lingering tang of smoke on the back of my tongue. I considered the tragedy of a chef this talented stuck micro-waving haggis out here in the middle of rainy nowhere. I looked up.

Cohen was not eating. He sat, hands on his lap, looking at the plate of lovely food as if it had offended him.

'Eat it, it's delicious.'

'I can't eat that,' he said to the plate, 'I'm vegan.'

'Eat around it then,' I said. 'Or eat something else. I don't care what it is. Have some bread and butter.' I knew it was stupid as soon as I said it. 'For fucksake, you're an adult. You can find food in a restaurant.'

Fin critically examined the side salad, lifting leaves with his fork and looking underneath for sides of beef secreted under the lettuce. He found the salad acceptable, actually giving it a little nod. Then he pushed the exquisite chicken dish away across the table, infuriatingly slowly. He pulled the tiny salad plate in front of him and began scooping mini morsels up on his fork, grimacing as he put them in his mouth. It was painful to watch.

'Fin, did you pass out in the car?'

'It's just low blood sugar. When I haven't eaten for a while I get a bit dizzy.'

'You passed out. What if that happens in the street? How would anyone know what to do for you?'

'I carry my passport, my doctor's number and a note about my blood sugar.'

He had a strategy for passing out and didn't seem to realise how bizarre that was. I pointed at his figure. 'No margin of error on you, is there?'

He glared at me. I didn't understand why everything I said about food was wrong.

'OK,' I said. 'Eat that and a pudding and I won't leave you here.'

He put his fork down and glared at me. '*That* is what you don't say.'

'What?'

'Talk about my body shape, try to blackmail me to eat. If someone has an eating problem you're supposed to encourage — '

'Son: eat if you want to get back in my fucking car.'

He froze. I could see from his face that he had been told bad things about me, doubted them, but now believed them to be true. 'Why did you drag me here?'

I smiled. 'Findlay, d'you think I'm stupid? I've got two kids.'

103

He was very offended. 'I've heard you were aggressive.'

'My girls are better at this than you.'

'At what?'

'Starting fights so they don't have to eat their dinner. I'm not looking after you. Eat or stay. Your choice. I don't give a fuck either way.'

We sat and ate furiously at each other, silently formulating insults and reproaches in time to the jig music swirling overhead.

I knew there was a train station in Crianlarich, not ten miles up the road. I could drop him there and he'd be back in Glasgow in an hour. I'd be free of him. But he wasn't dressed for standing on a concrete train platform in November. I was sure he'd fainted in the car and if he did that again, alone on an exposed train platform, he wouldn't be found until the next day. He could easily die of hypothermia.

My phone buzzed on his side of the table and he handed it to me. A text from Jess's phone.

'*Arrived safe and sound. Hotel nice and clean. Had a sensible dinner, love from Jess and Lizzie.*'

I texted back, '*I'd actually rather hear it from Jess herself thanks Estelle can you give her the phone back please.*' Didn't even use punctuation. Fuck her.

'*Hi mUM, its nice hotel. Were fine. JJxxx*'

My heart leapt and fell. Definitely from her.

I texted back, '*That's super! All ok here. Do try to have a nice time and take photos. Sleep well, darlings. I'm only a few hours away if you need me, Mum xxxxxxxx*'

'*Ok.*' Then an emoji of a swimmer.

I desperately wanted to hear more but didn't text a prompt. They should be in bed by now. I scrolled up through the old texts from her. She wasn't allowed to take the phone out of the house, it was just for play. I was looking for one that was more satisfying, longer and about anything. There really weren't any.

The waiter came up to the table with an oval dish and spoke to Fin. The chef had made a vegan stir fry, he hoped Fin didn't mind, they weren't going to charge us and the chef said it was his pleasure, he wasn't busy, he was trying out new dishes. They chatted about veganism.

For an anorexic being presented with a second dinner, Cohen was very gracious. He tasted it and said it was delicious, really amazing and asked to meet the chef. The waiter brought him out. He was pasty and young, with a shaved head and tumbling dice tattooed on his neck. Sweating with excitement, he chatted to Fin and said he was vegan too, or wanted to be vegan, I didn't listen. I don't understand why people monologue about what they don't want to eat as if it's interesting. They were chit-chatting, the chef asked for a selfie too and it didn't include me.

I busied myself on the phone, looking at the pictures on the *Death and the Dana* page.

Photo for Ep3

Harold J. Webb stood alone in a New York street. He was short, had a walrus moustache and was dressed in a grey morning suit, matching bowler hat, holding a silver-topped cane. He glared into the lens, his irascibility still crisp ninety years on.

Photo for Ep5

A black-and-white dotted image from a newspaper article.

A woman had been surprised by a photographer.

Two uniformed policemen held her arms tight and her hair swung out to the side. She had been yanked round to face the camera and was slack-jawed, wide-eyed with a slight double chin. Her hair was a cut into a rough mullet. The photographer was standing too close and the flash had bleached out her eyebrows, emphasising her heavy brow, making her look Neanderthal.

Was that Amila? No. The picture looked too old, was black and white. We hadn't got to that bit yet.

Photo for Ep6

Gretchen Teigler. This was a paparazzi snap from a while ago. She was walking along a sunny street, looking bland and unremarkable, in the beige uniform of American money: white sweater, slacks, clothes that flatter no one but denote membership as clearly as a gang tattoo. Her square face was framed by helmety blonde hair, sunglasses worn as a hairband. A chubby personal assistant walked behind her, carrying shopping bags. In the manner of dedicated PAs, she was dressed in an off-echo of her boss: same hair, cheaper sweater. She was looking at the back of Gretchen's head as if trying to anticipate her next thought. Dauphine Loire.

Dauphine Loire had once taken out a contract on me. I'd never seen a photo of her before. She didn't look murderous. She looked a bit nervous and very focused on Gretchen Teigler.

I saw PAs like that at Skibo. They were often codependents who found a calling that matched their condition, pandering to the unappeasable, working for little, defending with their lives. I found them a bit pathetic but Adam Ross pointed out that they often seemed happier than the wives or the children.

I knew that it would have been Gretchen who decided that the investigation should focus on Amila. I didn't believe Leon would kill his kids but was sure that Gretchen had decided who the official killer would be. This had her stamp all over it.

Gretchen's motive always bothered me. She couldn't be a villain because they don't exist. No one got up in the morning, rubbing their hands as they looked forward to a day of doing evil. She must have had some justification for the terrible, terrible things she had done. Everyone was too afraid to stop her or speak out. The press colluded, the cops went along with her, and if that didn't get her the outcome she wanted she sent the heavies in.

I went back to the podcast home page and looked at the picture of Leon and his kids again. He was happy then, just before, you could see it in his eyes. At least he had that. Looking at his picture made me want a cigarette and a warm night and a good friend to laugh and tell stories with.

I made myself close it and go to Twitter, open on the comments below the picture of Fin. Pretcha would be thrilled. Her pic had twelve thousandish likes and a lot of retweets.

People were pleased to see that the rumours of his death were untrue. Where had he been? Too thin, Fin! Looking sleek!

I scrolled back up to Pretcha's photo.

It wasn't a picture of Fin Cohen outside my house. It was a picture of me and Fin Cohen outside my house, a clear, sharp picture of my face with my scar visible. It cuts across my eyebrow. It is thin and white. It's distinctive.

The modern mania for photographs is hard on those in hiding. If you have a friend with a thin backstory who always wants to take the picture or slides behind the heads of others in group snaps, be kind to them. Camera phones are a bloody menace.

A little nervous, I scrolled down. There were exclamations of love for Fin, emojis, anorexia talk and then, quite far down, I hit a comment saying things I hadn't heard for a long time. My real name and a link to my story. Ten Fin comments further down a GIF of a dead cat nailed to my old front door.

Oh God.

My girls.

That was my first thought. Not that I was in danger but that my lovely unspoiled girls would find out about me.

I followed the link to an article about the case. It was eight years old, from a year after I had run. I'd read it before: it was about the other girl being found dead in a suspicious house fire while living under an assumed name. They mentioned my court case. I'd read it on the front page of a newspaper at the time, too afraid to even buy the paper. That was why I'd stayed away.

Fuck. I felt sick. I felt ashamed. I was shaking.

I leaned over the table, vinegar tears dripping into the creamy smears of sauce on my plate. The smell of garlic hit my nose and made me gag.

My girls would hear what they did to me.

Jig music jangled above my head, chit-chat jabbed at my ears. On Twitter, an emoji avatar told someone else to ring the police. They were trying to work out which city Fin Cohen lived in. Pretcha hadn't geotagged the photo, but it wouldn't take them long to find out.

A stranger told another stranger what should be done to me to teach me not to lie. Eighty likes. Fin better watch himself with a lying bitch like me. Someone with an avatar of the football club's logo said they could find me. Someone else said they would help. They decided to DM each other and dropped off the thread.

The next comment was 'Wow! Fin so thin!' thumbs up, from Japan.

'I need to go.'

Fin looked away from his adoring vegan chef and spoke very slowly. 'I haven't finished eating yet.'

'Box it up or stay,' I said and got up, dropped money on the table and hurried back out to the car.

18

I drove.

'What is going on?' asked Fin.

I couldn't talk. I couldn't look at him. I just drove. Thinking about the other girl. I knew they'd killed her. Gretchen Teigler killed her. I didn't feel sad about it at the time. I'd assumed she had everything I didn't have: support, family, resources, courage. I lived, she died, end of story. I honestly hadn't given her a second thought.

'Anna? Will you please tell me what's going on?'

I couldn't. I put the podcast back on.

Episode 5: Amila Fabricase, her Famous Mother and the French Obsession with Bread

This episode is about how the French police investigating the sinking became obsessed with Amila Fabricase to the point of charging her with three murders she couldn't possibly have committed.

There are a number of ways of looking at this. The kindest is that Amila's story was so beguiling and unfolded so pleasingly that the French police couldn't resist it. A more sinister one is that it was to deflect attention from Gretchen Teigler, who could be neither questioned nor crossed because she is so powerful.

I couldn't believe Trina Keany was saying these things. They were true but everyone else knew better than calling out the Emperor. Was Keany powerful too? Was she working for someone powerful? Was she stupid? If she was she was in terrible danger. I wondered if she knew that.

Perhaps at Gretchen's direction, the Dana's captain drew the focus to Amila again and again. He made public statements about Amila leaving, he gave interviews about her erratic behaviour on board, he hassled the police until they went to talk to her. But the captain had lost his ship while drinking in a bar with his crew and he let Leon pay the crew cash in advance of the voyage. This made him seem feckless and unprofessional, especially to other sailors. Maybe that was why he was so keen to have it resolved.

All of the police investigation centred on Amila and her story. But what a story! It's easy to see how they got sucked into the glamour, the death, the startling reveals. Amila's story was so compelling that a suicidal businessman must have seemed dreary by comparison. That's a benign explanation of how they overlooked all the other evidence of what happened on the Dana that night.

So, who was Amila?

Amila Fabricase grew up in Lyon, a city

obsessed with food. It is a city of restaurants and gastronomic theologians. It's where chefs go on holiday. The Lyonnais have loyalties to certain bakers and bouchons the way other cities have football supporters. Chefs and bakers and cheesemakers are celebrities there, admired and recognised in the street, and she was an integral part of that scene.

Amila was a baker. She left school young and trained hard. She was known and admired for her traditional breads. She and her partner, Sabine, were planning to set up their own bakery but neither of them came from money. They were still years away from raising their stake. This was used against her later, they said she was envious of the rich people she worked for, but aren't we all envious of rich people? Even rich people wish they were richer.

To raise the start-up money Amila worked as a chef on private yachts and Sabine was a chef for a Swiss banker. Three seasons later they had saved a third of their stake. It was slow but they were getting there. Amila was twenty-four, on the brink of a great career, when her headaches started.

They came and went suddenly, in flurries. Her right eye would swell and tears would course down her cheeks. She developed a weak shoulder from tensing in her sleep, a disaster for a baker. Time was running out.

Amila saw her family doctor about the headaches before she set off on the Dana.

113

He referred her to a specialist. She was tested for brain lesions and tumours. They found nothing. There was no known cause and therefore no treatment available apart from painkillers so strong they were disabling. Amila had to work an eighteen-hour day on board. She couldn't take them.

She texted Sabine the day before they docked in Saint-Martin and said the headaches were getting worse. She hadn't slept for days. Sabine texted back two words: 'Come home.'

As we know, Amila got off at Saint-Martin. She took a taxi straight to La Rochelle air-port and waited for the next flight to Lyon.

The Dana was heading out to sea as her plane lifted off from the runway. The Dutch containership was watching it. By the time Amila landed in Lyon the Dana was under the water.

She didn't go straight to the flat she shared with Sabine. She went to her grandmother's house, out in the countryside, because the doctor who was treating her was there. He gave her enough codeine to let her sleep for a full eight hours. She was very weak. She hardly got out of bed for days. On the third morning she was a little better, still groggy, but her grandmother was reassured enough to leave her alone in the house while she went shopping. Amila would be in custody by the time she got back.

The police came to the door and asked to interview her about the Dana. Amila didn't know it had sunk. She welcomed them in, thinking that Violetta's diamond necklace had been stolen. She said Leon was nice, but shouldn't have brought something that valuable on to a boat. She sympathised with the cops about having their time wasted. The police knew they were not there about the necklace but they didn't tell her that.

Amila gave them permission to search her house but asked them to be quick and finish before her grandmother came back. Her grandma was an old hippy and not entirely enamoured of the police. Amila was about to find out why.

The police were thorough. They didn't just look in necklace-shaped places but read through papers and examined computers. Then they called in reinforcements. By the time Amila's grandmother came back the cops had a search warrant and brought in sniffer dogs. They began to break through walls and lift floorboards.

They had found papers linking Amila and her grandmother to a string of murders and robberies. They later found a small quantity of explosives buried under the floor of an outhouse on the periphery of the property. They had proof that Amila Fabricase's name had been changed from her birth name: Rosa Luxembourg Berghoff.

Amila was Rena Berghoff's daughter.

Fin reached forward and paused the podcast. 'Why are we listening to this?'

My mind flooded with Gretchen Teigler and house fires and rape threats from strangers. 'PUT IT BACK ON.'

'Can we talk?'

'No. Put it back on, Fin.'

'I'm not interested in this. I don't know who anyone is.'

I'd have punched him unconscious if I wasn't driving. 'PUT IT BACK ON.'

'Who is Amila?'

'Put the FUCKING thing BACK ON.'

He saw me slap tears off my cheeks. I was driving too fast on a narrow, winding road. We were skirting the edge of the deep loch, no more than a cliff edge away from the black water. Trees overhung the road and the only lights were reflections from the road signs warning of sharp turns and cliffs and rock falls.

'You OK, Anna?'

'Please. Put it on.'

He put it back on.

In 1986 Rena Berghoff was a debutante at a Swiss finishing school when her father, an undersecretary at the French Embassy in West Berlin, died suddenly of a heart attack. She was seventeen.

Rena came to Berlin for the funeral and never went back to school. One biographer later said she had left 'undercooked'.

Berlin was a hotbed of radicalism at the time and Rena became involved with left-wing political groups. But she was a debutante, an aristocrat. There were rumours that she worked for the CIA, for the KGB, was doing an undercover investigation on leftist factions for Der Spiegel. No one trusted her. Rena didn't care. She wrote: 'The eternal companions of all clever women are mistrust and scorn.' Pretty astute for an eighteen-year-old.

By the way, if you're ever in Berlin and you see a woman wearing a T-shirt with 'Mistrust & Scorn' printed on it, that's what that is about.

Arrogance didn't make Rena more popular. She became a hate figure to both left and right. She gave birth to a daughter, refused to name the father and called the baby 'Rosa Luxembourg Berghoff'. This was widely ridiculed as pompous and offensive.

When the little girl was just one, Rena's politics spiralled out of control. An anti-apartheid demonstration outside the South African Embassy turned violent and a driver was shot, his car was stolen, and Rena and her faction were on the run.

They formed a terrorist group, Résistance Directe, and committed a string of bank robberies, a murder, took an industrialist hostage and brutally assaulted a German government minister. Their point was that the Nazis had never been purged from public life. They were still there, in high office. After two years on the run, they were all arrested in Hamburg.

Women terrorists attract a particular kind of horror. Counterterrorism officers regard them as more dangerous than men because they have often given up more, overcome more social conditioning to commit violent political acts. And officers generally train to avoid shooting women and children.

While they waited in prison for the trial to begin, all of Rena's comrades committed suicide, hanging themselves one by one. Rena didn't. By the time of the trial she was the only one left alive. The press characterised her a succubus.

Her trial took place in a closed court. The press were excluded to stop her hijacking proceedings to speak to the world. The photograph you can see on our website was taken as she stepped from a police van on the first day of her hearing: Rena didn't know her trial was starting that day. She didn't know where she was being taken. The picture was released to the worldwide press.

Found guilty at the trial, she was given eight consecutive life sentences. She issued a statement through her lawyer. She wasn't sorry. She would do it all again. She didn't even mention having a daughter.

Rena's mother cut all ties with her, secretly changed the baby's name to 'Amila Fabricase' and moved to the house near Lyon. At least that was what she said. At TREVI, the precursor to Europol, some detectives were convinced that fringe members of Resistance Directe had hidden out in the Lyonnais farmhouse for months.

They were watching the farmhouse until Amila was seven.

Amila didn't know her name had been changed. She grew up believing her mother and father were surgeons who died in a car crash. The police found her real birth certificate taped to the underside of a drawer in her grandmother's office. Interpol confirmed their findings. The cops knew who she was before she did.

France has draconian anti-terrorism laws. Amila was interviewed for twenty hours. She didn't really know what was going on. In transcripts of the interviews she still thinks it is something to do with the diamond necklace.

At this point no one knew why the Dana sank. Amila's only real crime had been to leave the ship at a fortunate time. But she was well known in Lyon and the local press called for her release. It was in response to this outcry that the cops leaked the Rena Berghoff connection and announced that they had found a package of explosives buried on the property with scraps of DNA on it that matched Amila's. Public sympathy evaporated. Only much later did they admit that the DNA of other members of Resistance Directe had been found on the package too and the incomplete DNA may have been Rena Berghoff's.

She was being held without charge until the police saw the wreck dive video and the hole blown in the bow. The damage came

119

from inside the engine room, in an area where there shouldn't be anything combustible. To them this was confirmation of the use of explosives. Amila came from a terrorist family. She had explosives on her property.

When a narrative chimes with pre-existing beliefs, it can seem so self-evidently true that all conflicting evidence is discarded.

Amila was charged with three counts of murder, among other things. She was tried under terrorism legislation, in a closed court, with lower evidentiary standards. They didn't even need to come up with a motive. It was just because of terrorism, that blank Scrabble tile that can mean anything at all.

Despite her cast-iron alibi, no appeal was ever lodged. Only months after Amila's conviction, Sabine opened the bakery they had been saving up for. Where did that money come from?

How did Amila turn off the Dana's radio and motor out of port and into the Atlantic when she was sitting in departures? How did she restrain the Parkers when she was in the air?

It has been suggested that she used the disabling painkillers to poison the Parkers. This makes sense. It would explain why they were sitting passively in a stuffy dining room, not eating, with the door closed. But how could she administer the drugs? She couldn't have put anything toxic in the

120

champagne: the bottle was opened after she left. She couldn't have poisoned the food: it arrived on board while she was in the airport. Remember, she didn't even know which restaurant the food was coming from. The captain arranged it while she was in the taxi to the airport. She couldn't have poisoned the plates or pots because she couldn't know what they would order.

This crime could only have been committed by someone on board.

The question the police never, ever asked was this: did someone on board do it? Specifically, did Leon do it? Why was he never a suspect? Was it because of his powerful wife? We'll explore this in the next episode when we ask: what's the deal with Gretchen Teigler?

Do you LOVE to cook but rarely find the time? Our sponsors, Fast'n'Fresh —

The episode ended as we reached the top of the loch. The music rose and fell as we drove along a straight road through a forest of pines. I turned the fog lights on, cutting through the pitch-dark, turning the road ahead into a grainy computer game.

Gretchen Teigler paid Sabine off. It seemed impossible that someone could get away with all of this, do all of this, walk around and breathe and marry and shop and do all of this. And Hamish was in Porto with Estelle and I wasn't going to live with my girls any more and my picture was on Twitter with my door in the background, my front fucking door, where my kids lived, where a fire could happen, a suspicious house fire. I was driving faster and faster.

'Anna? I think we need to talk.'

'Shut up.'

'Why are you driving so fast? Where are we going?'

'Adam.'

'I don't know if you're safe to drive.'

'Fuck off.'

' . . . '

'Fuck right off.'

I can't quite recall what happened then. The road went blurry and there was a crunch, a skid and a loud 'BOMP' and the car stopped moving forward. It gave out a grinding growl.

I looked over. Fin Cohen's body was slumped over the dashboard but his face was missing. I had killed him. I blinked. His head had been swallowed by the airbag.

19

'Fin?' I threw my arm out and slapped his shoulder, adrenaline-clumsy. 'Shit! Fin?'

He jerked back, gasping, a diver coming up for air.

'Are you dead?'

The question was redundant but he assured me he wasn't dead anyway and I told him that neither was I.

Neither of us was even hurt and the car was fine. We were both very surprised. I was so surprised that I was trembling too much to drive for a while. So we sat quietly. Cohen folded the airbag neatly and sat it on the dashboard like a dishcloth he wanted to dry.

He kept saying it would be all right, like an idiot. He was trying to be reassuring but all I heard was how naive he was and how I shouldn't have bothered force-feeding him in the restaurant. He had been pictured with me. He had no idea of the shitstorm we were in. Teigler didn't care about truth. No one did. And what was Trina Keany doing telling the truth in a world where that would get you killed in a house fire? We were in terrible danger. She was powerful and vicious.

But Fin thought I was upset about Hamish and Estelle and I did him the kindness of letting him think that. He said that they had been having an affair for months. I think I knew that.

He knew from the start and he had stayed away from me because he didn't want to be implicated in their deceit. It started when he was first hospitalised.

'My eating removes me from life, sometimes. I wasn't there for her,' he said.

I looked at him and said it was kind of obvious. He nodded, ashamed. All of that seemed very small and luxurious so I said, 'Well. We've all got our thing.'

'I heard you read obsessively.'

I snapped angrily, 'Is *that* what she says?'

Unwilling to fight he held his hands up in surrender and looked away. He took a deep breath.

I looked out of the windscreen. The night was pitch black. I must have slapped the headlights off. The only sign of civilisation a little window of yellow light far up a distant hill. Above us the dark sky was a blanket of fulminating charcoal. My girls would find out what they did to me, those men. Those things they did to me back then. My little girls. I wanted them ignorant and innocent. I wanted them to go swimming and eat vegetables. That past life had felt like something vivid but imagined, something that happened to someone else, centuries ago, only now it wasn't. The break between my two lives had been so complete. I was just dealing with what was before me, not what was behind me, day to day, hitting my marks.

'I mean, Anna,' Fin said carefully, 'you will meet someone else. You're *still* an attractive woman.'

The whole situation was suddenly absurd.

Sitting in a crashed car with a starving man and my life shattered, Gretchen Fucking Teigler back in my life, and Leon, dead. But Fin thought I could still pull. There was always that. Absurd.

I started laughing. And sobbing. Great bubbles of snot bursting from my nose. I banged the steering wheel with an open palm until it hurt. This went on for a long time, until the skin was raw.

Fin Cohen sat still. He reached forward at one point and touched the carefully folded airbag, as if to check it wasn't going to blow up in his face again.

Finally, I managed to stop laughing. I wasn't shaking any more either. I wiped my face dry with my sleeve and looked out of the window. God, what a fucking mess.

'I want a cigarette.' I didn't say it to him, I just said it.

He reached into his pocket and took out a beige leather tobacco pouch, a flat wallet held closed with a thong. It was quite a beautiful thing, old, very soft and smooth. He rolled a very thin cigarette and gave it to me and lit it for me with a lighter.

Some cigarettes are nice, some are exquisite, this was more than that. It was a reunion with my old bad-ass self. I hadn't smoked since I left Skibo.

I breathed in, drawing grey stain down through my lungs, enjoying the damage it was doing me. Could I disappear again? Just run away and start again for a third time? But Pretcha's photograph showed my front door.

That's where they would look for me and if they didn't find me they would find my girls.

I could go ahead and kill myself, that seemed reasonable for a second, but then I realised that Pretcha's photo would be the last sighting of me. The tweets below told the story of who I had been. Hamish would find out about my past and one day he'd have to tell the girls. When they grew up they'd go looking for me and read the newspapers and the court reports. That's how they would remember me. Not kissing their hair or cupping warm water to rinse soapsuds off their little backs. Not waiting at the school gate in the rain for them. They'd remember their mother as beaten and victimised. A troubled fantasist, a lonely drunk, mad, no wonder she killed herself. And I'd seen how my dad's suicide hollowed out my mum, how hard it was for her to get past it. Because of what he'd done, suicide was my reflexive thought when I was in a corner. I'd be passing that on to them.

What else could I do?

I couldn't ask the police for help. Gretchen Teigler was too powerful. I wanted to slap her, run at her and slap her face. It gave me a little lift to think that. I'd been running away from her for nine years and thought about running towards her. Turn up on her doorstep and confront her. There would be no reason to go after the girls if I turned up at her door. It was dangerous but remember, I was suicidal. It was a fantasy at that point. She was reclusive and paranoid. I didn't think I would get anywhere near her.

I asked Fin for another cigarette and he gave me one. I smoked and imagined Teigler's face, her cheek pinking from a slap, what I might say to her.

'We need petrol,' I said, restarting the car.

I backed out of the ditch, the wheels scattering stones over the tarmac.

'Headlights,' said Fin.

'Oh, yeah,' I said, flicking them on. 'Because then we'll be safe.'

We drove in silence.

I was exhausted, lost in thought, almost relieved, to be honest, contemplating something life-threateningly reckless. I've met people that nothing much ever happened to. They live in the same place, they go on holiday, come back, eat food, day after day. No ups, no downs. I used to wonder if they were lying or unobservant or had somehow arranged their fate that way. But it's just random dumb luck. Too much has happened to me. Too many lives. Too many events. I can't take in any more.

'Why *do* you read all the time?'

Fin's voice startled me. I'd actually forgotten he was there.

'I don't read *all* the time. Sometimes I listen to audio books.'

'Estelle said you'd read while you were changing for yoga and sometimes she'd leave you at home and come back hours later and you'd still be in the hall, with your coat on, reading.'

'Isn't it good to read?'

'Isn't it good to watch your weight?'

That was unexpected. He was making a joke.

I asked, 'When did your food thing start?'

He sighed. 'The band got big. Everything went crazy. I just got focused on that one thing. I could control it and I couldn't control anything else. It's hard to feel so judged and criticised when your identity is just starting to form.'

'No carapace,' I said and he liked that.

I told him that I read to self-medicate. That I find the world a bit much sometimes. Podcasts are like reading when you need to use your eyes and hands, and he said yeah, yeah, that's kind of what his eating was like. Self-medicating. But then it took over and he couldn't stop. 'It's a chemical spiral. It gets so that it feels like the only thing that matters. Controlling it. Eating isn't like a book, though, you can't just put it down.'

I didn't say so but I've read books I couldn't put down, not always because they were good either, I just couldn't stop reading. Once I was reading a book and finished it by mistake (I hadn't noticed the last 140 pages were an index) and then had nothing to read. In a blind panic I went back to the start and read it again.

'Well,' I said, 'at least you've got one thing that makes you feel good.'

'Yeah,' he smiled at me, 'I've got one comfort and it's killing me. It's all so public. It feels as if there are lots of consequences. People see it, young people, and when I'm failing I feel responsible for things I can't control. And I don't want being sick to be all I'm known for, you know? Being ill to be the only thing I put out in the world.'

'Maybe you like the attention?'

'Hm. 'Shy Man in a Spotlight'. Not sure I do.'

He was quoting their biggest hit at me, which I thought was quite crass.

'Why did you come to my door, Fin?'

He shrugged. 'I was walking around for hours feeling sorry for myself. I've been trying to be less self-obsessed. I was nearby so I tried to think about someone else. It's part of my spiritual practice. Trying to be other-centred.'

'Does it work?'

'Sometimes? I'm here. I could still be out walking and hating myself.'

'And instead look at all the fun we've had: there have been fights, you've been threatened with chicken and we've had a car crash.'

'A smashing day out. You're pretty obsessed with that podcast. What's that about?'

Well, I was too tired to make up a story so I just told him the truth, that I met Leon when I worked in a hotel and how I just liked him and felt he was being maligned in the podcast, that Leon was nice, a bit daft, a bit feckless, but not overtly nasty. Gretchen Teigler was a bag of poison. She'd destroyed lives before, I knew she had, but she was so powerful that no one ever said anything. As I told him this I felt my craving to see Adam Ross grow, Adam who could read between lines and didn't need everything explained to him in exhaustive detail.

I drove on and got Fin to watch the dive film. It freaked him out so much that he made me pull over for a minute. It was probably more intense for him because he was watching it in a moving

129

car and it was dark outside and his body was eating itself.

'Did you see that light coming from the boy's mouth?'

He nodded. 'Is he speaking?'

'No. It's a reflection of the diver's light, from his head torch.'

'I'm going to be sick.'

But he wasn't sick. We waited until he felt better before driving on.

When we got going again I told him Gretchen Teigler was almost certainly responsible for Amila taking the blame. She had blocked investigations before. She was rich and powerful and thought she was above the law.

'Did you meet her at the hotel?'

'No, I've had dealings with her but never met her.'

'You have any evidence against her?'

'She doesn't leave evidence.'

He didn't seem convinced. It did sound a bit mad. I told him to look at the photo of Leon and his kids on the website. He did and said, 'Oh God, look at them.'

I loved the way he said that, as if he really looked at them, read their gestures, saw the tender interplay.

I took a left at a deserted crossroad. 'And that was taken an hour before he's supposed to have killed them. I mean does that look like a man who's planning to kill them?'

Fin was still looking at the picture.

'It doesn't, does it?' I continued. 'He's smiling. He's happy. The daughter, Violetta, she's wearing the necklace he bought her. Look at those gorgeous kids, at how proud Leon is of them.'

He hesitated and then said, 'Who took the picture?'

'What?'

'They're all holding champagne glasses, you can see everyone's hands. No one's using a selfie stick. The phone isn't resting on anything so it's not on a timer. If only the three of them were alone on board, who took the picture?'

20

Parts of Fort William had been pedestrianised since I was last there and the road system was unfamiliar. We had to park quite far away but I found Adam Ross's door by memory. It had been several lifetimes since I was there.

His flat was on the top floor of a converted Georgian merchant's villa, overlooking a beautiful little square. The council had tried to make the space into a gathering point for locals, furnishing it with plant pots, paving and a large steel bench in the shape of a comfy chesterfield sofa. The steel sofa had little puddles all over it and represented the hollow hope of comfort afforded by the square itself, which was a conduit for winds and whipping rain.

We stood in the bitter cold and looked up to dirty windows with rotting curtains sagging in them. I had a sick feeling Adam was dead. His health was precarious, by which I mean he was a lifelong heroin addict.

The front door was heavy and low, down a step from the street because the floor of the square had been built up over the years. His name was still on the door.

I pressed the buzzer. No answer.

'Not in?' asked Fin.

I was so far back in time, in such a specific set of emotional memories, that I was annoyed to find Fin with me.

He stood with one hand tucked into the pocket of his jacket, just the fingertips, as if he was modelling in a catalogue. He was shivering from his belly again, embarrassed about it, again.

'Are you shivering because you're too thin?'

He looked scared.

'I'm not going to nag you, just tell me. We'll get you some jumpers or something.'

The door buzzer suddenly echoed around the empty square, amplified on shop windows and the steel sofa, sounding as if it was coming from all around us. I pushed and the door fell open and down, sagging on loose hinges. We stepped into the concrete close.

When the housing association bought the house they kept the facade but rebuilt everything else. The close floor was concrete, painted oxblood red up to waist level. The stairs, which I suppose were once an elegant twist around the turn of a hall, were squared off and paired with a plastic banister. The downstairs lightbulb was out and we ascended from the dark into a soft light. Adam Ross was standing on the landing, hanging over the banister, too excited to wait indoors, same as always. He was grinning wide, showing his bad teeth.

'Annie, ya fanny!' he called down on my head. 'How old are you now?'

'Adam! Look at the wrinkles on me!' I said gleefully, lifting my hair to show my washboard forehead.

'Mental!' he grinned, meaning an old friend from a decade ago appearing on the doorstep at ten o'clock on a midweek night. 'You're a middle-aged hausfrau who's losing her looks!'

'My man just left me for someone younger,' I said and we both laughed.

Lovely thing about Adam, and why I loved him, was that he was kind to me when it mattered and he had seen a lot too. It's hard to be among vanilla bastards all the time. Normal people can get genuinely upset about a bad haircut, cross words, sick cats. It's hard not to roll your eyes and say the wrong thing. I often said the wrong thing — wake up, shut up, grow up. These are the wrong things to say when people are sad about some minor cruelty or sentimental incident. But Adam Ross was as damaged as me. He didn't need to be shielded or protected and he knew what not to pick at. A fellow traveller. You could say anything to him. That is rare and very precious. Most of us demand a tiptoe or two. I hadn't really driven all the way here for information I could probably find on the internet. I really just wanted to get out of there, and to rest my eyes on Adam.

I'm struggling to describe his appearance.

You know when you squeeze a tea bag out and leave it in the sink, it looks spent and crumpled. But if you leave it in the sink to dry out for days, perhaps in a warm environment, it becomes almost unrecognisable as an ex-tea bag. The edges bleach to white. The inside desiccates. These sorts of things had happened to Adam.

I think we had both assumed the drugs would have killed him by now. He worked as crew on private yachts, then as a sailing instructor, then a fisherman and then a trawler man. These are not careers enhanced by the use of soporifics. I worried about Adam and checked him out on Facebook every so often. He only posted when he got clean. His time-line read like a digital clock that needs new batteries:

Ninety days!
Seven days!
Twenty-four hours!
One year!
Ninety days!

The comments below were always positive and encouraging but over the years the supportive comments grew fewer, got shorter and more formulaic. Like most addicts, he was fucking infuriating.

'How do I look?' He held his skinny arms out and pulled some bodybuilder poses.

'Spiffy as ever but, honestly, Adam, really quite fucked.'

'Aw, I know. Thanks anyway. Come away in.' He stepped back to let me through, saw Fin on the stairs and blinked hard at the sight of him. 'Is that Fin Cohen?'

Cohen didn't know what to say. He looked to me for guidance but I didn't know either. I went into the flat.

Adam's girlfriend had been living with him when I knew him before, I used to visit them, but all her stuff was gone now. I wanted to ask about her but couldn't remember her name. The flat was very tidy, everything was in neat piles and the carpet had track marks from a Hoover.

Fin and I walked into the vibrant orange living room and sat down next to each other of the sofa. Adam stood in the doorway, rubbing his hands together, pretending that Fin Cohen wasn't sitting in his house.

'Well, can I get you a wee cup of tea and a biscuit, maybe?'

'No, Adam, I just wanted to ask you about something technical.'

'Good,' he said, 'because I don't have any biscuits or tea or coffee.'

Then he stood in front of us, crossed his ankles and dropped, cross-legged, to the floor.

'Do you remember Leon Parker?'

'Did he work at the castle with us?'

'No, he was a guest, there with a club member called Lillie Harkän. She was Dutch. Very good-looking. Snippy.'

'Don't remember either of them. Did they come sailing with me?'

'I don't think so.'

'Ah, I wouldn't know them then. Does McKay know you're about?'

'Albert McKay?'

'He asked after you when you left. Earywigging for snippettes. Even asked me once if I ever heard from you, which, you know . . . it's big for him.'

Albert McKay was not known for being emotionally engaged but he took an interest in me for some reason. He was the manager of the castle. When he sacked me he did so reluctantly. He said I did not have the 'right personality for service', which I considered a great compliment.

He said we had to be nice to our guests meaning we shouldn't hit them. Still, he had always given me references afterwards and many of them were glowing enough to verge on the fraudulent.

'I was thinking about going to see him.'

'He'd love that,' nodded Adam. 'What do you want to know about sailing anyway?'

I told him about Leon's yacht, a sixty-foot schooner, how he was supposed to have cast off himself. Adam said yeah, you could do that alone. It's not that complicated. I said that he hadn't turned the navigation lights on, had left the radio off and sailed out to the Bay of Biscay at night. Adam said that was dangerous. I said I know, they all died. Had Adam seen the insurance company film of the wreck? They found the family's bodies in the dining room. Christ no, he said, sailors don't watch shit like that. That's for civvies. I said OK, here's something I was wondering about: Leon paid the crew, in cash, at the *start* of the voyage.

Adam waited, turned his head sharply, tipping his ear towards me, waiting for more. He tittered, '*What?*'

'He paid them in cash at the start of the voyage.'

He snorted and shook his head. 'No, he didn't.'

'He definitely did.'

Adam shook his head and wrinkled his nose. '*Whit?*'

'He gave them full payment, up front.'

He laughed. 'No one would ever do that. You get paid monthly, into a bank account from an offshore company. Do you know who crews these boats? Folk like me. Would you give me cash and expect to see me again?'

'But, Adam, you're — ' I didn't know how to formulate it so that it didn't sound derogatory. A drug addict? A junkie — I hate that word. I hate people who use that word.

Adam knew what I was struggling with. He nodded at his skinny legs, flexed his hands. A chunk was missing from between the knuckles where he'd had an abscess. The scar was tight and deep. Fin was looking between us.

'I've got a wee bit of an addiction thing going on,' explained Adam. 'And it's not exactly conducive to honesty in all your affairs.'

Cohen nodded that he understood. His gaze flitted around the poor room, making sense of it.

'Anna, no one pays a crew in cash up front. They've got every reason to fuck off. It's hard work, long hours.'

'But Leon did that, so the question is: why would he?'

Adam laughed at me. ''*The question is*'? The fuck are you on about? You investigating it?'

Fin was quite excited. 'We were listening to the podcast and then I looked at the photo from when they were supposed to be alone on the boat but it's not a selfie. There had to be someone else on the boat.'

'Ooooh,' Adam grinned, 'Like you're armchair detectives now?'

'Yeah,' said Fin.

'Good for you.' He gave a patronising nod to Fin and then looked at me and laughed. 'The fuck, Sophie?'

I laughed with him but calling me Sophie was a stupid slip. I tried to bluster my way out of it, 'I liked Leon! They say he killed his kids but I don't think he did. I'm trying to find out what really happened.'

'Hmmmm. Yes.' Adam grinned. 'Sweet, sweet justice.' He knew there was more to it than that. He knew there was a lot more to it and he waited for me to tell him, nodding a soft prompt. Adam didn't even notice that he'd called me Sophie. Fin had though. I could see him watching us, waiting for an explanation.

Adam's eyebrows were leaping up and down.

They both wanted explanations but I didn't want to tell Adam about Gretchen Teigler or the other girl. And I didn't want to tell Fin who Sophie was.

Adam kept nodding and I nodded along, belligerent, waiting out the awkward moment. Then we both laughed.

'Well,' I lied, 'so, you know, what else is there to do on a Monday night?'

He laughed at that as well.

During all this to and fro and knowing laughter Fin was just sitting there, taking it all in, thinking.

Adam stopped laughing and glanced at Fin, and gave me a stern look, telling me not to drag Fin into trouble without telling him what was going on. It was obvious he hadn't a clue. Adam was damaged but he was also decent.

'So.' Adam considered the problem. 'Something you might want to think about. A crew won't get on board if there is a sniff that they wouldn't get paid. That's two or three months of your life. Sometimes, if the chief is a twat, you worry that they'll dock your wages for, you know, doing things wrong.'

'Like what?' asked Fin.

'Being late back from shore. Refusing duties, breaking things. Stuff.' He shrugged. 'You can end up basically paying *them* at the end. So, would the crew be worried? Was he broke?'

Fin said, 'Or suicidal and liked the crew, that's why he paid in advance?'

'No,' I insisted, 'he wasn't suicidal.'

But Fin corrected me. 'We can't know that. You hardly knew him.'

Adam tipped his head and frowned. 'Ah, come on, we've all thought about it.'

'The crew said he was very calm.'

'Yeah,' said Adam sadly. 'You know sometimes, when people have decided to do it, they're very calm just before. Kind of saintly. I've seen that a few times.'

We looked at Adam, a husk of a man. He lived in a high-stakes world. I'd seen him RIP friends on Facebook, always young people, always grinning in blurry photos. He'd saved my life once. He'd probably done it for other people too.

His eyebrows rose in a question. 'Was Leon broke? Because banks'll freeze your account. Maybe he wanted to make sure the crew got paid and didn't know if the money would be there when he got back?'

'He wasn't broke,' I said. 'Gretchen's rich.'

'That doesn't follow,' said Fin, dismissively. That kind of annoyed me.

140

'Albert'll know,' said Adam. 'Albert knows who's rich like I know who's holding. You should go to Skibo and see him. He's still there.'

He was right. Albert McKay would know but I didn't know if he would tell me. He was manically discreet. It would take some teasing to get it out of him.

21

The heat had left the car by the time we got back into it. With the stale smell of cigarette smoke and the burst airbag it felt like walking back into a party where a lot of regretful things had been said and done.

We shut the doors and looked out at Ben Nevis, haughtily ignoring us in the distance.

'Why did Adam call you Sophie?'

'Adam?'

'Yeah.'

'Did he?'

'You know he did.'

'I didn't hear that.'

'He called you Sophie.'

'Oh! That's his ex-girlfriend's name.'

Fin hummed and hesitated. 'I wouldn't have put you two together, to be honest. He's quite . . . I don't know.' He gave a mini cringe as he did up his seat belt. 'You're quite middle class?'

I laughed. 'Am I?' Keen to change the subject, I pulled on my seat belt and said, 'Anyway, I don't think Leon was broke. His wife is one of the richest women in the world.'

'But they signed prenups.'

'Even if Leon was broke I know he wouldn't kill himself.'

'You can't be sure.' He was being rude again. He didn't even know Leon.

'Yes, I can.' I sounded too adamant and I

couldn't know. Just a few hours ago I'd nearly done it myself. I think what I was saying was that Leon was a good man. I needed to believe that but maybe I needed it more back then, when I was so friendless and frightened. This felt like an echo of that time and I'd survived. Maybe I could —

'Anna, you're even lying to yourself now.'

'FIN, CAN YOU SHUT THE FUCK UP?'

He turned to me and he was smiling, not the reaction I expected because I had shouted pretty loud and used a curse and hoped, really, to scare him into being quiet.

But it didn't work. He said gently, 'Look, you're too invested in this. You hardly knew him. What's really going on?'

'Forget it.' I started the engine.

'What even is Skibo Castle?'

'It's a luxury holiday resort in a castle that belonged to Andrew Carnegie. Adam and I worked there. Albert's the manager there, he knew Leon.' I pulled the car out into the road. 'Albert knows everyone, he works in the luxury sector. It's his job to know all the latest gossip about wealthy people. He has an encyclopedic knowledge about them, knows more than the gossip mags ever will. He'll know what people are saying about it.'

'Why not just phone him and ask about it?'

'He's old-fashioned and very well mannered. He's too discreet to risk talking on the phone.'

'You're going to ask for reassurance that Leon wouldn't kill his kids?'

'I'm going to ask about Leon's finances and

Gretchen Teigler. He'll know. I know he will.'

Fin tapped his fingers on the steering wheel. 'Anna. What are we really doing? Are we just running? I'm up for that by the way, if that's what this is.'

'I want to clear Leon's name.'

'And this has to happen now? Today? After what happened this morning? Come on,' he sneered. 'Just be honest with me.'

'Look,' I pulled up at the side of the road, 'I didn't ask you to come with me. Why don't you get out and get a hotel or something? Just go home.'

Fin sat still, looking out of the window placidly. Then, as if he had just remembered, he took out his tobacco pouch and rolled two cigarettes. He offered me one. I took it.

We lit up. I stopped smoking years ago and remembered now how completely disgusting and utterly compelling it was, how my blood pressure rose when I inhaled and how it made my mood ricochet around.

He gestured to the road ahead. 'Drive.'

'I think you should get out.'

'I can get out any time. I'll get out later. Drive.'

So I drove and smoked and loved it and wished I wasn't smoking.

'Really, I don't get why you're still here, Fin. You could have left at the restaurant or got a hotel in Fort William.'

I waited for him to say some sappy shit about being worried about me. I didn't expect him to say what he did.

He exhaled and smacked his lips. 'OK. I couldn't get a hotel because I haven't got tuppence. I can't even use my cards any more. So either you drive me home or take me with you.'

'I can give you money to get home.'

'D'you want me to go home?'

I didn't know. I didn't really want to be alone but he wasn't much fun to fight with and that was all I had going on at the moment.

'Anyway,' he said, 'I've been in hiding for a while, but now people are looking at me again. They're aware of me and I don't want to seem broken. You know? I need to be doing something, d'you know what I mean?'

'No.' I was irritated and he was excited. It wasn't a good combination.

'What I'm saying — I think you know what I'm saying — let's go on an adventure, investigate, follow up that thing about who took the picture. I'm thinking we could make a podcast about it. Put it out on Facebook and Twitter.'

'No!' I found that idea really alarming. I was kind of shouting and driving too fast, trying to frighten him, I think, but he was having none of it.

'Ah, come on, it'll be fun. The case is interesting.'

'No!' The road was narrow and I was driving very fast, faster and faster, panicky driving.

'Slow down!' He pointed up ahead to a sign warning of sharp turns in the road.

I did slow down. 'I mean, why? There's nothing left to say.'

'You've got enough to say about it. Has anyone asked who took the photo yet? I mean, what if we're good at this? We can live-stream and tweet links, it'll be fun.'

'Look, Fin, you don't listen to podcasts. It can go very far wrong. You accuse the wrong person and they sue you, you can make a mistake in reasoning and get piled on and trolled for it. People will persecute you for having a linguistic tic — '

'A tic? Like what?'

'One presenter used to say 'hnnn' after every second word — 'angryhnnn', 'going forwardhnnn', 'in other words-hnnn'. He didn't have a sound engineer to edit it out or tell him. The guy had to leave social media because every time he posted anything a thousand people would reply 'hnnn'. It's brutal. Podcasting is like comedy or football, everyone thinks they know how to do it but they don't. They don't have a fucking clue. And you need a network to attract an audience.'

He held up his phone. 'We have got an audience. They're waiting for me to say something.'

'Stupid.' A bigger audience was the last thing I wanted. 'You don't know what you're talking about.'

He was unfazed by me. I think he might have dealt with a lot of aggression from Estelle. She's quite fiery too.

'It's just a terrible idea, Fin. You have to make them in the studio for sound quality.'

'Rubbish. Nothing is done in studios any

more. If I put this little mic into the headphone jack I can get very good-quality sound. Look.' He took a small black suede drawstring bag out of his pocket and reached into it, taking out a little mic no bigger than my thumb. 'We used this to record song ideas on the road. The sound quality is so good one guy released an album he recorded with it.'

'Absolutely not. If you do that I'll dump you by the side of the road.'

'Dumped twice in one day.' He brushed a speck of ash from his tweed sleeve.

'God, you're so fucking preening.'

'And that aggravates you?'

'It does. The button done up to the top, the perfectly buffed shoes. It looks as if you've got nothing to do all day but admire yourself. You're honestly not that good looking.'

'Personal fashion isn't a celebration, it's a defence. It's the armour of everyday life.'

'Well, you've got too much fucking armour on.' I wasn't being very nice at this point. I was alarmed by the podcast conversation and how blithely Fin had suggested drawing even more attention to us. It wouldn't take a genius to trace me to Fin and Fin to Estelle and then find out she had gone to visit her family in Porto with my girls.

He sighed and then out of the blue he said, 'Have you ever heard of Bill Cunningham?'

'No.'

'He said that, about fashion being armour. I was thinking about him because he lived above Carnegie Hall.'

147

'*The* Carnegie Hall?'

'Yeah. In a bedsit. Lived there for decades. They let out rooms above the hall as studio apartments to artists, back when no one wanted to live in New York. He was a fashion photographer, invented street-fashion photography. He was amazing but never really cashed in on it. He said, 'They can't tell you what to do if you don't take their money.' I like that. I think about him a lot.'

'Did Estelle like that?'

He laughed and looked out of the window. Then he laughed some more. 'Poor Estelle. She really didn't know what she was getting into.'

I could have said the same about Hamish but I wasn't as kind as Fin.

We drove and smoked and had another argument about something irrelevant to this story. We were enjoying ourselves. We stopped at a petrol station in Inverness to buy drinks because our mouths were foul from smoking. I made him eat half a chocolate bar and watched while he swallowed it. I told him if he fainted again I'd stop the car and roll him into a ditch and drive away. He said that seemed quite strict but entirely fair.

Back on the road we hit the bright suspension bridge across the Moray Firth.

'This is so far,' Fin muttered. 'I mean, what could a hotel manager possibly know about that's worth going all the way up here for?'

I picked up my phone and put on the final episode of the podcast. The Gretchen episode.

22

Episode 6: What's the Deal with Gretchen?

In this episode I want to talk about Gretchen Teigler and Leon Parker.

These murders were committed by someone on board. Leon had the means, the skills and had orchestrated the situation. He could have done it. To me, that's an obvious observation, but he wasn't investigated. The question is — why? And the answer is almost certainly — Gretchen.

Every generation thinks the world will end with them. Whether it's the Black Death, Judgement Day or nuclear war to wipe them out, humans have a hard time imagining a world going on after their death. Maybe because, if the world does just rumble on, nothing we do really matters anyway. We're not that important. But some people are. Gretchen Teigler might be. Her money, her history, her connections are so extensive that when she dies the world might just give up and fold in on itself because Gretchen is a direct consequence of many of the major events of the twentieth century.

She was born at the crossroads between two great fortunes and, aged just twenty-three, inherited more money than the GDP of half the world's states. Unlike most rich kids, Gretchen hasn't spent and enjoyed her money. In fact, in the years since she inherited she has tripled her fortune through aggressive deals and questionable investments, using methods most people would baulk at.

She is an extraordinary woman. She is fantastically rich and never, ever speaks to the press. She never has. She refused to even appear in her school yearbook. When she graduated from high school she submitted a photo of Eleanor Roosevelt looking particularly toothsome instead. That was prescient for a seventeen-year-old in late-1980s California. But she had good reason to be wary of public attention. Rich kids were being kidnapped all over the world and the Teiglers were loathed. She had three generations of reasons to be wary.

It began like this: in around 1900, a small German man left his home town of Weil in Freiburg and walked to Paris. There, he set up shop and began selling face cream. A lot of people sold face cream, the market was crowded, but Otto Teigler had discovered, long before it was well known, what is now called the Veblen principle. If Otto made his face cream shockingly expensive then people would buy it as a status symbol. What the cream did or didn't do wasn't really important. They weren't really buying cream. They were buying exclusivity. Women who could afford the cream wanted to boast about having it. Men bought it as ostentatious gifts for wives and lovers. Celebrities wanted to be associated with the cream and were happy for their names to be used in endorsements.

Otto understood the forces at play well enough to keep the formula secret. He built and advertised a laboratory where chemists were paid high salaries to develop new products. His face cream outsold all others and Otto Teigler made a fortune which he used it to promote his one true passion: fascism.

German Nazism recruited from the working classes but Teigler's fascism was a Veblen product: he made it exclusive. At first he established a league of prominent, well-to-do right-wingers. They hosted elaborate fund raising dinners, balls, concerts. These rich, glamorous people then attracted an army of less wealthy but socially aspiring supporters. They, in turn, brought in even less wealthy supporters until the league had an army of impoverished angry blackshirts.

1930s France was awash with immigrants. From the south came half a million Spanish refugees fleeing the Civil War. From the north and the east came Jews, driven from their homes by Nazis and pogroms. Otto Teigler provided the French government with vast funds to repatriate the Jews to Germany. He started a newspaper designed to incite violence against Jews and the Spanish. Following the Nazi's invasion,

Teigler became a prominent supporter of the appeasing Vichy government. Then the war began and we all know how that went.

But the aftermath of the war was telling.

Soldiers begin fighting for a cause and finish fighting for their comrades. This was no different. After the war Teigler's main concern was for his fascist league brothers.

In the chaos and recrimination of peace, when any woman who accepted a drink from a German soldier was punishment-raped or had her head shaved in public, Teigler and his comrades protected each other. France needed investment and Teigler Inc. built factories. It employed fellow league members to run a workforce made up of the blackshirt army and over the following two decades Teigler Inc. blossomed into a worldwide brand.

Otto and his wife, Therese, had one child, a daughter named Françoise. She had grown up in the belly of the regime. Now eighteen, Françoise attended smart parties and movie premieres, was pictured waving from airplane steps at glamorous locations. Everything she did was a Teigler Inc. endorsement because the tagline always read 'sole heir to the Teigler fortune'. Then, abruptly, in 1961, Françoise dropped out of view. No one in the Teigler camp ever mentioned her again.

This is what happened to her: while attending a house party in Monte Carlo Françoise turned down an invitation to a night at the casino. There were twenty or so people in the group and everyone was keen to go except for Françoise and one other guest. She was bored of the casino and the other guest, a young man her own age, didn't approve of gambling. They were left alone for the evening. He was unlike any man she had ever met. He was intriguing, had a lot of unfamiliar ideas about politics and the history of Europe. He was from a wealthy Chicago family, his name was Freddy Klaerche and he was a rabbi.

Less than a week later, Françoise and Freddy ran away to California together. They were married for twenty-seven years.

The Klaerche family were just as conflict-ridden as the Teiglers. These Chicago industrialists were a vast, fractured clan who sued and countersued each other over trivialities. Françoise and Freddy stayed out of it. They lived modestly, happily and had only one child. They named her Gretchen.

Growing up in San Diego, Gretchen had no contact with her grandparents. Her parents died within a year of each other, father of a degenerative muscular condition, mother of a stroke, leaving her alone in the world aged just twenty-two. She has always been intensely private, which is what makes her first and only foray into public life so strange.

Her grandmother, Therese Teigler, was widowed and elderly when her estranged daughter died. Seventy-nine-year-old Therese Teigler could not attend the funeral because her young boyfriend was jealous and didn't like her going out of the house.

Therese met Anton von Beuler at a charity fete. Twenty-six and very handsome, he was working as a waiter for the catering company. At the end of the fete Anton helped seventy-nine-year-old Therese from her wheelchair into her car, climbed in next to her and they went home. Six months later he was still in the house and boasted that his bank account was hundreds of thousands of Francs heavier.

This is a problem most of us do not have: the super-rich are surrounded by flies. They attract predators. It is both a hazard of being very rich and what motivates others to get very rich. The dying super-rich attract more flies than most, or maybe they don't have the energy to bat them off. Some are blind to the complexity of those relationships, but some aren't. Some like it. For some people these power differentials are a reason to get rich. Therese seemed to enjoy it. She didn't leave the house any more because Anton didn't want her to.

Her staff called the police but they couldn't remove von Beuler because Therese said she wanted him there. Her lawyers tried to have him evicted but she had signed a letter consenting to him doing whatever he wanted in the house. Then von Beuler began removing artworks from the house and keeping them in his own storage unit. He said they were redecorating.

154

A rumour began that she had changed her will, disinheriting Gretchen and making von Beuler her sole heir.

Gretchen was twenty-three at this point. She had never met her grandmother but, hearing of Therese's intentions, she flew to Paris on her own initiative. She waited until von Beuler was out and had the butler let her in to visit her grandmother.

Gretchen quietly drank her tea and talked to her grandmother about the weather and holidays and health while, all over the house, a private security firm planted cameras and microphones.

Two weeks later Gretchen returned, retrieved all of the equipment and released the footage, unedited, to the media. That was a strange choice. There were blow jobs between members of staff, drinking, pilfering. She could at least have cut the footage of Therese being washed by a nurse or using the commode, but she didn't. Those intimate episodes were not what caught the press's attention though.

The film showed bankers and accountants coming and talking to a confused Therese about her accounts, her tax liability and her offshore investments. Therese was dodging tax on a massive scale and had been for decades. The Teiglers had finally done something to offend the French.

Things moved quickly then: Therese's new will was nullified by a judge and von Beuler was charged with abus de faiblesse

— conning a frail person. He was made to give everything back, the money, the shares, the art. Ironically, the most valuable pieces in the Teigler art collection were by two Spanish asylum seekers and an Italian Jew: Picasso, Dali and Modigliani.

Everyone who worked for Therese was sacked and replaced. She was dead within four months and, in accordance with the reverted will, Gretchen inherited everything. She was fabulously wealthy, on paper at least.

When she moved into the Teigler mansion in Neuilly-sur-Seine she discovered that von Beuler was not the first handsome adventurer with his hand in the pot. There was very little left and they were running everything through the books. Offshore accounts were frozen and back taxes were billed. Gretchen was suddenly not very wealthy at all.

She set about rebuilding the fortune with the help of her legal advisers. The firm she chose had taken over an Italian football club in administration. Now Gretchen decided to invest in football. Her career in football finance has been controversial to say the least. One Italian club dissolved into insolvency six months after she withdrew her investment and the pension fund was found to be all but empty. This happened several times, twice in Greece, once in a minor league Spanish club. Football finance is a strange grey area. Although heavily regulated, the large sums generated some-times mean that unscrupulous investors are attracted to it, using shell companies and accounting tricks.

So: this next part is very difficult to dis-cuss. Legally, the suggestion of one fact causing another fact cannot be implied or we could be sued. So, this part has been phrased carefully by our lawyer and I am now going to read it out to you word for word:

'Twelve years ago a young PA called Dauphine Loire came to work for Gretchen Teigler. Loire has barely left her side since. The two women are very close.

'Unrelated to this: around the same time a whistle-blower in a Spanish football club made allegations about financial irregularities. Despite events which might, cumulatively, be regarded as a campaign of intimidation, the man con-tinued to make allegations online and in interviews with local journalists. The whistle-blower claimed to work for the accounting firm which audited the football club.

'Fact two: this whistle-blower was threat-ened with legal action by the parent company of the football club.

'Fact three: the man died. His house caught fire but an unexpected torrential rainstorm quenched the flames. Fire investi-gators found his body only partially burned. At post-mortem he was found to have been murdered before the fire began. His throat was cut. If the freak storm had not extinguished the fire, the murder would *never have been uncovered. That murder remains unsolved.*

'Unrelated to that fact is this: a well-known print publication was sued last year for wrongfully speculating about that death. That print publication lost their case, paid damages and has now ceased to exist.'

It was the closest thing I had ever heard to outright allegations against Gretchen Teigler. Trina Keany was either very brave or very stupid. It was a small-time podcast. She probably didn't have access to a legal department. If she had an editor or a parent company protecting their capital she would have been stopped from saying it. I thought she was making a dangerous mistake.

But we're not going into all of that. That's nothing to do with our story.

Anyway. This was ancient history when Leon and Gretchen started going out together. They were fifty-seven and forty-eight respectively, had moved in the same social circles for some time before they were romantically involved. They were married in Paris. There were two witnesses: her PA, Dauphine Loire, and a secretary in the office of le marié.

Gretchen didn't respond to press enquiries about her wedding. Leon said they had got married and were very happy. It took everyone by surprise. No one even knew they were dating.

This was no marriage of convenience. It changed both of their lives fundamentally.

In the first few months of their marriage Gretchen was being seen in public and even attended a couple of parties. She began to travel for pleasure, always with Leon. They visited Switzerland and India. They travelled to Freiberg, met distant family and they went out to Parisian restaurants in public, that is to say she didn't have them shut down for a private meal but ate in front of other people, with other people, apparently at Leon's behest.

Leon put his Sandbanks house on the market, asking price twenty-one million. He was moving to Paris to live with Gretchen.

If Leon was good for her, Gretchen seems to have been a good influence on him too. He had always been an absent father but he now made time to see Violetta and Mark away from their mothers, sometimes with Gretchen, sometimes alone. They developed relationships. Both kids admitted that these interactions were not easy, they were getting to know each other, working through resentments and difficulties. Violetta seems to have found it particularly hard. There was a lot to get over. She told friends that she didn't like him, he was vulgar and dumb and stupid. But Leon persisted.

Is it possible that these lifestyle changes got too much for Leon? He was in his late fifties, Gretchen was in her late forties.

Change is hard. Leon seemed to be review-ing his life, picking over everything that had happened to him. What if he didn't like what he saw? Could he have been suicidal but afraid of leaving his kids behind? There was no guarantee that Gretchen would sup-port them.

It is fair to say that Gretchen is attention-shy and the exposure of an investigation into Leon's death may have seemed too much. She didn't apply for the generous insurance on the Dana, perhaps to avoid the exposure of opening the case again. Or maybe she is just the richest woman in the world, was grief stricken and asked her staff to overlook the debt. Neither the police nor the press approached her, it was as if she had been cut out of the story all together.

There are so many threads left hanging in this case.

In an interview given to a German TV network, a local St Martin man, who rented his Airbnb room to Mark Parker the night before the Dana arrived, was walking on the dock on the night of the sinking. He told the reporter that he saw a girl in a stripy dress cast off the ship. He said she had long blonde hair. This interview has now disappeared from the TV company archives and was only ever mentioned on Reddit by people who saw it broadcast at the time.

Amila and Sabine had saved only one-third of their stake to open a bakery.

Just months after Amila is convicted Sabine opens a bakery.

And what happened to the diamond necklace? That was never mentioned again.

I said at the beginning of this series that when you look at the facts of this case, the court's findings were impossible.

This is what I think happened: I think Leon deliberately orchestrated that night so that he was alone with his two kids. He could sail. He knew the Dana. He had access to the engine room and could have planted the explosives. He also had access to the food and the champagne.

He planted the explosives and drugged the champagne. Then he told Mark to go downstairs, maybe got Violetta to cast off and go downstairs while he stayed in the wheelhouse. I think he piloted the ship out to sea and set the course. If the drugs were starting to have an effect he may have become confused and forgotten the radio and the lights. I think he got the kids into the dining room, closed the door, served the food and, after they all passed out, the explosives in the engine room finished the job.

Leon killed his kids and himself that night. Sad, but obvious. Gretchen Teigler may have been grieving, she may have been heartbroken, but so are all family members when a murder happens. Whether she made it explicit or implicit, the sheer power of her name directed all of the investigation away

161

from her and those around her. Because of that, an innocent woman languishes in jail. Amila Fabricase will be sixty-one before she gets out of prison. Her partner Sabine is standing by her.

Thanks for joining us for this true crime series here on the MisoNetwork.

Do you enjoy cooking? With Fast'n'Fresh —

I switched it off.

'What?' asked Fin. It was only then that I realised I'd been muttering to myself.

I tutted, 'Teigler.'

'Dreadful,' he said. 'Why did she do that to her grandmother?'

'Well, that's just a taster. Trust me. She's done much worse.'

'Like what?'

There was too much to tell and we were fast approaching Skibo Castle.

'Look,' I said.

Fin sat up as we took the turn from the main road. The estate wall was low. We could see into the perfectly maintained grounds and buildings. I could almost smell the money, or at least the absence of other smells, which is perhaps what money really smells like.

23

I drew up at the barrier and pressed the inter-com. Having worked there, I knew what would be happening inside. The security manager in the Stewards' Hall would be checking the bookings and sign-outs. Probably using an iPad now, but it was an actual book in my time. He or she might be frowning, wondering who it could be at eleven thirty on a Monday night. Check-ins tended to run from Friday to Friday. He would be looking at the security screen, see me and Fin smiling into the lens.

The intercom crackled. 'Good evening, madam.' They said this to let me know they could see me. 'How may I help you?'

'Hello, um, I used to work here and I was passing and, I know it's late but I was wondering if Albert McKay is still the manager?'

'And your name is?'

'Anna McLean.'

'Could you wait a moment, please, madam?'

'Certainly.'

The mute was employed and we were alone.

''McLean'?' asked Fin.

'It's my maiden name.'

'I didn't think you and Hamish were married.'

'We didn't get married, but I changed my surname to Hamish's for the kids.'

'Oh.' He mumbled, 'You seem to have a lot of names.'

He obviously hadn't read the tweets about me. There weren't many compared to the ones about him, he must have just scrolled past them thinking they were irrelevant but I wouldn't be able to keep it from him forever. I made a note to get my lies in order.

The voice crackled awake again. 'Come down to the main house please, madam. Mr McKay said you know where the side car park is.'

The barrier lifted and we drove on a road of flawless tarmac, passing stables on the right, a paddock on the left, heading up an incline. As we crested the small hill the scene opened up as if scenery flats were being raised from below a stage.

First the hills across the water rose into view, pale and round. Then the sea became visible on the left, molten grey with the winking lights of oil rigs in the bay for repair. They stood ankle-deep in the shallow water, like giants wading, home for tea. Lastly, the castle rose up from behind a screen of strategically grown trees.

Fin gave a low 'whoa' and I felt a spark of pride as if it were my own house.

The castle was turreted and asymmetric, gloriously uplit by spotlights hidden in the shrubbery. It was built of vibrant yellow sandstone and had lights on in every window, each dressed with matching curtains. Despite the scale, it looked welcoming, like we had been invited to someone's lovely home for a party.

We drove past and around to the side car park. This was strictly for residents only and was surprisingly empty, just a couple of large cars. I had never been there in November. We got out, locked up and crunched across the thick gravel to the main door. A stone portico, big and high enough to shelter a horse-drawn carriage, shielded the door. The giant storm doors sat open to a stone vestibule with a small cloak-room for wet clothes and muddy hiking boots.

The uniformed doorman greeted us very formally and opened the elaborately engraved glass inner door, inviting us into the house proper.

He left us to go and find Mr McKay.

The central hall of Skibo Castle, I have to say, was the most laughably opulent bit of domestic architecture I've ever seen. The room was two storeys high with an elaborate carved wooden gallery running all the way around, leading off into the bedrooms. A giant wood log was burning in the oversized fireplace and giving off a soft heat. Two red sofas flanked it, sitting on a giant Persian rug. But the stairway is where the whole room went nuts. Straight across from the entrance a massive butterfly staircase had a big church organ under its left armpit. The copper organ pipes glinted, reflecting the lazy fire behind us.

At the half-landing, where the stairs bifurcated, was a giant wall of stained-glass images commissioned by Andrew Carnegie. These depicted the good works performed *in vivo* by Carnegie. It didn't show him ordering Pinkerton men to shoot at strikers or dodging Frick at parties. It didn't show mutilating accidents in smelting plants. It showed Carnegie in a frock coat, smiling among adoring workers, doling out advice and being admired by the poor. Once, quite drunk, I stood in front of it with Adam Ross and we laughed for fifteen solid minutes at the many layers of stupidity.

There is so much screamed symbolism in the hall, it was a mercy that I was never there for Christmas.

The doorman came back in and shepherded us through a little door to the dark servants' corridor. Most of the house is given over to hidden corridors for servants to scurry through and stay hidden. We walked down to Albert's office door. The doorman gave it a cursory knock and opened it.

The office was small; a coal fire glowed in the grate. Bookshelves of grey box files lined the walls. The desk was immaculately tidy, nothing on it but a pen and a notebook, closed. Not even a computer. Albert McKay stood up from his desk and gave a small bow. 'Miss McLean,' he said, as if I had just left the room and come back in again for my scarf.

I swear he was wearing an exact copy of the clothes I had last seen him in nine years before: a white shirt, waistcoat, green moleskin trousers and brogues.

We both fought off warm smiles.

'Hello, Mr McKay. This is my friend, Fin.'

Albert came round the desk and shook Fin's hand. I could see Albert assessing Fin, looking him up and down, pricing his clothes.

'Mr Cohen, it's very nice to meet you.'

Of course he knew who Fin was. It was

Albert's job to know who every potential visitor was. His interest in Fin was deferential which meant that he hadn't researched him and didn't know Fin was penniless.

'What a lovely place,' said Fin politely.

Albert thanked him. 'Shall we go to my house,' he said, but it wasn't a question and he didn't ask me why I was there, which seemed strange.

He lifted his jacket from his chair and led us out and down a corridor to a back door.

Outside, we skirted a windless wall of the castle and cut across a grassy verge to a wide private road that led all the way through the grounds. Giant redwoods lined the driveway. The grass on either side was so green and neat that it looked fake. The grounds were very grand, much more so than the house. The castle was set in the Tidy Wilds, a countryside without the smells or rabbit shit or mud. I liked it. I don't really like the countryside.

I said to Albert, 'It's very quiet, isn't it? I was surprised they let us in through the main house.'

'Mr Ross called to say you were coming up with Mr Cohen and I told them to let you in.'

'I need to ask your advice about something.'

Albert hummed. 'I thought so . . . Wait until we get into the house.'

We took a turn off the main road, down to the left, on to a path that overlooked the glass dome over the swimming pool. We looked down and I nudged Fin so he didn't miss the sight of it.

It was dark inside the round glass dome. It looked like a steampunk spaceship neatly parked on the banks of the lake.

'How is Adam?' asked Albert.

'Not dead.'

Albert shook his head, 'A Lazarean miracle, that boy. Keeps OD'ing and being brought back from the dead. His poor mother.'

'God, what he's put her through!' I said, but we were both smiling. Adam was so likeable that even OD'ing sounded like an amusing foible.

We were some way down the road before I remembered that we had parked back at the castle. 'Should I move my car?'

Albert thought for a moment. 'What kind of car is it?'

'BMW.'

'What year?'

'Last year. It's an X5.'

'Fine, leave it. We're quiet at the moment.'

Hamish's car was fancy enough to be parked in the Skibo guest car park. He would have been pleased.

Albert led us along the road for a short while and then cut across a side lawn. Frosty grass crunched underfoot. Fin looked up and gave a gratifying coo of appreciation.

The cottage had been built as one of the members' luxury lodges but Albert got to live there because there was a problem with the sauna which was somehow never fixed.

The walls were red-stained slatted wood, left rough at the edges, giving the outer walls an organic, undulating texture. A green porch ran all the way around and the porch overhang was supported by green-stained tree-trunk pilasters, the nubs of amputated branches still discernible.

Albert walked up to the porch and stopped at the front door. His hand hesitated on the handle. Fleetingly, I wondered if he had a boyfriend living with him, or a miniature horse for a wife or something, and felt he should introduce the fact before walking us in. But he said nothing and opened the door.

I was hyper-vigilant again. I hadn't had that since I left Skibo. It may have been returning here that brought it all back after all these years. It was very uncomfortable. Everything felt like a potential threat. It was hard to filter noise and sights.

There was no one in there. It was very plain inside, no personal effects or photos anywhere. It looked like a show home but that was Albert's style. Lux-functional.

He shut the door behind us and asked, 'Sherry, anyone?'

I teased him, 'Who drinks sherry?'

'I do.' He smiled. 'Tea then?'

We settled on that and followed him into the kitchen, which I don't think he liked. There was a single meal from the castle kitchen defrosting on the worktop. It had the calorie count written on the cover and I thought this might be what he was embarrassed about.

We sat at the kitchen table.

'So, what did you want to ask me about, Anna?'

'Do you remember a Dutch club member called Lillie Harkän?'

He sang suddenly in a rich baritone: 'Lillie Harkän, sweet Lillie Harkän,' to the tune of 'Lili Marlene'.

I joined in and Fin looked confused.

169

Albert explained, 'Ms Harkän was a rather negative lady — '

I clarified: 'She was a whiny bitch.'

Albert rolled his eyes in an all-too-familiar gesture and told Fin, 'A rather negative and, sadly, unfortunately mannered lady. Rarely was there an interaction with the staff that did not end in acrimony on her behalf. And so, when we returned to staff quarters to find that softer pillow or whatever, we would sing 'Lili Marlene'.'

'Instead of saying what a cow she was.'

'Because that leaves you in a bad mood and unable to deliver service to the next guest.'

'But she was a really grumpy cow. I mean, nothing pleased her — '

Albert swiped me silent with his finger. 'That's enough.'

He wouldn't allow us to say rude things about the guests, even if they were awful. He loved the rich and powerful, he loved the royal family and film stars, he thought they had privilege because they were better than us. He adopted their snobberies and dressed like them. He was the perfect servant, like a functional form of Stockholm syndrome. Adam and I could never have done that. We had no future in service and Albert had spotted that in both of us.

'Anyway. What about Ms Harkän?'

'Well, when I worked here she came with a boyfriend called Leon Parker, do you remember him?'

He flashed me a warning look. When I was young that would have been enough to shut me up. But I was older.

'Do you remember him?'

'Hm. Leon Parker was married subsequently, wasn't he? Not to Ms Harkän.'

'He was.'

'He came to a rather sad end, Mr Parker, I believe?'

'Do you remember him?'

'Only vaguely. I believe we sent him an invitation to revisit shortly after his reported wedding. He didn't respond.'

'He must have been very rich then?' I said, nodding towards Fin.

'Actually, it was his wife we were interested in.' Fin leaned forward. 'Gretchen Teigler?'

'Hm.'

'Did she come?' asked Fin.

'No.' There was a cloud in Albert's mood now; he ground his jaw and snarled a little at Fin. He didn't seem to want to talk to him any more. I knew he had something to tell.

I tipped my head at him. 'Have you met Gretchen Teigler?'

He scowled at me. 'Leave it.'

'You have! What's she like?'

'Very powerful. Leave it, Anna.'

'Sorry, is there a loo down here?' asked Fin.

Albert told him it was upstairs, through the bedroom at the top of the stairs. But I knew there was a toilet just off the kitchen. We watched Fin walk out, heard his feet on the stairs, heard the bathroom lock click shut.

'Albert, do you know Gretchen Teigler?'

'No, but *you* know Gretchen Teigler, don't you?'

'What — '

He held up a hand to silence me and waited until he heard Fin flush. Then he craned towards me, his face suddenly flush, and whispered:

'Aren't you in enough trouble, Sophie Bukaran?'

24

Fin came back downstairs and found us in a completely altered mood. It wasn't jovial. Albert was frowning and I was frozen with shock. Albert told him we'd decided to go for a walk in the grounds to see what had changed since I was last there. He should wait here. Won't be long. He didn't explain why Fin wasn't invited.

It was raining a little and my expensive leather coat wasn't made for hillwalking. Albert lent me a wax jacket from his cupboard.

We walked out, leaving Fin sitting in the kitchen, bewildered and drinking tea, fiddling with his phone. Fin caught my eye and raised an eyebrow encouragingly, thinking I was going to ask searing questions about Leon and the *Dana*. I gave him a stiff smile. I didn't know if I was coming back, or if I would see Fin again and I was sad about that, which was unexpected because he was very annoying.

Outside, the wind had picked up, flurries of rain swept in from the sea. We walked straight uphill in silence, in the dark, as if it was a chore or we were going somewhere specific.

I can't avoid this any more. I have to explain who I am, where I came from, why I ran. A long-held silence is hard to break. You may have to strain to hear. You will have been told this story before but only in one way and not in this way.

But you know, often with uncomfortable stories like this there is a chasm between lip and ear. You might not be able to hear it at all.

25

If I told you their names you'd think you know me. You don't. I'm not going to talk about that night at the hotel in Soho. I will not name the footballers. I will not specify which London club they played for. You can go elsewhere for all of that.

I will not talk about my injuries, internal or otherwise, or about what happened in court, what was said about me or my history or my mum. My mum was a good mum. She did her best. My failings are mine alone. I will not talk about the jury taking under an hour to deliberate on nineteen charges.

At the beginning people begged me to talk. I was offered money. They emailed and phoned and came to my door. *Human interest. Your side of the story. What really happened. You have a responsibility to other girls.*

It wasn't a tactical decision to stop telling my story, it's just that every time I told it everything got much, much worse. I came to think of it as an incantation, a lyric curse I brought down on myself. But when I stopped telling it everyone turned on me, speculating about my motives, about girls 'like me' and what was wrong with us. They said the right to anonymity should be withdrawn in failed rape trials. Then I was named on the Internet.

The flames were fanned by one of those

contrarian columnists. You'd know her name. Her byline back then was '*She says what everyone else is thinking*'.

I wondered: *is* that what everyone else is thinking?

She said that it was consensual. All of it. Even the violence. Some girls like it rough. She said I was envious, that I wanted a footballer boyfriend, money and fame, but that I woke up in that hotel room and realised that they had used me instead of the other way round, and I set out to destroy them. That's when I went to the police. She pointed out how much damage my spite could have done: billions lost in broadcasting rights, bankrupting a financially precarious football club. Thank God for investors like Gretchen Teigler, willing to bail out a beloved UK institution. I could have ruined careers, finished marriages, damaged children. She is still working, that journalist. Still gleefully opining.

Chat shows and the phone-ins were full of discussions about the case for weeks. These girls. These girls, what are they doing, going out, dancing, envying?

Even my supporters didn't really want the truth.

They only wanted the bits that suited their agenda. They were only listening for the crimes of their enemies. I was a jumping-off point for stories they wanted to tell anyway. I was a disappointingly unhelpless victim: my mum was a professor at SOAS. I had an unconditional offer from Balliol. I was very drunk. I still don't think that means they had the right to rape me.

The first time I told the story it was to the police. That was the most memorable time because I heard it back when they played it in court to prove how much of a liar I was.

My lip was swollen and split and I was in shock. I sound like someone else entirely, stuttering, slurring, hesitating over details, changing the colours of suits and carpets.

The police interview took place in a very small grey room with a steel table bolted to the floor. There was me, two women and a camera. One of the women, DS Patricia Hummingsworth, asked the questions. The other one looked bored and sat back in her chair and stared at me.

Patricia tried to be kind at first. I liked her. I told her what happened.

She looked at my split lip. 'Did *they* do that to you?'

I touched it. 'This?'

She nodded, head tilted, sympathetic. 'Yes. That. Did they do that?'

'No, I think I did it before I met them. I fell over on the stairs because I was a bit drunk.'

She blinked and withdrew across the table. When she opened her eyes the warmth was gone. She was never nice to me again. I actually wondered: how did falling over mean consent? She wanted to know how much I drank that night. I tried to remember but, obviously, it turned out later, I'd had a lot more than I thought. This was a big mark against me, as if being drunk in public took away my right to the protection of the law.

Was I from a well-off family?

I remember how jarring that conversational segue was. Was I from a *what?*

She repeated it: was I from a well-off family?

Well, I don't know. My mum had just died, single parent, just died and she didn't have money. We didn't have money. I was out that night because my mum had just died and I was trying to cheer myself up.

Would I say I was feeling reckless that night?

Feeling what? I didn't know what was going on.

The questioning got fuzzy, broken up, it was all about my state of mind and how I felt when I saw those famous men. I don't follow football. They were wearing suits; I thought they were bankers. I asked her: why are you asking about me? What's that got to do with what they did?

Then she asked if I had a boyfriend.

Oh thank God, I thought, she wants someone to come and get me.

No, I said hopefully, I don't have a boyfriend at the moment, but my friend Tasha can come for me. She has a car.

No boyfriend currently, though? Nice-looking girl like you?

I thanked her for the compliment. That's very kind of you but no, I'm not seeing anyone. But Tasha can come and get me. She can drive . . .

Sophie, how did you get that scar on your eye?

This? I fell off a bike when I was a kid. Now, looking back, I know what she was asking me: had I been attacked before? Did I make a habit of being victimised?

She asked if I had gone out looking for a boyfriend last night.

Oh God. I suddenly saw it all from her side. A fall-down drunk, a smashed lip, out on the prowl, saw blokes with money and a car and fame and mothers who are not dead.

It was too late to stop telling. I couldn't lie. I was drunk. My mum had just died. I'm entitled to get upset and drunk without being raped and beaten by four men. But I couldn't take it back, and the next thing I knew, we were in court. And then it was finished. Not guilty. There's a famous photograph of one of the footballers wearing a Prada suit, punching the air outside the Old Bailey.

Afterwards.

Everything snowballed. It was everywhere, on chat shows and social media, and everything was about me, why I lied, when I lied. It was never about them. They didn't lose sponsorship deals or work. Their club gave them full support.

My name was leaked online, then my address. My house was egged. Eggs breaking on window glass sound like shots fired. A girl spat at me in the street. Men gathered in my garden when the pubs closed and sang the club anthem up at my bedroom window and laughed. Mum's car was burned out in the middle of the night. The cops wanted me to move. I didn't want to. I'd lived there with my mum and she was gone. All the things she'd touched were there.

Early one morning I heard screaming in the street outside my house. A woman was pointing at my front door. Someone had nailed a cat to it.

It was a small grey cat, a skinny little kitten, not yet fit to meet the world on its own. The cat had a nail through its head. A trickle of black blood ran down our yellow door. The picture was in the newspaper. That was too much: people care about cats. I was relieved. I thought people would finally see what this was like. They didn't. They said I did it myself, for attention and sympathy. I was a monster.

It's hard to lose faith in people when you're young. You never get over that, not really. I hid. I even hid from my friends.

So, this time was horrible but it did feel as if it would pass. Until the other girl came forward.

I first heard her on the radio at home: reports that a witness had come forward in the rape case. She had been in the hotel suite that night and was giving the police a statement. I didn't remember another girl being there. Would she corroborate my story? If she did would they retry the case? I couldn't live through that again. Or would she call me a liar, was she a stooge from the football club? If she did would they charge me with perjury? Would they jail me? I had no money for bail or lawyers.

Paralysed by indecision but needing to do something, I went into the kitchen to find some food. Eating at all was an achievement most days. I focused hard on this one task: I would fry an egg to make a sandwich. I pulled the pan out and poured in too much oil by mistake. I turned the ring on. I went to the fridge for eggs. I broke one and let it slide into the softly bubbling oil. I watched it. Suddenly my mobile rang and made me jump. It was behind me, on the table. I turned my back to the cooker, picked it up and looked at the screen.

DS Patricia Hummingsworth.

I can still hear the eggs splutter in the pan behind me. My finger hesitating over the answer button, my heart racing.

Hot oil spluttering and the phone in my hand, buzzing terror. That was when I felt a calloused hand close on my throat. I saw his dim reflection in the window: dark hair, narrow face. The man was tall and broad, he lifted me up by my waist and neck just as I hit the answer button on the phone.

Patricia heard it all. She later gave evidence at the inquiry into my disappearance. She heard me gurgling and choking. A strangled scream and a heavy, metallic thud. Then she heard the phone go dead. When they arrived at the abode (cops talk like this), they found signs of a struggle but Sophie Bukaran was missing. Blood everywhere, kitchen in disarray. The findings of that inquiry were that I was presumed dead.

It turned out the other girl had corroborated my statement. That night, she was passed out in another room, forgotten by everyone. She woke up and heard me screaming for help, begging them to stop. She saw everything but didn't come forward immediately. She was ashamed because she heard me screaming and just hid.

As soon as she gave it, someone leaked her statement to very bad people. Minutes after she gave it, they knew that the case would be retried. They knew before Patricia even called to tell me.

They knew billions would be lost, unless I wasn't there to tell that story again. I was nineteen. I was loathed. I had no family. I was disposable. A disposable girl.

What happened in the kitchen that night is blurry because I've never told anyone about it but this is what I recall: my feet leaving the floor, the sensation of choking, my phone falling to the table, the man lifting me by the neck and waist, holding me tight to his body as he swung me away from the phone. My arms flailing, hand closing on the frying-pan handle. He dropped me and reached back into his waistband for a knife. I spun round, swung the pan at him and sprayed his face with hot oil.

Hot oil stuck to his skin. He reeled, staggering with hands over his face. I clubbed his head with the pan, over and over, screaming brute noises. I saw an unfamiliar big knife on the floor and kicked it away.

There is a peculiar, sour kind of intimacy in being attacked. I could have identified his hands from a line-up of a hundred. I knew his smell and the earlobe on his right side. His smell, a blend of cigarettes and stale sandalwood, comes to me still, full, total, and makes me want to run.

He was down but I kept hitting. I kept hitting even though he wasn't moving. There was a lot of blood, very red. I couldn't stop. I kept going until my arms were trembling with exhaustion. I think my mind was back in that hotel room with those men, all the wild panic and terror from then was being taken out on an unconscious, blood-splattered man. I saw some of the burned skin on his jaw slough off revealing the flesh underneath and pity made me stop. He was still breathing at that point. I'm pretty sure he was.

What could I do? I didn't think I could call the police, they'd find a way to blame me for this too. His breathing was shallow, his eyes were swelling, a cut bloomed on the bridge of his nose. Blood pooled behind him on the floor. He lay very still.

Who was he? He wasn't a football fan making a point. He didn't have a football top on or say anything. He was dressed in dark clothes and hadn't shouted threats or anything. He just wanted me to be dead.

I searched his pockets. A photo of me, taken in the street outside my house. Bus tickets. Tesco receipts. A fat envelope, unsealed, full of fifty-quid notes. Ten thousand pounds, I found out later. Inside the envelope I found a business card for Teigler Inc. A phone number was pencilled on the back with 'D.L.' scribbled next to it. I'd heard of Dauphine Loire. I knew who Teigler Inc were.

I glanced down and saw the colour was draining from his face. I thought he was dying. I ran. Up to the bedroom: grabbed pants, passport and a coat. On the way out I kissed my mum's photograph, held it to my heart. I couldn't take it: this was her house, she belonged here. I kissed her again, put it down and ran.

My passport was new. I thought of running to France, but I didn't know who was after me. If it was Dauphine and the Teigler organisation, France would be the worst place to go.

So I pulled up my hood and caught a train to Charing Cross. I walked up to Euston and I caught a sleeper train to Fort William, somewhere I'd never even heard of. I hid in a crappy hotel for weeks, coloured in my distinctive scar with eyebrow pencil, kept my hood up and cut my hair. I spoke little but when I did I affected a genteel Scottish accent. Accents are important signifiers of authenticity and I got good at that one. I became as close to invisible as possible.

I had been hiding out for three weeks when I met Adam Ross in a supermarket. It was so long since I'd spoken to anyone that my voice sounded strange and strained. It didn't matter. Adam was OK with strange. He was shivering and sweating. He was the sickest alive person I'd ever seen. He started talking about crisps or something, I can't remember what he said. It was ten in the morning and he asked me if I had any money and I said I had some and he said would I buy him some drink? Not 'a drink', not 'drinks'. I thought it was a charming regional phrase but soon found out that Adam literally meant 'some drink'. An unspecified amount of anything with alcohol in it. He'd spent all his money on heroin and needed something.

It was a chance to practise my accent. It still wasn't very good but Adam isn't judgemental. We had a great afternoon in that pub. I didn't even drink much. He did.

He said there were jobs going where he worked in the summer, if I wanted one. I was amazed he was employed. The job was live-in, on a private estate with very high security. I said that sounded perfect but I didn't have papers or want to be found. Adam didn't ask why. He just shrugged and said, aye, OK, look; Fort William is full of tourists passing through, leaving coats and rucksacks lying around unattended. He'd get me a new ID if I wanted?

And so I became Anna McLean and I got the job. I stayed a week. Then another week. A month. Eight months in the end. In time I drifted to Glasgow, met Hamish and had the kids. I had a home. For years nothing happened. No one was interested in me.

I loved Hamish. I need to say that. I can't always remember why any more but I recall the feeling and it was real. The money and the stuff, the pay-off for being a rich man's wife, that wasn't why I was with him. I was there despite the money. If you've ever had to run you know that stuff is just stuff. Even rich people can only stand in one room at a time.

When I got pregnant I remade myself again. I'd stopped smoking and swearing and hitting people with trays. Now I became mild. Anna McDonald from Glasgow was on the parents' council, campaigned for a new lamination machine for the school office. I shopped and read a lot. I couldn't go abroad because my passport was in the wrong name so I said I was afraid of flying and we holidayed in Cornwall.

That was the best life of all my lives.

But as the girls grew the strain began to tell. Old Anna was scratching away from the inside. Resentments came back first. Then the aggression and that was hard to hide. Reading and listening to stories in the early morning helped me get my mask on straight.

Estelle Cohen was the first person to see me. Trophy wife to trophy wife, she saw the conflict and layers, that there was more going on. As I came out of the stupor of early motherhood Sophie started coming back. That was who Estelle saw.

Now I have no mask left. I am not Anna McDonald née McLean, soft-spoken younger wife from Somewhere-Outside-of-Aberdeen. I am Sophie Bukaran, the disposable girl, and I am not yet dead.

The disposable girl should develop a drink problem or take drugs. She should become the victim of someone else, somewhere else. At best she becomes a campaigner against whatever she was a victim of. Nothing can happen to her that doesn't refer back to the attack. She has been branded. The event owns her. She can only ever exist in reference to it.

But that's not true because the world is full of us. One in five. We are as perennial as love. We go about our business, raising kids, running countries, starting wars and solving crimes. We don't tell our stories because, if we've survived, that can only mean that what happened wasn't so very bad after all. It never means that we are fucking amazing.

I am fucking amazing.

When I was nineteen I ran so fast I left a branding behind. And I have stories to tell that are more than titillating details or pleas for your pity.

This is just one of them.

26

We walked up a hill overlooking the sea.

'Albert — ?'

'Not yet.' He strode on ahead.

Albert knew who Sophie Bukaran was. He'd heard, somehow, about Gretchen Teigler. I knew that the further we got from the house the worse whatever he had to tell me was. My heart rate slowed to a treacly bump, a familiar numbness crept over me. The body develops a tolerance to adrenaline. At a certain level all that remains is a paralysing ennui.

Heavy-footed, I followed him to a copse of trees on a hillside. He sat down in deep shadow, scanning the horizon. I copied him.

We were looking out over the Firth and the North Sea. The lights of Dornach glinted in the distance and a faint, sour smell of fermented barley wafted over from the Glenmorangie distillery. Far away, a toy town car rolled over the bridge, twin headlights cutting through the dark. There was a time when I was so watchful I could tell the size of a car from the sound of the engine.

Albert reached into his pocket and took out a packet of cigarettes. The brand was Marlboro Lights, a big favourite from twenty years ago. It was a middle-class brand, low tar, and that spoke of an aspiring quitter who had smoked heavily at one time.

'Didn't know you smoked, Albert.'

He took one out for himself and handed me the packet. 'Should try to quit.'

I took one and gave it back. 'I just started again today.'

'How are you finding it?'

'Disgusting. I love it.'

He half smiled as he lit up. His eyes seemed sad but it was dark and his face was hard to read. I could see that his jaw was tight, his lips bloodless.

I asked him, 'How long have you known I was Sophie?'

'Since Leon Parker was here with Harkän.' His voice had dropped. 'He asked me if Gretchen Teigler was a club member. He'd been chasing her for quite some time, I think. He said you knew her name, asked if I had mentioned her to you. It was quite sneaky the way he did it. I said yes, I had, but I hadn't. I did a bit of research after that. Traced you.'

'It was that easy?'

He looked at my scar and touched his eyebrow. 'That's a fairly distinctive mark. The police posters were everywhere. Do you know what happened to her?'

'Gretchen?'

'Not Gretchen.' He cast me a reproachful look. 'The other girl. She hid but they found her. She wasn't as good at it as you. You have quite a talent.'

'Who found her?'

'Who do you think?'

We sat with that for a while. Then Albert said:

188

'She was quite a troubled person. She had a drugs problem. She grew up in a foster family.'

What difference did her background make? Albert meant no harm but he made it sound like a mercy killing. The murderer's difficult background would be relevant, not hers. I was dismayed by Albert parroting that crap at me. But he worked in a luxury resort, he sucked up to rich people all day, he dressed like them, toadied to them, shared their values. He really wasn't the most critical of thinkers. We probably needed to stay off the subject of politics if I was going to keep liking him.

I sat and smoked and talked myself out of saying anything to correct him. The sweat from the hill climb was cooling on my clothes. The wax jacket held it against my skin.

'I'm quite disappointed in Leon for telling you that,' I said, actually talking about Albert, 'I liked him.'

'Did you?'

'Didn't you?'

He shrugged. 'He was my age. As a contemporary I'd judge him a little differently from you.'

'How would you judge him?'

He pressed his lips tight and shrugged. 'On the make. Relying on his charm. A good nose for money, a bit desperate.'

'Desperate, like he was broke?'

'Well, I think he was very wealthy at one time, but not any more.'

'I liked him, at the time I thought he was, you know, a guest but maybe, under other circumstances, he could have been my friend.'

He gave a cynical smile and drew on his cigarette. 'They're not your friend, Anna. Ever, ever, ever. Remember that.' He looked at me for a while. It felt quite final, as if he was looking at me for the last time, and he said very quietly, 'Keep your head down, get away from that bloody Cohen bloke. He's drawing attention.'

'I don't want any trouble.'

'Keep out of sight or you'll get it. Teigler can't afford any complications like you suddenly appearing in public, not right now. Her company has finally taken a controlling stake of the club. They now own two square miles of undeveloped land in central London. Can you even imagine the value of that?'

'They can't sell off a stadium. There'd be a massive public outcry.'

'They won't. They'll manage it badly and be forced to sell it to pay their debts. It'll take a long time. It's all legal, but at a very delicate stage right now. This is the worst time for you to reappear. You need to hide, especially now the feminists are involved.'

'The *what?*'

'The feminists. You're a hashtag — #JusticeForBukaran.'

That explained why I had dropped off Fin's Twitter feed.

'Well,' he continued, 'The feminists are amplifying it all, calling out the people threatening you. They've traced IP addresses and they're naming them. They'll make it impossible for you to keep your head down.'

I wanted to say that rapist footballers and

billionaires and hired hit men were the people who were making things difficult for me, not allies. But he was like an uncle to me, and politics is not always for the kitchen table. I had to say something though, so I said quietly, 'I don't think 'feminists' is a proper noun.'

Albert smiled at that. We smoked our cigarettes. It hurt my throat so I drew it in deep and looked out over the sea. I struggled to remember why I liked Albert. I had felt safe here because of Albert. I remembered his patience when I couldn't find Anna McLean's national insurance number. I was nervous about it, kept my bag packed, ready to run. A month into the job he stopped asking for it and said that HMRC had sent him the number. I was too afraid to ask what happened.

I asked, 'Did you hide me? That thing with the national insurance number . . . '

He smiled, so wide and unguarded that, for the very first time, I saw he had a dimple in his cheek.

'Well, it was nothing,' he said humbly. 'I'm glad you made it. Let's go back down.'

We stood up and brushed ourselves off. Albert kicked the flattened grass to hide the marks we had made. I watched him and wondered why we had come all the way up here for this conversation. He could have whispered all of this while Fin was upstairs. We were here so that no one ever knew Albert had helped me, because there would be consequences for him if they did. He'd protected me and I hadn't even noticed. He had been the friend I thought Leon was.

'Albert.' I put my hand on his forearm. 'Thank you.'

He stopped breathing and tensed as if I had tasered him. It was an electric moment.

What I meant was thank you for giving me this extra time. For my girls. For the moments of peace I have known. For the books I got to read. For my flawed and cowardly Hamish, whom I still love, for Christmases and all this extra life. The years he gifted me felt like a story I told myself as I bled to death on the kitchen floor in my mother's house.

He blinked hard at my hand until I took my hand away.

We tramped downhill, hard on the knees as descents often are, heading back to the cottage. A lone rabbit darted across a dark field. It was lovely to be back in the hills, under a big grey moonless sky. Air to breathe. Abrupt freedom in an ancient, half-forgotten land full of lies and people who don't belong.

As we walked back down I thought more about the national insurance number. Something bothered me. The chronology was wrong. Albert got the number a month after I arrived here but Leon didn't come until seven months later. Had Albert always known who I was? Did he recognise me when I turned up for the interview? Why not say so now then? I looked at the back of his head and decided not to ask. The intimacy of my saying thank you was awkward enough.

We followed a line of trees, skirting the drive, making our way back round to the kitchen door.

The cottage glowed, warm and inviting.

My toe was dipping into the pool of light around the cottage when Albert stopped me dead with a raised hand.

We could see through the French windows into the kitchen.

Fin was sitting at the table, clutching the arms of the chair, looking up, looking scared.

In front of him stood a brawny man in dark clothing. He was holding a hunting knife to Fin's face.

27

We snuck up to the house, keeping to the shadows.

Fin was speaking. The man was speaking but his voice was so low I couldn't hear what he was saying. Fin's voice was uncharacteristically high.

'No! No, what?' said Fin, 'I came here with a friend to see someone. No, I didn't know why, I didn't even know where this is, not really. No! I don't have a gun! Why would I have a gun? This is my phone!' He held it up to show the man. 'What are you doing with that big fucking knife?'

Flush to the wall, still in the dark, Albert reached for the door handle. I expected him to kick his way through the door but he didn't. He just opened the door, not even terribly quickly, stepped into the kitchen and shouted, 'YOU!'

The man swung round to face us. He was nothing to do with the castle. Skibo security men dress as ghillies, in discreet off-the-peg outdoorsy gear. Tweed coats and green trousers. This man was dressed in nondescript black clothing, like the man in my kitchen all those years ago. Dull, dreary clothes that no one would remember seeing, jacket and trousers that evoked no associations or comment.

He looked at me, dead-eyed. 'Sophie Bukaran.'

From the corner of my eye I saw him slide the knife into a leather sheath on his waistband. It caught the overhead light and flashed. Fin was very close. He was staring wildly at it.

''*Sophie Buchanan*'?' Fin stood up. 'What in the fuck is actually going *on* right now?'

The man lifted his hand almost languorously and jab-punched Fin on the solar plexus. Fin gasped and dropped back into his chair like a kitten swatted off a lap.

I ran across the room — 'Don't you fucking touch him!' — and reached over to shove the man away but he smirked and grabbed my elbow joint, pinching pressure points until I was seeing white flashes. My knees buckled.

He reached back for his knife.

'NOT IN HERE, PLEASE.' Albert spoke loud and slow.

The grip loosened on my elbow. The man looked at Fin wheezing and holding his chest, looked around the room, and saw how consequential that might be. He gave Albert a small bow and Albert nodded towards the front door, walked past and the man followed, tightening his grip on me, taking me with him.

We filed out of the kitchen. Fin stood up but I glared at him to sit back down and stay. The man saw my warning and hesitated.

'What's the point?' I said. 'Look at him. He's half dead anyway.'

He might have trouble managing both of us even with Fin looking so weedy. The space between his thighs was big enough to accommodate another thigh. The man huffed a laugh and tightened his grip on my arm, yanking me out of the cottage and down the steps, hurrying to

195

catch up with Albert.

We headed into the shrubs, following a path between old hedges. Albert was in front of us. He didn't glance back. It was a strange walk, not long but tense. Each passing second I expected Albert to lead us across a trip wire, turn and shoot, turn and karate-chop, like an old-fashioned hero. But with every step Albert did nothing. Time slowed down.

I was ignoring the obvious. Why did Albert's hand hesitate on the door handle on the way into his house? When did he realise I was Sophie? Why did he make me go up the hill?

We were passing a line of dark trees when Albert looked back. I thought he was signalling to me. He wasn't. Albert and the man locked eyes. Too long. An understanding. They had a plan.

Albert had taken me out walking to give the man time to get into the house.

He knew I was Sophie Bukaran all along. Albert was never with me. He hadn't given me a job and good references, he'd been holding me and keeping track. I was a bargaining chip and he was cashing me in while my value was high.

'Albert?' I pleaded. 'He's going to kill me.'

He couldn't meet my eye.

I shouted at him, 'You soulless fucking lickspittle. He's going to fucking kill me.'

The nape of Albert's neck blushed and he hurried on ahead.

We walked into the staff car park. Albert raised his hand, pressed a fob. A car winked through the dark and we walked over to it. The hand tightened on my arm.

Refusing to look at me, Albert opened the back door of the car and stepped away. The man cupped the top of my head and pushed down, shoving me into the back seat roughly. I landed on my side. He lifted my feet and pushed them in. He stepped back and raised a hand to slam the door.

Then, out of nowhere, a hill fell on us.

28

The door was gone. The men were gone. The night was still. I scrambled upright and saw the car door skidding, free-style, across the ground. It came to a stop. I heard a groan. A body was on the ground thirty feet away, moving in the dark. Twin red lights blinked and reverse lights came on.

It was Hamish's car. The lights had been off and the engine was so quiet that I'd had no warning of it coming towards them at fifty until it ploughed into us and ripped the door clean off.

It backed up wildly, spraying gravel in a wide arc, and pulled up next to me. The front passenger door flew open. Fin Cohen was in the driving seat. I leapt out of the back seat and clambered in.

Fin drove off at high speed before I'd shut the door. I slammed it and held tight to the seat as car alarms — seat belt undone, door open — all blared in the cabin.

In the side mirror I saw Albert get up and stagger, head in hands, and the knife man roll over on the ground, clutching his arm.

Fin drove up and over the little hill heading for the main gate. The barrier was down. It was a heavy metal barrier, an anti-terrorist measure — I remembered it going in. We'd never get through it. But Fin took a sharp left, crashed through the wooden fencing around the paddock, drove across rough grassy ground for a hundred yards and then crashed through another part of the fence, completely skirting the metal post, made it out on to the road.

He took a skidding right-hand turn, scraping in front of a heavy goods lorry before flicking the lights on.

We sped away from the lorry's indignant horn, heading for the bridge over the Firth of Dornoch and the south.

Aware that the airbag folded on the dashboard was on my side now, I fumbled my seat belt on.

Fin was wild-eyed. 'Phone the police.'

'No. No police.'

'I just ran over two men, Anna. We have to call the police.'

I grabbed his elbow. 'Please, Fin, please, no police.'

'Why did he call you by Adam Ross's girlfriend's name?'

'I don't know.'

'Did you and Adam rob that place?'

He was miles out.

'For money for heroin?' he said, drifting further still from the truth.

'Yes,' I said too quickly for it to be a credible lie. I should have hesitated. 'Yes, we did.'

He didn't believe me but kept driving, bent tight over the steering wheel, alert to the rear view, watching the road, keeping the kerbs in his eyeline. We reached a stretch of the A9 that was long and straight. If they were following they couldn't fail to find us.

'We can hide in here for a bit,' I said. 'Pull in left.'

The Glenmorangie distillery did a good tour. I'd been there several times even though I don't like whisky much. But I knew a spot around the back we could hide in. We pulled down the steep turn with the lights off and parked. I said I thought we should wait, let them pass.

We sat in silence for a moment.

'So,' said Fin, eyebrows high, 'I don't believe that about Adam.'

'Why?'

'You're not an addict.'

'You don't know that — '

'I don't like you enough for you to be heroin addict. You're not the type. But I take it you left that job under something of a cloud?'

'You're a good driver,' I said, weakly trying to change the subject. 'Have you got any tobacco left?'

He fumbled the tobacco pouch out of his pocket, handing it to me, tugging it back as a bargaining chip. 'So. Who is Sophie Buchanan?'

He'd misheard the name. He wouldn't be able to google me.

'Just a name I used at one point.'

He stared incredulously, as if he was seeing me for the first time. 'Are you a thief?'

'No.'

'An industrial spy or something like that?'

That sounded like a good lie to go with but I was in shock and wouldn't be able to spin it convincingly. 'It's about . . . ' I didn't know what to say. 'Things that happened a long time ago.'

'Anna, he had a bloody big knife. And, as you are no doubt aware, I am knife-to-the-face phobic.'

He was being very formal, I think because he was so scared.

'I didn't know that was going to happen.'

'We should call the police.' He reached for his phone and I grabbed his hand.

'We really *shouldn't* call the police.'

His eyes raced across my face. 'I haven't the faintest fucking idea what you're getting at. Was Knife-man the police?'

'No. The cops are good guys but — ' I saw my leather coat lying in the back seat. Fin must have found the car keys in the pocket back at Albert's cottage and run to the guest car park. He had pulled out on to the drive. He could have left and kept himself safe but he didn't. He doubled back and came for me. 'Why didn't you just drive away?'

'Haven't got any money for petrol.'

'Oh.'

'I considered it. I knew I'd feel really guilty.' He was honest. I admired that. 'We're not really here because you think Leon is innocent, are we?'

I sighed. 'It's a bit more complicated, yes.'

'Tell me a short version.'

I struggled to find a starting point. 'Well, I'm not really from Aberdeen.'

'Right.'

'I'm from London.'

'Mm-hm. D'you know that guy with the knife?'

'No.'

'He's not your ex?'

'Never met him before. Someone's sent him to get me. To kill me.'

'There's a 'contract' out on you?' He smirked. 'What the fuck? You're a housewife!' I hesitated too long and he said, 'OK. If you decide to stop lying and tell me what the fuck is really going on, I'd really appreciate it, but will *they* call the police?'

I smiled. 'No.'

'McLean, Buchanan, McDonald. I will find out who you are, you know.'

I laughed. 'No way. You'll starve first.'

'Don't hold your breath. Estelle's been waiting for that for years.' He looked at the dark drive out to the road. 'Let's chance it.' He put the lights on and restarted the engine.

He took my goading in good part but I instantly regretted it. I tried to go back and temper it. 'You don't have to starve.'

His smile was strained. 'It's not a lifestyle choice.'

'People overcome addictions, you know.'

'Oh, do they?' He said flatly. 'Interesting. Well done, them.' I think he'd had that conversation quite often. Possibly with many different people.

He pulled up the steep drive to the road and nudged cautiously forwards, looking left and right for the telltale glare of lights on the horizon. He pulled out carefully and gathered speed on the road. Fin resisted talking about himself. With a sudden pang I realised I was missing Hamish, who talked about himself all the time.

'You will proper hurt yourself if you don't eat more.'

'Yeah,' said Fin, frowning and watching the rear-view, 'Fucking thanks for that. That's really helpful.'

The road was empty.

'But you will.'

'Who is Sophie Buchanan?'

'You will damage yourself permanently.'

'What's your real name?'

We had reached a companionable deadlock and drove in silence. For a brief moment the North Sea opened up on the left. Lights from a row of oil platforms glinted in the dark like misplaced Christmas trees.

Albert told me to get rid of Fin and keep hiding. It would suit him and Teigler if I did. I thought about the other girl, my shadow-self, the me-shaped vacuum at my side. She hid and she died. It wasn't safe to keep hiding but the habit was so dear to me. I wasn't ready to give it up.

I thought of Leon marrying Gretchen Teigler. Was that so bad? Maybe he didn't know about her. But I listened to my thought process and noticed that I was desperate for Leon to be a good man and he clearly wasn't. Everyone knew what Gretchen was like. When I thought back, at the way he told his tales, looking away, stealing cigarettes from someone working a chamber-maid's job, he wasn't sharing stories with me. He was practising for another audience. God, I was awful at choosing friends.

We drove quietly down the dark road as I considered all of this.

'So, Anna-Sophie, how far from those men is far enough?'

'Very.'

'I don't suppose you brought your passport with you?'

'I did, actually.'

'OK.'

It took a while for me to realise we were heading to Inverness airport. I couldn't fly. My passport was a dead person's and would set off alarms at every Border Agency desk in the country.

But that crisis was an hour away so I sat back and enjoyed the drive.

29

The airport was small. The calm sea was on our left, an empty car park in front of us, the bright airport building on our right. A runway ran between the back of the terminal and the fast road to Nairn. Through the glass walls of the building we could see a steward sitting at a desk, puffy-faced and caked in make-up, getting through her early shift.

We went in.

She said there were no international flights until the next day but we could get to London and connect from there?

We stepped aside for a chat and Fin said we could hide out at his friend's castle in France, near Clermont-Ferrand. Maybe we could go there via the Île de Re? We could retrace the Parkers' movement in the town, go and see the Airbnb man and ask him about seeing Violetta about the person he saw on deck that night? I said yeah, that'd be great, I'd love to do that. I was agreeing to everything because I wasn't going. I was going to run.

I bought us two cheap tickets on the first flight out. I didn't need to use my passport because the flight was domestic, leaving for Gatwick at 6.20 a.m. It was four in the morning. We had over two hours to wait.

We sat on seats and I nodded along as Fin messaged Trina Keany to ask if we could quiz her about Leon's financial situation. Maybe we could buy her a coffee? He signed it 'Fin Cohen'. The currency of celebrity. Most of us would just ask the question. But I agreed to all of this and more because I had no intention of getting on the plane.

Fin was tired. He wanted to go through security and hang about by the departures gate, drinking machine coffee and dozing on the chairs. The airport was very small. Once I was through security I'd be trapped. I said I needed a bit of time alone and I'd go and move Hamish's car to the long stay car park. He was suspicious of that and insisted on giving me his phone number and made me call him so that he had mine.

'So, was it a Van Gogh?'

'What?'

'Did you steal a Van Gogh from them?'

'Yes.'

'Hm. Worth it then.' He sighed and stood up slowly. 'I need to lie down or I'll fall down.'

I stood up with him. 'I'll move the car to somewhere less obvious.'

He said, 'I don't know if you've flown with this company before but you *have* to get here thirty minutes before the flight time or they won't let you on.'

I nodded.

'Seriously. I've been refused at security while the plane was sitting at the gate.'

'OK.'

I watched him go through to departures. A lone security guard waited patiently, shifting from foot to foot. I could see past the conveyor belt, through the frame of the metal detector, to rows of seats and glass windows overlooking the small runway. Fin walked over, handed his ID to the security guard, emptied his pockets, took off his shoes and shed his jacket into a basin. He gave me a tiny wave and went through.

He was a nice man really.

I went back to the car.

A gale was whistling far off in the North Sea, lifting white horses near the shore. I pulled my coat closed and stood to look, opening my face to the wind.

Out there, hundreds of miles away, my girls were safely tucked up in little beds, lashes resting on fondant skin, soft hair sliding off pillow cliffs. When the sun came up they would choose a cereal and drink milk and go swimming. My children were safe. It was all that mattered to me.

I would run, draw whoever came next away from them. Maybe the other girl had kids. Maybe she thought of them when the men came for her. Maybe her last thought was about her kids and maybe she felt grateful that they were safe.

The bonnet of Hamish's car was buckled where it had smashed the door off the other car. I ran my fingers along the gash at the side and got back in.

I started the engine, leaving the lights off and reversed through the empty car park until I reached a drop-off point. Fin might come out to look for me. If I left now and he found me gone he might call the cops. I wanted him safe. I decided to wait until his plane took off. If he came out I'd find some other method of getting away from him.

I put the radio on to a soul station and listened for a while, trying to revive my comforting thoughts about the girls. I couldn't quite get it back. I knew other men would come for me because I had reappeared and they'd keep coming for me until they made me go away forever. It was about money, unless Albert had been lying about the stadium sell-off, but I didn't think he was. He didn't think it mattered what he told me, expected me to be dead by now. It felt too boring and specific to be a lie but I googled the football club. They were indeed renovating their stadium. A statement from the board of directors said they were looking forward to reopening in three years' time.

I first noticed the headlights in the corner of my eye: a car coming off the main road, taking the airport turn too fast. Judging from the wide axle and high roof, it was a Jeep.

I got out of Hamish's car and shut the door, crouched down and backed off between two nearby parked cars. I watched.

The Jeep cut across the empty car park and stopped near the main entrance. A figure in black got out and jogged into the terminal. As he walked along the bright inside concourse I saw it was the man with the knife. His left jaw was red and swollen. He looked very angry.

The security guard at departures took his phone and scanned an e-ticket, checked a credit card for ID and ordered him to take his shoes off and put them in a basin on the conveyor belt. It took him an age to get them off. Lace-up combat boots.

I rang Fin and whispered, 'Hide. Knife-man's coming in.'

He hung up.

I waited, watching the Jeep from the side of the cars. It moved to the nearest disabled parking space and waited, engine running. In the light from the terminal I could see Albert was driving. He looked my way and sat up suddenly. He peered. He had spotted Hamish's car.

Suddenly a light went on inside the Jeep and Albert reached down to pick up a phone. He was taking a call.

Now very bright headlights were approaching and a bus glided in from the main road. It did a full circuit of the airport car-park one-way system before coming to rest right in front of the entrance. Albert was still on his call but watched the bus carefully.

A few passengers tumbled off and disappeared into the side door of the terminal. Workers. There was no one waiting to get on but the bus idled, engine rumbling.

Albert hung up. He looked at Hamish's car again. He looked at the bus.

A slow-moving luggage cart trundled around the pavement side of the building, parking parallel to the bus. The cart driver climbed out, walked up to the bus door and waved hello to the driver. The bus driver waved back, pressed a button and the side of the bus opened to a cavernous boot. The cart driver walked back and started loading the big boxes into it.

Albert watched, bending forward in his seat, frustrated that he couldn't see. Then he got out, leaving the Jeep door open, and hurried around the bus to see. But the cart driver had finished loading and slapped the chassis of the bus twice, signalling to the driver who pressed a button to shut the boot. The panel closed over just as Albert arrived round the side. He hurried back to the Jeep.

Our plane was taking off in thirty-three minutes. I wanted to call Fin again, check he was safe, but he might be hiding and his phone might not be on silent and I might give him away.

The bus drew out, coming straight towards me, lights brushing the top of my head. I lay on my stomach and rolled underneath one of the cars. When the bus passed I raised my head and saw a second set of lights: the Jeep was following the bus away from the airport terminal. They thought we were in that boot.

As they passed I saw that Albert wasn't alone. Knife-man was in the passenger seat.

I waited until the lights were past me, until they hit the roundabout, and then I rang Fin again.

'I'm hiding in the ladies' toilet,' he whispered. 'Where are you?'

I ran to the terminal.

The security man glanced at my ID and waved me through. I arrived with dramatic speed into a small grey departures hall of sleepy passengers. I found Fin was standing between two drinks machines, looking flustered. 'Have they gone?'

'Think we're in the boot of the bus. Chasing it back to Inverness.'

Just then a hi-vis-vested man at the desk called the flight through the tannoy. The room wasn't big enough to warrant a tannoy, he could just have said it.

We queued, showed our tickets and were directed out to a propeller plane on the tarmac. It was small, a puddle hopper, just three seats across inside.

We sat next to each other. I was shaking, felt sick, so wired I could have ripped all the chairs out of their brackets without breaking sweat. It was incredibly hard to sit still.

Fin took out his phone, checking his Twitter account. Pretcha's photo was up to seventy thousand likes but no one was talking about me any more.

I took out my own phone, carefully keeping the face pointed away from Fin, and searched #JusticeForBukaran. I was surprised and incredibly touched. There were threats and insults but other people were challenging them, saying nice things about me, that I had courage, that I was young, that I had been lied about. Really, some of them were too nice and talked about me as if I were a sainted martyr. People were overtly mentioning Gretchen Teigler, saying disparaging things, linking over and over to articles about a cop called Patricia Hummingsworth. Patricia had been jailed six years ago for taking bribes from Gretchen's PA Dauphine Loire. Loire fought the case and was found not guilty. I shut the article and turned off my phone.

I glanced at Fin's. He wasn't just looking at comments below Pretcha's picture, there was a fresh post from Fin, uploaded fifteen minutes ago. It was an audio file. The likes and retweets on it were rolling up in the thousands as we watched. He smiled at it, terribly pleased. 'I recorded it in departures, before that man turned up.'

'Is it a song?'

'No.' He put his phone on airplane mode. 'It's a rough podcast about Leon Parker. Eight minutes? Not much more than that. Easy, just a voice recording about Skibo and some screen-shot images but it's already doing really well.' He showed me the tweet. It had seven thousand likes already and the count was rolling up all the time.

The stewardess was standing over us, smiling and looking at Fin's phone. 'Have you put that off, sir?'

He pressed the button and the phone went blank. 'Off,' he said, smiling back.

'Thank you.' She walked back up to the front of the plane, sat in a flip-down chair facing us and did up her seat belt.

'Fin? What have you done?'

He shrugged innocently. 'I just said that Leon didn't kill himself. That someone else was on board and took the photo . . . ' His voice trailed away as he read my expression.

'Fin, if there was someone else on that boat then they've murdered *three* people. You just broadcast the fact that we know.'

The propellers started as the plane taxied to

the runway. It was deafening.

'I THOUGHT IT MIGHT BE FUN.'

'DID YOU?'

'A BIT FUN . . . '

The nose of the plane tipped sharply up, the tone of the propellers rose to a shriek and I shouted as loud as I could:

'YOU'RE A VACUOUS IDIOT!'

30

My heart was still racing as we landed, a heady mix of indignation and exhaustion.

Gatwick was bland and enormous. We traipsed down blank corridors, up dreary escalators, through white doors. I was wildly alert to every man in dark clothes, every shady corner, every fresh jolt of the luggage conveyor belts.

Through arrivals, we found ourselves in a row of cafes and shops. Fin led us into an open-sided Starbucks. He went up to order, taking his place at the end of a glacial queue, leaving me to listen to his podcast.

It was shit.

The sound quality was awful, the air con whirred in the background, you could hear people buying cans from the drinks machine and the toilet doors slapping shut. It lasted for eight minutes. His voice was soft and conversational. He said he was going through some 'tough stuff' and had gone off on an adventure with Anna McDonald, his 'friend', which made me sound like a girlfriend he didn't want to admit to. He told the story briefly and then he said we were investigating the *Dana* sinking, following on from the *Death and the Dana* podcast, that we didn't believe Leon had killed himself or his kids. He brought up the thing about the photo — who took it? We thought there was a fourth person on board that night and that we were planning to find out who, to solve one of 'life's li'le mysteries'.

He rounded it off with, '*So, until next time, mystery fans.*'

He came back with two coffees and a muffin. I pulled the earbuds out and dropped them on the table. He sat down, opened the muffin and tore it in half, eating a mouthful. He nodded at his phone.

'What do you think?'

''*Life's li'le mysteries*'? It's a triple fucking murder.'

By now the tweet had thirty thousand likes, the count was escalating ridiculously fast.

He took another bite of his muffin. 'Trina Keany said she'll meet us this morning — '

'Shut. The. Fuck. Up.'

He ate the whole muffin himself. I didn't want any. It was vegan and tasted of despair anyway. I sipped my coffee. My head hurt. I didn't know whether to slap him or just get up and walk away.

Beyond the open Starbucks, flocks of passengers floated past. Families came out of baggage reclaim with enormous wheeled bags, cranky and tired from long-haul flights. Business people scurried by with briefcases.

I went back to my girls for comfort. My girls, on holiday. Waking up, tumbling from beds I had never seen. Whispering to each other about what was going on with their dad, worried about me. Sneaking up and putting on the television before breakfast, as if it was a Saturday. My girls —

'I find you an incredibly angry person, Anna.'

'Shut your anorexic fucking nuts, Findlay.'

'Oh. I stand corrected.'

I slapped his phone. 'What are you doing, advertising yourself on there?'

'I'm making a little amusing thing for people. A distraction from the misery of existence.'

'About my dead friend?' That wasn't my real objection, but I was pissed off and very much wanted to win the argument.

It stunned him quiet for moment before he parried, 'You started it. You made me listen to a story about his death.'

He had me there.

'Look,' he said, 'I'm not being malicious. I'm just trying to bring a little joy to the world. People on Twitter are claiming that I'm dying — what does that say to other people with anorexia? I'm not dying. I'm living and being interested in the world. It matters because people are looking at me. I'm coping with a very difficult situation. Soon the word'll be out that my wife's left me, that she's having a baby with some rich old lawyer. It's humiliating but *I'm* coping with that. I want them to have something else to say about me, even if it's that I ran over your old boss and, by the way, I still don't know what that was about — '

'What?'

'Why I had to run over two men to get you — '

'No. Back more.'

'My wife's left me?' I saw him slowly realise that I didn't know. 'Having a baby . . . ' His voice trailed off.

My hand was still on his phone. He reached forward and put his bony hand over mine. 'They didn't tell you. Oh, Anna.'

A baby. No. They didn't tell me.

We sat there for quite a long time.

Fin finished his coffee. Mine went cold. I went cold.

After ten minutes or so he stood me up and walked and then we took a lift down. He bought tickets and we got on a train. The train set off.

The carriage wasn't busy but someone recognised Fin — I saw her do a double take and look away. She tried to take a photo of him on her phone, smirking as she held it up for the shot, pretending to read something. It was so obvious and she was smug and mean about it, it made me feel even worse.

When she got off I whispered, 'Couldn't the baby be yours?'

Fin didn't answer for a long time. His breathing was irregular. I felt he was only just holding it together and didn't want to press it. We passed through two stations before he spoke. 'You don't understand.'

I did a bit, but I could see it wasn't volitional. Did starvation do something to his sperm count or make him impotent? There was no way of asking that wasn't insulting.

A baby.

They would stay together. They would form a new family. Estelle was great, Hamish was lucky, the girls would be delighted with a baby, but Fin and I, we were finished. We were extras in our own lives, marginal asides to the people we loved the most. I felt as if I was sliding off the side of the world. I started crying. Fin took my hand and held it until I stopped.

Then we held hands as we sat on the rickety train, rolling into a grey November London. It wasn't romantic. It wasn't sexual. We held hands like Hansel and Gretel on their first night in the forest. We were both sad and I think we were both grateful that someone else was there, someone kind.

31

I wasn't planning to meet Trina Keany. I just didn't want to be alone. Somehow though, her resistance to us made me feel a burning loyalty to Fin and our ridiculous project. Or maybe I was just playing a part and got very into it.

I was ambivalent when we turned up, is the point. By the end of it I'd have walked through a wall for our right to broadcast his next ramble. That was why I went into the travel agent's afterwards and bought two flights to La Rochelle.

We were walking up a busy side street off Oxford Circus when we saw Trina sitting outside a cafe. She was alone at a little metal table, reading something on her phone. It was narrow and noisy and the pavement was littered with bins and trestle blackboards. It wasn't a street anyone would choose to sit out in but there was no ashtray on the table and she wasn't smoking.

Trina was young and slim, chocolate-coloured skin with a lot of freckles. Her hair was black, worn in dry twist-outs, frizzy at the ends. A blue lanyard hung around her neck under her grey suit jacket. Even from quite far away, she seemed agitated.

She looked up, spotted us walking towards her and her eyes brightened for a second at the sight of Fin. She obviously recognised him, but then her face snapped shut, her lips tightened and she got her defences up. I didn't think the meeting was going to go very well. It was fair enough. Fin had put out a podcast contradicting her, and he did it without contacting her about it first. It occurred to me that, for all his formality and old-world charm, Fin could be mercenary.

We all introduced ourselves, shook hands and pulled up chairs. Her lanyard was for the BBC building round the corner.

Fin apologised for negative reactions she had received to his podcast response. She shook her head and chewed her cheek.

'Doesn't matter,' she said, though it clearly did. 'People are downloading us to find out what it is you're contradicting. You've bumped us up the charts.'

The familiar timbre of her voice, her intonation, it took me back to the kitchen before everyone got up, to the bathroom with Hamish banging on the door, to the desperate drive up the lochside. I couldn't stop looking at her lips, wishing she would speak again.

Fin said, 'So you work at the BBC?'

She nodded. 'Admin. Not making anything.'

'But you want to be a broadcaster?'

She frowned. 'Look, dispensing with formalities: you can tell the bitch that I won't take it down.'

'What?'

'I am surprised it's you, honestly, because I've always liked your music.'

Just then the waiter came out and interrupted us. We ordered tea. Trina waited sullenly, glaring at the table and at me. She was very blunt and angry. I won't lie: I liked her a lot. The waiter went back inside and she said, 'Is she paying you? Or are you celebri-friends? Is that how it works?'

'Who are you talking about?' said Fin. 'Gretchen Teigler?'

'Not that one.' Trina said. '*She* got you to make it, didn't she?'

The growl of a bin lorry engine in the next street reverberated on the windows of the buildings around us.

'Sorry,' said Fin, shouting over the traffic. '*Who* are we talking about?'

Trina clicked her tongue and sneered, 'OK, then.'

The tea arrived on a tray and we all sat and watched the waiter put it down, spill the milk on the brushed-metal table, clean the table, take the money, feel in his pocket for change. During all of this Trina Keany was agitated, juddered her leg under the table, her eyes darting as she mentally rehearsed the next bit of the argument.

The waiter left and Fin tried again. 'Trina, sorry, what do you think is going on?'

'Ha!'

'Why did you agree to meet us?'

She thought about it for a moment. 'Why did you want to meet me?'

I explained that we wanted to ask her about some things in the case, that we had unanswered questions, but she was making faces all the way through, expressions that related in no way to what I was saying, and I just sort of petered out and gave up.

Fin took over again. 'For example: what

221

happened to the necklace?'

She narrowed her eyes. 'You know perfectly fucking well.'

'NO, WE DON'T KNOW.' This was me shouting in exasperation, but the street was so noisy I don't think I sounded particularly angry, just very clear.

'Gretchen Teigler was sent the necklace IN THE POST.'

We were both shouting now and it wasn't for the purposes of clear diction.

We were all lost in the conversation but Fin was lost. 'Gretchen Teigler? It *is* her now?'

Trina turned to him. 'AS IF YOU DON'T FUCKING KNOW.'

He held his hands up. 'OK. Everyone needs to calm down.'

'So,' I said, 'you think Teigler sent us?'

Trina sat back. 'Are you going to say she didn't?'

'Trina, look.' I held my fringe up, showing her my eyebrow. At first she was confused but then she looked at me closely, examining my scar.

We locked eyes.

She looked away and mouthed a curse. She turned back slowly to me and said quietly, 'I'd like to talk to you about that.'

I muttered, 'I don't talk about that.'

'Everyone thought you were dead. Where have you been all this time?'

'Hiding.'

'The other girl — was she with you?'

I shook my head. 'We never met.'

She hissed at me: '*It's Teigler again.*'

222

'I know,' I said. 'I couldn't believe what I was hearing you say on the podcast. I couldn't believe you had the guts to call her out.'

'I didn't know I was calling her out. I've never heard of her before.'

I might never get to speak to her again so I just blurted it out: 'Trina, no one tells the truth about her. No one stands up to her. I can't tell you what it meant to me yesterday.'

She was suspicious of that. 'So what?'

'So, thank you. Also, you have a lovely voice. Nice tone.'

She nodded at the pavement. 'Well. That's nice but I didn't know not to say those things. But thanks.'

Fin wasn't following this conversation and he was straining to hear us over the noisy traffic. He suggested we go for a walk. Trina said OK, she had forty minutes left of her lunch. We walked east to a quieter street and kept going.

Fin said to Trina: 'We got interested in the story because my friend, Anna, was listening to your podcast and knew someone you mentioned in it.'

'Your friend 'Anna' knew someone?' She smiled from one to the other. I shook my head softly and she realised that Fin wasn't being facetious, that he didn't know.

'Anna was friends with Leon.'

I nodded. 'I knew Leon nine years ago, way before he married Gretchen. He was going out with a Dutch woman. I worked in a hotel that they stayed in. I don't think he did it. I'm sure he didn't kill himself.'

'*Nine* years ago you didn't think he would kill himself? That's wishful. It's an impulse not a fixed character trait.'

I suddenly knew she was right. It was a passing impulse. It was a circumstance. I'd never thought of it like that. I was so relieved at that possibility: I hadn't inherited my fate. I didn't need to pass it on to my girls. None of it was inevitable.

Trina whispered, 'You think I was wrong?'

'I think Leon had come close but didn't do it. He's been in worse situations and didn't do it. I think there was someone else on board the *Dana* that night.'

'No, I mean, was I wrong to arrive at a conclusion? Usually true crime podcasts finish up by saying 'we may never know'. It's such a cop-out. That's what I thought. That's why I was definitive and said it was him. Now I'm more convinced than ever that she covered it up.'

'Weren't you frightened of a backlash?'

She sighed. 'Honestly, I had no idea about Gretchen Teigler. I mean, I knew she was rich, she came from a strange background, but who could know she'd be like that? I didn't even blame her in the podcast, I just said that her power could have distorted what the police did. It's not that controversial. I'm fucking terrified of her now though.'

'I'm sick of being terrified of her.'

We were in a broad street with a lot of speed bumps, trees, a softer soundscape. Ahead of us Fin stopped and turned to an open gate, waving us to him. We followed him into the forecourt of

224

the British Museum.

Up the stairs and through the door, we stopped at the desk and the security guard checked our bags. We walked through a metal detector, emerging into the strange, grey twilight in the glass-covered courtyard. We wandered westward and sat on a bench, Fin and I on either side, Trina Keany in the middle.

We were looking at the back of the Rosetta Stone set upright in a glass case. The tourists were gathered on the other side of the glass, looking towards us but not seeing us.

'It's Teigler,' she told Fin. 'She contacted me about the podcast.'

'Gretchen Teigler threatened you?'

'Not directly. She sent someone. They ordered me to take the podcast down. 'Upsetting to the family,' she said. 'Unethical disregard for her feelings.' All that stuff. She chose that cafe where we just met because it's so noisy.'

'So that you couldn't tape her?'

'Exactly.'

'And you chose it so we couldn't secretly tape you?'

She gave an apologetic shrug. 'I didn't know who you were or who you were working for. She was very threatening. She offered me money to take it down. I refused and she threatened to get me kicked off the network. Then they went to see the owner and he told them to fuck off and then they tried to buy the network off him for forty grand. He's from a rich family, thank God, didn't need the cash. I'd have caved. Anyway, the podcast is the number-three download today because you said it was a bucket of crap. The more prominent it is the safer I'll feel.'

'I didn't say it was a bucket of crap.'

'You kind of did.'

'We loved it. We just disagreed with your conclusion. Forty grand doesn't seem like much.'

'Really? I think it's a lot. Podcasts don't make money.'

'But you're sponsored.'

'Barely covers studio time. We don't get paid. Patreon is a big waste of time unless you've got profile.'

'You're making them for free?'

'Yeah. I don't mind, I love doing it. You don't have to convince a committee of bored execs while your enthusiasm wains. You can just make it and put it out and people can listen or not. It will change but that's what it's like right now.'

'I love that,' nodded Fin, smiling warmly, 'like the start of rock and roll.'

'Someone'll find a way to make them pay and it'll be professionalised, but we're not yet and we're very vulnerable. We don't really have editors or corporate structures to check what we're saying or warn us. Teigler is a nasty nut job but if no one is allowed to say it publicly, how the hell am I supposed to know? You try not to slander or insult but you can't get it wrong by accident with scary rich bastards and just apologise. It doesn't work like that.'

Suddenly, she stopped and stiffened at the sight of a woman walking in a gallery nearby. For a moment Trina watched her and then relaxed. 'Not her.'

'Is that like the person who came to see you?'

'Yes. Slim, blonde, neat, you couldn't really describe her, just bland, icy manner. Gave me the right creeps.'

'What did you say about Violetta's necklace?'

'I only heard that after I'd finished the podcast. I was going to add it in later but you could spend forever revising these things. Gretchen Teigler was sent the necklace a week after the *Dana* went down. It came in the regular post, in a padded envelope, and she threw the envelope away before she knew it was significant.'

'That's a lie.'

'Yeah but that's the story she told the police. Gretchen was in Paris when the *Dana* sank, in case you're wondering.'

'Did you hear anything about Leon's financial situation?' Fin asked.

'Yeah, Leon was bankrupt. He bought the *Dana* cheap to resell back in England. Had a buyer. He was just sailing it from Corfu. But he was totally broke.'

'No,' I said, 'he owned a house worth millions.'

'Mortgaged to the hilt,' said Trina. 'He was trying to sell it. People get desperate. You should be asking about Amila. I've got a picture . . .'

She found it on her phone. It was a cut-out from a magazine article, a photo of a slim, dark woman in immaculate chef whites, standing in front of the window of an old-fashioned *bouchon*, gold lettering sweeping across the glass behind her. Over her forearm was the handle of a wide wicker plate, tipped towards the viewer to show off the bread. The bread was the object of interest, both to the photographer and to the woman. She smiled pacifically down at the bread basket. The caption in French read 'La Dame du Pain'.

'Is that her?'

'Yeah. Something happened to Amila, I don't know what. She isn't appealing the case. I don't know if she's being forced not to or blackmailed or just getting bad legal advice.'

I went to the loo and Trina followed me. I knew she wanted to talk. She waited until we were both washing our hands and she caught my eye in the mirror.

'Fin Cohen doesn't know what you're doing, does he?'

He didn't and I felt bad about that.

She shook her hands dry. 'You know what happened to the other girl who came forward in your case?'

'Yeah. That's why I stayed away.'

'Well you were wrong to. They had to identify her body from her dental records. She shouldn't have gone into hiding. They were the only people really looking for her. If I was her I'd have gone and stood next to the fucking Queen and shouted it all through a megaphone.'

We left on good terms, promising to keep in touch. Trina hugged me and whispered that I was a hero. She meant well, but heroes are usually dead. We parted in the street and promised to keep in touch.

We booked flights for the next day, then we

went and found a run-down hotel. It smelled of cabbage. Two rooms were stupidly expensive but I paid for them with my resettlement cash.

I plugged my phone in to charge and lay across the bed, falling asleep with my shoes and coat on.

I slept like the dead, like the other girl, and I dreamed of coming apart under the sea and not caring any more.

32

Passport control was at the dark end of a long corridor. I wanted Fin to stand well away from me. I was using Sophie Bukaran's passport, and if I had been declared dead I might get hauled off. I didn't want him implicated.

He knew something was up and didn't want to take separate lines so I made it a game, like tricking Lizzie into eating broccoli by saying they were trees and she was a giant. Let's make it a race, I said, make it fun. Fin smiled and said, yeah, but he was humouring me. He didn't really understand the game.

He was on the other side of the ribbon, waiting for his window, standing on one leg, scratching his arm, fiddling with his phone. I tried to mimic his insouciance but it came out stiff and odd. I hopped about, scratching at myself, stood up tall, swallowed a lot.

Fin tried to make a joke across the barrier but I ignored him. He looked a bit hurt but then he was called forward to his window.

'I win!' he called back to me.

I shook my head and looked away as if he were a mad stranger. There was only one person in front of me, a white backpacker with blond dreads and an ethnic-print patchwork shirt. He slouched over the counter. The customs man ordered him to step back, sounding fierce and firm. He looked at the hippy's passport, looked at the hippy, looked at the passport.

The backpacker made a joke and laughed. The customs man didn't laugh. He held the backpacker's eye as he fed the passport into the chip reader and slapped it down on the counter with an eye roll. The backpacker took it and hurried away.

My turn.

Damp and breathless, I stepped forward and handed over Sophie Bukaran's passport. He put the page down on the scanner and looked at me, he looked at the photo. He looked at me. He waited. A light changed below him and he put the passport back on the counter. I lifted it but he tugged it back. Remember to renew next year, madam.

Thank you.

Fin was waiting for me on the other side. 'OK?'

I nodded. I was trembling.

We floated through duty-free. Chocolates and handbags. Bright white lights. The shops were beautiful. Everyone moved in an orderly dance, skirting one another with perfect poise.

My passport worked. I had eight months left on it. I could go anywhere. All over the world I could hear doors swinging open, doors on to beaches and fields and cities. Athens, Paris, Jaipur, New York. New York! My passport worked. I could go anywhere.

Somehow, we ended up in a shop full of watches. A young woman asked Fin for a selfie. She took it and walked away without saying thank you or goodbye but Fin didn't even seem to notice.

'People are so rude.'

He was very calm about the whole thing. 'They don't mean to be. They forget that you're a person. It's just the deal. I was so young when we got famous, I wouldn't have consented if I'd known what it would be like but it's done now. I sold my face for a pittance.' He shrugged. 'Anyway, people are giving their faces away for nothing now.'

We walked on, revelling in the luxury mall atmosphere.

'They've got vegan chocolate,' said Fin dreamily, looking across to a big fancy shop.

I followed him into a purple-and-gold shop where you could choose the chocolates individually from a big glass cabinet. It was hard to hang on to the indignation because of the passport. I had never dared to dream of travelling.

'Which one do you want?'

I pointed vaguely at a small nutty one and watched him catch the server's eye. My God. I had the option of running again. Not to say I would do that. But the possibility was elating, like finding an air pocket in a car I was drowning in.

Then we were outside the shop and Fin was eating a very big chocolate he clearly didn't want. It was the size of a child's fist. He took a bite, licked his lips and hummed, chewing and chewing and chewing.

I shoved mine in my mouth and chewed it a bit and swallowed. It was horrible, a sort of oily chocolate, and mine wasn't even the vegan one.

'Nice, isn't it?' he smiled.

'I'm not fussed about chocolate.'

I was swithering about whether to tell him about the passport, let him share in the joy, but it was a complicated story and I was more practised at not telling it.

Fin put the rest of his chocolate in his mouth and I suddenly saw a man across the concourse filming us on his phone. I turned away and watched the man's reflection. He was smirking as he filmed, aware that Fin was a famous anorexic eating a big chocolate. He seemed to think it was funny. I looked at Fin. He knew he was being filmed, he wanted people to see that. He was doing it for the benefit of people he would never meet. People who might get better. I could see from his eyes that it pained him to eat it, that he was incredibly anxious, but he did it anyway. It was a brave performance and it was humbling to witness.

'Fin, I need to come clean about something.'

'Hmmm.' He was still pretending to enjoy the chocolate but his eyes were brimming.

The man stopped filming us and moved away.

'My name is Sophie Bukaran — does that mean anything to you?'

'No.'

'I was raped by four footballers in a hotel ten years ago. It was a big case. They were found not guilty.'

He didn't know what to say. He watched my lips as if he was waiting for a tasteless punchline.

'Gretchen Teigler owns that football club. After the case ended someone tried to kill me in my house and I ran. Everyone thought I'd been

233

murdered. Several people have died in suspicious house fires. They all stood in Gretchen Teigler's way.'

Fin looked as if he might be sick but he managed to mumble, 'Sophie Bukaran . . . ?'

'That photo of you and me on the steps outside my house, it proves I'm alive. They can't take the chance that I'll speak out again, not now. That's what was going on at Skibo.'

Fin blinked hard. 'Look, could we go and sit down and you can tell me this again?'

'Yes.'

'Anna, I'm going to be sick.'

'No, you're not. We'll just walk very slowly and I'll rub your back and tell you the story.'

33

It was warm and bright in Saint-Martin.

We stood on the dockside, stiff from the plane and the taxi ride. A breeze was on my cheek, the faint smell of fish and soap mingling on a warm caressing wind. I felt very far away from everything.

The setting felt hyperreal because I was here twice: in the imagined town from the podcast and the real place, moving through history and imagination and reality. All the Saint-Martins seemed equally matched and clashed and melded in my mind. That was where the prisoners filed on to ships bound for Devil's Island. There's the five-star Hotel Toraque. This was the street Violetta and Mark walked down to go and meet their dad. Leon passed just here with his kids, heading off to get beer and Fantas.

Fin felt it too, but not as much as me. He hadn't listened to the story as if he was in it, and there was an extra layer of wonder for me because of the passport and the possibilities ahead of me. I was out of the UK for the first time since my mum died. I could go anywhere. Everything felt new and fresh.

Fin said, 'Fancy a coffee?'

I slipped my arm through his. 'I'm hungry.'

He said he could probably manage to eat something. He was eating. He wasn't enjoying it but he was making himself. It was hard to watch him.

We found a cafe on the busy dock, sat outside and the waiter gave us big menus. I ordered a croque-monsieur and asked if they did vegan food for my friend? The waiter tutted and was generally very irritated by the mention of veganism for some reason. He prodded Fin's menu. You can have that, that or that. Basically fries and salad. Fin said OK then. The waiter snatched the menus and stomped off as if we had ordered his mother's eviction.

'Bit annoyed,' I observed.

'A Frenchman who has tasted vegan cheese?' suggested Fin.

We looked around. Everything was stylish, understated and a little bit twee. This is what we saw: the hotel on the dockside was a converted warehouse. It was a squat, three-storey building with a turreted stairwell and Moorish tiles around the door. The rooms had large windows with balconies looking out over the dock.

My imagined dock was completely wrong. In my mind it was a harbour of straight lines but this was a tear-shaped inlet. In the middle stood a small island, cluttered with modest fishermen's houses, warehouses, boat sheds, all converted into restaurants and holiday homes. A brick walkway led across to it, cutting the harbour in half.

Only small craft could dock in the harbour. The tide was out and the boats lolling in the mud were only ten or twenty feet long. The *Dana* was sixty feet long, too long for the dock and too wide for the narrow harbour entrance.

We smoked and speculated. Could the *Dana* have been docked over there? Could it fit there? I had imagined it right here, in the very centre of town, next to the cafes and bars. We scanned for the rooftop restaurant that had overlooked it as it set sail but we couldn't find that either.

Fin suggested they might have docked further away and arrived on a smaller boat?

No, because remember the gangplank was metal and Amila came clattering down it and everyone looked. The *Dana* must have been here somewhere.

Fin got his phone and mic out and said he was going to do a quick update about Trina Keany being threatened and Amila's bakery. I'd been thinking about what Trina said about the other girl.

'I think I should out myself,' I said. 'Just say I'm Sophie. The people who are interested will put it together. It might be safer than hiding.'

'You sure?'

'Yeah,' I said, though I wasn't.

Fin fitted the special mic to his phone and we introduced ourselves. I just said I was Sophie Bukaran, I see from Twitter that some of you have heard of me. Then Fin did a straight, off-the-cuff ten-minute update. It was quite impressive to watch. He listened back to it twice.

When the food arrived he made me take a picture of him eating chips. He posted it without asking me. I didn't think it was a good idea to identify our location but he said we'd be out of there by tomorrow.

'They have planes and everything, Fin. They've got people everywhere.'

'OK.'

Fin didn't really believe me when I said we were in danger. I think he thought Skibo was a one-off.

The reaction on Twitter was immediate: people commenting on the photo and retweeting, expressions of support for me, for Fin, for women, for whatever. Fin sat and ate, watching the numbers scroll up and up.

'Fuck. People know it's Saint-Martin.'

'We better get out of here.'

'Let's give ourselves two hours. Loads of tweets about the ghost in the video. Why do people believe that?'

'People are idiots,' I said.

'Yeah.' He sounded unconvinced. 'But we should mention it.'

'We should debunk it. I think I know exactly what happened.'

'Really?'

'Mark Parker was playing a joke — ' My phone jangled in my pocket.

It was a text from Jessica. She was fine and having a nice time. The swimming pool had a tree in it (this done in emojis). They ate (emoji of a pizza). Estelle spewed (sad face).

I texted back — '*I love you!*' (I put in emoji hearts here because she likes those.) '*I miss you like crazy! Got time for a chat?*'

She didn't answer. I don't know why I asked. She doesn't even like speaking on the phone to her friends, but I was desperate to hear her little voice, to hear Lizzie's giggle. Then my phone rang. It was Jess calling and I answered, excited, but heard Hamish. He sounded very angry. I didn't want to speak to Hamish.

'What the hell are you doing in France?'

How could he know that? I realised he must be following Fin on Twitter, or, more likely, Estelle was following Fin, saw the photo, knew we were together and told Hamish where we were. If Hamish found out about Sophie Bukaran he might use it to get the courts to refuse me visitation.

'Are the girls OK?'

'Anna, answer me. Are you in France?'

'Kind of.' I don't know why I felt so guilty.

'I have two things to say to you: do NOT spend all of that money.'

'I'm not.' But I was.

'It's for the new flat. When that cash is gone I can't access any more for six months without incurring a penalty. You've always been so frugal and sensible, what the hell is going on?'

'Why did you call me on Jess's phone?'

He wasn't listening. 'Secondly: how the hell can *you* be in France? You wouldn't leave Glasgow for the last three years! And who is Sophie Bukaran? Is she with you?'

'Well, you're in bloody Portugal, Hamish.'

He went off on one about the money again. I didn't shout back though, I didn't defend myself or counter-accuse. I didn't think anything could be said that would profit either of us. I listened, imagining Sophie, not Anna, listening to a rant from this mad old stranger. I thought Sophie would have told him to fuck off. I didn't think

239

she would feel ashamed and cowed the way Anna did.

'Hamish,' I said in my London accent, 'I know she's pregnant.' And then I hung up.

I felt nothing but tired. Not being goaded into an argument with Hamish felt like an ending. A real end to the thing. A door closing softly on a shoddy mess.

Jess's phone called me again but I knew it was Hamish. What a cheap move, using her phone to make me answer. I didn't answer. I didn't have time for his headfuckery right now.

Fin worked his way through the chips and salad, watching the likes and retweets rack up, like the seconds of our lives passing.

'Has Estelle called you?'

He shook his head.

'Have you called her?'

'There's nothing to say.'

She was following him on Twitter. She was talking to Hamish about him. She was probably listening to the podcast, but I think Fin knew that. I think, really, she was his audience for the chocolate-eating and the chips. Maybe that was why he was with me, doing this at all. The whole performance was aimed at her. I couldn't hate him for it. I pitied him because it was over between Hamish and me, but I didn't think it was for them.

I paid and he got up. 'Come on, let's go and see if we can find anything.'

We sauntered casually away from the harbour when what we should have done was run and kept on running.

34

The streets were pedestrianised and cobbled, brushed with a layer of sandy dust like the leavings of a hot summer. The locals were dressed for an Arctic winter, in scarves and jumpers and gloves. I was sweating. We walked half a mile to the bar where the *Dana*'s crew had watched football. Fin wasn't sure we'd get a friendly reception, he baulked at the door, but I went straight in and ordered a demi beer.

It was a narrow galley with a yellow Formica bar. A television hung high on the wall at the far end. The barmaid served me and saw Fin loitering outside the door. She waved encouragingly at him to come in. He said, no, no, it was OK. Then she offered him a bowl of peanuts as an inducement, as if he was a shy woodland animal, and we all laughed about it.

I got him a demi and he came in and drank some.

'You are Fin Cohen. A musician?'

He said he was. She said her friend was the manager of the Hotel Toraque. His name was Hector and he had texted her to say that Fin Cohen had been spotted in town. He was a crazy fan. She rolled her eyes. A crazy super-fan.

I tried a few questions but she wasn't keen to talk about the *Dana*. She said she only started working here a year ago anyway, came from Warsaw and knew nothing about it. The crew

241

were here all night and that was all she'd heard.

It felt like a triumph of sorts, getting a reluctant witness to speak, and I tipped her, though it isn't the custom in France, and she took it because she was Polish and well travelled enough to know I wasn't trying to be rude.

We went off to find Mark Parker's Airbnb.

We had booked it while we were waiting to board at Heathrow. The listing said it was '*situé au coeur de la cité*'. It looked grim in the photos. It boasted 'bed type: real bed' but looked like a single futon. A decorative fan was pinned on the wall at a strange angle, possibly as a cover-up for a damp patch. No pets. No smoking. No parties.

We found the street very quickly. It was broad, with stone benches shaded by shedding pine trees. The house was down a side alley.

It needed a coat of paint. Stratified black dust had settled on the white lime-washed walls. The front door was plastic, cheap and moulded to look like wood.

I knocked and we listened. A mop handle clattered to a stone floor. After a moment the door was opened by a young, very tall, bald man and I introduced myself as his tenant for the evening.

'No luggage?'

'No.'

He opened the door to the wall. 'Come in.'

He led us up a dark corridor, past a mop propped in a corner as if it was in time out. We came to a small door and he opened it, turned to us and shrugged.

'*Vous avez payee, mais . . .* ' He gestured to my expensive leather coat and shrugged again.

The room smelled bad and looked awful. The window was dirty and a corner crack was mended with yellowing Sellotape. The stone floor was still wet from the mop. It stank of tangy synthetic lemon.

I smiled at him, which surprised him. 'I'll pay you for three more nights, in cash, right now, and then my friend and I will leave and you'll never see us again.'

He looked at us, from one to the other. 'For what?'

'We want to ask about Mark Parker.'

'Why?'

'I want to know about his luggage.'

As I say, he was tall, about six five, and had to stoop in the low corridor. He looked over our heads regretfully. 'This island is so small,' he said. 'There are much people here who don't want to talk of these things. It's difficult . . . '

He wanted more money.

I said, 'OK, never mind. You keep the payment for tonight and sorry to have bothered you.' I turned to leave.

'*Non!*'

I turned back.

'Come in here.' He waved us towards a bigger door that led into a kitchen.

The house was small and narrow. To accommodate the addition of a kitchen, the back of the house had been knocked through and a boxy glass conservatory built on. This room smelled weird too, the same kind of lemony weird. I began to think the smell was coming from the man.

243

He sat us down on a mottled pink-and-grey sofa and I counted out the cash. When he was sure it was ·the right amount he nodded and began:

Mark Parker booked that room only one week before he is arrived. He was lucky to achieve this room. Many have said it is not a good room but it is good enough for one night and is well priced. Very cheap. Why not? People of no money cannot stay here now it is a rich place. Cheap places are necessary, are they not?

They are, indeed. Did he remember Mark arriving at the door?

Certainly, he did. He remembered very much detail because afterwards it came to his realisation that this person had died.

It happened like this: Mark was a little bit late because the bus from the airport had been delayed. Later in this day it was heard that a crash is happened on the road bridge. Anyway, anyway, not relevant to this.

So it was that Mark was a little bit late, but not important. The door is knocked, he open the door and it is Mark Parker there, outside. Mark shows his booking on the phone and they say, oh, little bit late, never mind, sorry for this, OK. Come in.

What was he wearing?

T-shirt of *The Omen*. Yes, said the man, he must be a big fan of horror! The next day he is wearing a T-shirt of *Drag Me to Hell*: very good movie, old-school horror, Sam Raimi is, of course, genius. So, anyway, Mark is come in.

Did he have a bag with him?

Yes! A bag enormous! I show him this room and say wow! Such a big bag! Very small room. But is very thin bag.

Was it a surfboard, or a boogie board?

Thinner. He pinched his finger and thumb together to show that it was paper thin. But, he said, at the end of this bag (here he made a cupping/weighing gesture) is lumps, like T-shirts and clothes. I have to pass him this bag into the room! Very narrow door.

What did you think was inside the bag?

Hm. A plastic-stiff feeling.

A laminated poster?

A what? What is that thing?

'Laminated poster' is surprisingly hard to mime. I had to use a letter from the breakfast bar and said, 'Paper with plastic on it.'

'Ah, *feuilleté?*'

I didn't know if that was right: stiff. Not bending. Plastic?

Certainly. What was it, in there?

Have you seen the film of the wreck?

Certainly, he nodded. I see it, although not so much a fan of horror. Mark is fan, very much, very big. Me, I prefer sci-fi.

Fin said Sam Raimi was married to the daughter of Lorne Greene, who, of course, played Commander Adama in the original *Battlestar Galactica*. The man was delighted by that morsel.

So, but why are you asking this? Was it movie stuff inside?

I said Mark was into movies, he loved horror and I expect he would have already seen *The*

Haunting of the Dana.

'Oh.' He rolled his eyes. 'This film is a shit.'

'Yeah, so I saw the dive film and know lots of people think the face of the boy in the cabin was pasted into the film afterwards. But I saw bits of varnish moving in front of it, from the side, so that doesn't work. I wondered if the image could have been a poster of the kid in the movie.'

'No,' said the man, 'not possible. That ship was in the sea for one month and a poster would — ' He made a crumble gesture, as if he was rubbing money at me.

'Not a laminated poster,' I said. 'If it was good laminate. Could that be what you felt in the bag? With the T-shirts and shorts? A laminated poster?'

He thought about that. He looked at the ceiling. He rubbed his finger and thumb together, remembering the sensation of the bag. 'Ah! But that, it is absolutely possible!' He looked away and imagined it. 'Yes! *Feuilleté.* That, it is possible!'

'Another thing,' said Fin. 'Soon after the *Dana* sank you gave an interview saying you saw someone on the deck of the *Dana* that night — '

'No!' He held his hand up to stop the line of questioning. 'No!'

Neither of us quite knew what he meant. Was he saying he hadn't seen that or we shouldn't ask about it?

He stood up. 'You must go.'

I thanked him and we got up. We promised not to tell anyone that he had spoken to us. Fin bowed and thanked him for his courtesy. The man was moved by this for some reason and kissed Fin several times.

On the way back down the narrow corridor he apologised for his English. Better in German.

'You don't want to talk about what you saw that night?'

'Some things — there is not enough money to talk about. Frightening woman come by — threats. *Drag Me To Hell*, eh?' He opened the door to let us out. 'I am sorry.'

He slammed it shut behind us.

35

We sat down on a stone bench in the bright square. Fin called up the dive film on his phone, replaying the part where the boy's face appears. Detritus floated past the outer frame of the picture, across the boy's dark eyes. When the water flowed in from the corridor the current in front of him quickened. The diver's head torch reflected on the gloss surface, causing the flash of light from the boy's mouth. It was a laminated poster. We were pretty sure.

Fin asked me how I had spotted it and I told him I knew as much as there was to know about lamination. Price point, thickness, longevity, lamination textures, which paper sizes they could accommodate. If it was a laminated picture it would need to be A3 size, possibly A2. Most machines could only laminate up to A4. He must have used an office services shop for one that big.

Fin was impressed with my reasoning. 'Wow. You know a lot about lamination.'

'Yes, the parents' council took that purchasing decision on the basis of a very thorough report.'

'Mark must have had it made in Southampton. Maybe we could trace the shop where he had the lamination done.'

Fin tweeted out a question: we thought the 'boy' in the wreck dive video was a laminated poster of the actor in the original *Dana* film.

Anyone in Southampton know if Mark Parker used a lamination machine in an office services shop there? I think we both felt quite hopeful and competent at that point. I've always enjoyed the promise of a hanging question.

The ghost story didn't mean that much to either of us but it meant everything to a lot of other people. The interested-in-ghosts community was enormous. Suddenly, Fin was being followed by fifty people at a time, a hundred people, a thousand. They were commenting, retweeting, talking about ghosts and the still from the video, sending pictures and GIFs of the boy. It was overwhelming and changing so quickly, it was like trying to read a poster on the side of a speeding train. Fin struggled to make sense of it for a bit and then gave up in exasperation. He actually turned his phone off. He was running out of battery anyway.

Fin nodded back to the Airbnb. 'Was he threatened not to say he saw Violetta casting off?'

'Well, he'd just deny it if it wasn't true. Who'd warn him not to talk about something he didn't see?'

We looked around at the quiet square. It was beautiful. The stone was pale, the light bright, the air was warm. An old man passed by on a child's bicycle, his knees wide to the side, clutching a paper bag of groceries to his chest.

'Fin, I really think we need to get out of here.'

'What a shame. It's so pretty.'

The museum across from us was shut, we couldn't hear any traffic, though cars were parked here and there in the street. A woman walked at the far end of the square, crossing our eyeline and heading down to the dock. She seemed the epitome of Saint-Martin: tall and slim, cool glasses, wearing a grey cashmere poncho with mustard trim. Her dyed blonde hair was pulled up in a perfect ponytail at the crown. I gave the girls ponytails like that and after fifteen minutes they had stray hairs dangling over their ears, escapee curls at the nape. God, I yearned for the sight of them. I took my phone out and looked at some photos and films to keep me steady.

'Missing them?' asked Fin.

'It's agony.' But I watched a film of the girls in the garden and it lifted my mood. I knew they were safe. I watched a film of them failing to ride bicycles. Children in stories can always ride bikes. Mine find it impossible. In the film they were wobbling along on stabilisers in front of the house, Jess whining, 'I can't!' and my exasperated voice shouting from the behind the camera, telling her to just shut up and bloody pedal. Sometimes being a mother isn't quite what you think it's going to be.

'Come on.' Fin stood up and brushed pine needles off his backside. 'Let's go back down, see if we can find where the *Dana* docked and then get a taxi to the airport.'

We walked down to the harbour, passing the bar again, and found ourselves among a glut of shops selling potpourri and stinking glycerine soap. We backtracked and got lost in a winding lane. This one was full of boutiques.

Fin stopped suddenly. He was looking down a

narrow alley that led to a pretty courtyard of converted stables. Standing on a plinth in the middle was a large bronze sculpture of a fat cartoonish baby ecstatically raising his chubby arms to the sky. We went towards it and found ourselves surrounded by designer clothes shops on a bijou scale. Decals around the edge of the window advertised who they stocked: Gucci, Chanel, Burberry, Missoni.

'Missoni,' whispered Fin.

The shop surround was pale blue. It looked expensive. The window display was a single dress on a velvet hanger and a rustic wooden stool with 'not for sale' handwritten on a card.

We opened the door and stepped into a small room with a lone rail of four dresses and a woollen hat on a plinth. At the far end was a wooden table, possibly the comrade to the stool in the window. Behind it sat a woman with grey hair in a tousled bob. She wore a bright yellow dress and had cat-eye glasses made of clear plastic hanging on a matching plastic chain. She made me want to go straight out and buy a yellow dress, dye my hair grey and develop an astigmatism.

She put her glasses on and looked us up and down, nodded faintly at Fin's shoes, took her time over me. She priced my wide-leg Margaret Howell trousers, Agnes B. shirt and the coat.

'Bonjour.'

'Hello,' said Fin but she didn't take her eyes off me.

'This leather coat — taupe, it's by Marni, yes?'

I nodded. She gave me an approving nod.

'You stock Missoni?' asked Fin.

'No.' She took off her elegant glasses and stood up. 'Not any more. Too expensive for here. Now we stock M for Missoni, the cheaper label.'

'Too expensive for *here?*' I asked.

She smiled. 'Here, it's very low-key. It's not Monaco. Only French come here, no Russians.'

I thought that was quite racist but asked, 'When did you stop stocking Missoni?'

'Oof! Twelve years ago.' She waved at the name of the shop painted in faint grey behind her, *Ela, de 2004*. 'A few years after we opened.'

'So, you weren't selling Missoni two years ago, only M for Missoni?'

'Yes, only the cheaper brand.'

'Are you the sole stockist of M for Missoni in Saint-Martin?'

She looked suspicious. She pointed at me with one arm of her glasses and turned to Fin. She drew a circle around him with her specs. 'Hm, *Violetta Parkour.*' She wasn't looking at me any more, she was looking at Fin. 'You are Fin Cohen.'

He bowed. 'I am.'

She made a circle by her ear. 'I listen to this thing you're doing. People here, not happy with you being here, bring it all up again, I think it's good. Off-season, it's very quiet here. Bring people in, maybe. But some here are very hostile.'

Fin asked, 'Did she buy her dress here?'

She nodded her head from side to side, meaning yes.

'But the reports were that she spent a

thousand euros. M for Missoni dresses aren't that much. How much are you charging?'

She smirked, flashing deep dimples at us. She really was a gorgeous-looking woman. It's dismaying to meet someone in their sixties who is better looking than you will ever be. I was thinking about this when she raised her hand, holding up her thumb and forefinger.

'She bought two?' I asked.

Tiny nod. 'The same dress. Twice.' She seemed quite pleased about the sale.

'Why would she buy two?'

She shrugged. 'She loved the dress? Good price? *Nettoyer a sec?* Sometimes rich people who travel will buy two because they can't have a piece cleaned quickly. I don't know. I was very happy.'

I could see that. 'Two the same?'

'Same design but one size 36 and one 42.'

'Didn't you have the 38 or 40?'

'Of course. But she wanted those sizes.'

'Did she try them on?'

'Just the 36. Fit perfectly.'

'Did she pay cash?'

'*Non.* She charged it to the hotel. I called and they said fine.'

She was barely looking at me now, she was blatantly flirting with Fin. I might as well have been invisible. My pride was a little bit bruised by that, not that there was anything between Fin and me, but she didn't know that and I was standing right there. They made eyes at one another. Fin thanked her and bowed. She curtsied back. The atmosphere between them was so charged you could have stood a fucking spoon up in it.

Outside we walked back to the lane of soap shops and headed back to the harbour.

'Two dresses,' I said. 'Two different sizes.'

'Why is that important?'

I explained: look at the picture on deck. She's nowhere near a 42. One of the dresses she bought was much too large for her.

'I still don't know what that means.'

'Fin, there were two women on board wearing the same distinctive dress. There *was* someone else there, *they* took the photo. That's why no one noticed the extra person moving around on the boat, because they were wearing the same dress.'

'The crew didn't mention that.'

'Neither did Mark when he texted his mum. Maybe they snuck on later or maybe it was someone they knew? Like Violetta's mother? Anyway, Monsieur Airbnb didn't see Violetta, did he? He saw someone wearing the dress. It could have been her or the other person.'

We stopped at the mouth of the lane in front of the busy dock. Fin grabbed my arm and pointed out to sea.

A large yacht was docked outside the harbour. It dwarfed the little buildings. It was beautiful, white with two high masts and brown-frosted glass that made it slightly old-fashioned.

He pointed at the ship and traced the skyline with his finger to a flat roof that overlooked the deck. A forlorn string of light bulbs hung from a corner pole, flapping gently in the wind.

It was the rooftop restaurant.

The scene opened up now: Violetta and Mark walking down here, right in front of us, in the heat of a July afternoon, crossing and heading for the outside wall of the harbour as the *Dana* docked. I could hear the clatter of Amila's feet on the metal gangway echo around the harbour front, feel the confusion among the drunk crew as they arrived back in the dark to find the ship gone. I was deep into these imaginings but Fin was deeper still. I glanced at him. His eyes were hooded, his cheeks lightly flushed, his mouth hung open. Then, beyond him I saw a man, head down, barrelling down the street to the dock.

He was three hundred yards away. He was big, a full head above the milling crowd, wearing a battered leather jacket, baggy jeans, clothes that were too cheap and washed out for here. He had a brawny red face and tight fists swinging at his side as he walked away from the open door of a taxi. He was scanning the street, looking for someone. I knew instinctively that he was coming for me.

I put my arm around Fin's waist and guided him casually away in the opposite direction.

'Excuse me?' he said indignantly.

'We need to go.'

He didn't like being touched or me pushing him so firmly. 'Get off.'

'Fin, trust me. Move.'

I was looking for somewhere to hide but we were beyond the shops and bars. I headed for the Hotel Toraque.

36

Breathless, I shoved Fin through the door into the hotel.

'I saw a man, like the Skibo man. I'm sure — '

'You gave yourself a fright?'

'No, I think he was here looking for us. Down the dock. He was looking for us.'

'Was it the Skibo man?'

'No. Different man. He was looking. He was all wrong.'

He put his hand on my shoulder and actually patted me. 'It's OK. You got a fright. It's OK.'

'He was looking for someone, really staring.'

'OK. OK.' He patted me again.

The lobby was empty. A small log fire crackled in a huge fireplace and a telephone rang somewhere in the distance. Behind the reception desk stood a dapper, grey-suited man with a name badge. It was Hector. He had a dark quiff and an elaborate facial hair arrangement, part neck beard, part moustache, that would be impossible to describe without a drawing. He stood, frozen, his eyes fixed on Fin.

'Find-Lay Cohen,' he whispered, voice raw with emotion.

Fin stepped towards the desk. 'Um, hello?'

'You are Findlay Cohen.'

'Yes. I wonder if you could help my friend and me? It seems we're slightly hiding from someone.'

'Of course.' He touched his hand to his grey-suited chest. 'This would be the honour of my life.'

He led us into a windowless back office with a small desk and three chairs, then turned and shut the door very carefully behind us. He looked at Fin with an intensity that was disturbing.

'Findlay Cohen . . . '

Fin tried to smile.

'Hector,' I said, 'we're being followed by someone. He wants to hurt us. He's a big man. We're scared.'

Hector's face darkened. 'You will have nothing to be afraid of here. If anyone comes here to hurt you I will . . . ' He lifted a letter opener from his desk and demonstrated giving an invisible intruder an upwards stab to the heart.

We both suddenly noticed that we were in a very small room with a strange man to whom Fin Cohen had come to mean something dispropor-tionately significant. It didn't feel any safer.

'Well — ' Fin lowered the dagger by the point — 'there won't be any need for that sort of thing. Kind of you to offer, maybe. Can we call a cab for the airport?'

Hector realised that he had gone too far, put a hand on his stomach and reined in his emotions. 'Of course. Of course! Sit down, I will call a taxi. Sit, please.'

We took the seats across from his desk. Hector picked up the phone and gruffly ordered some-one to get a cab and bring it round the back. Then he sat down and gazed at Fin across the desk. 'Your music . . . ' he said, 'has meant a lot

257

to me. At my wedding, my wife . . . your song 'Never Again'.'

'At your wedding?' Fin squirmed in his chair.

'At our wedding. It was transcendental. It is the honour of my life to meet you. When I heard you were here, in Saint-Martin, I couldn't believe . . . I just couldn't believe that . . . '

He made a gesture of his frontal lobe exploding. Fin sensed an opportunity. 'Hector, you know why we're in town?'

Hector nodded. '*Oui.*'

'Violetta stayed here, didn't she?'

'*Oui.*'

'Were you working here then?'

'*Oui.*'

'Did you meet her?'

'*Oui.*'

'What was she like?'

'Pretty, young, excited to be in the hotel. Very excited by the bathroom and the drawing room, by the soaps and fruit baskets and so on.'

While Hector was answering questions his eyes were wide and fixed on Fin. It was as if he was trying to fit more Fin into his brain. Fin was so uncomfortable that his face was aquiver. A smile twisted into a frown, morphed into fury as if the unsuccessful smile was convulsing on his lips.

'She had a suite?'

'*Oui.* The Washington. The very best. She did not belong in the very best suite. She was pretending she did but, clearly, she was a poor person.'

I smiled at a fellow fraud's failure and asked,

258

'How would you know that?'

'Cheap clothes. Also, she was so happy with the suite. Rich people take it for granted or complain. That suite is *magnificent*.'

Fin asked, 'You sent all her belongings home afterwards?'

'*Mais oui.* Those tourists were coming in. We don't want that here. We sent it back.'

'Do you have the address you sent them to?'

He flipped open his laptop and typed in his password, looking away for a moment. Fin took the opportunity to draw a deep breath. Hector found the file and swung the laptop around so that the screen was facing Fin. I took a picture of the address in Venice.

The phone on his desk rang three times before he picked it up. '*Oui.*'

He hung up. He stood up, and with tears in his eyes he said, 'Findlay Cohen, our meeting is at an end.'

Fin stepped around the desk and Hector kissed him very formally on both cheeks. Possibly to stop Hector looking at him like that, Fin threw his arms open and hugged him. Hector was so moved that he let out a little cry.

Finally, he pushed Fin away regretfully and led us out to the backyard through a side door. A taxi was waiting. He leaned in the driver's window, gave him an order and we got in the back seat.

The driver greeted us and pulled out. I slunk down, watching over the rim of the window for the ruddy man, expecting him to leap at the car, shoot at the car, stop us somehow. But we made it out of town and hit the wide road that cut across the island to the bridge.

We were driving out of the town, no one behind us, just casually driving away. Hector helped us, the dress-shop woman helped us and it was all because of the podcast, because Fin was famous and we had an audience. It felt like a fairy tale, where everyone you meet is kindly apart from the bad guys. Not like real life at all. It would be a window of goodwill, we were a novelty, but, just maybe, while people were still interested, we could use the podcast to expose Gretchen Teigler.

Bristling with hope, I leaned over to Fin and said, 'I think we should go and face down Gretchen Teigler.'

'Anna, be honest with me: are you on medication?'

37

'I'm not on medication.'

'Like, psychotropic medication of some kind?'

'I'm not mental, Fin.'

'I didn't say you were mental.'

'That was a kind way of saying it but the question is the same.'

We were driving fast along a wooded road, approaching a small flat town and a sprawling camp site. Trees petered out and the horizon opened up as we approached the road bridge. The land spread its arms to the sea and the bridge to the mainland soared softly up into a blue sky, hung with colourful windsurfer kites.

Fin looked tired. 'You can tell me.'

'I saw a man.'

'Sophie/Anna, I really like you, I do, and I know you're paying for everything, but this is exhausting.'

'What is this about? You think I imagined that man?'

'I'm not saying there wasn't *someone*, I just . . . maybe you overreacted.'

'Fin, why do you think they were taking me away at Skibo? What do you think they wanted?'

He shrugged. 'To talk to you?'

'Yes, a man brought a knife to a conversation. You don't understand: there's history here. They think I'm going to tell my story about the rape again. It would be so bad for the club, there are billions at stake. Our lives are in danger.'

His raised a sceptical eyebrow. 'My life isn't in danger.'

'Fin: *you ran him over*. You witnessed them taking me away at Skibo. You're a threat now.'

'OK. Thanks.' He covered his eyes with his hand and kept it there. 'Fuck, you're hard to be around.'

'Am I?'

'I mean, *obviously* something happened at Skibo. Was he arresting you though? I don't know.'

'With a hunting knife?'

'Well, this man that we are apparently running from, I mean, I didn't see anything.'

'Oh, well, if you didn't see anything then it doesn't exist.'

'There's no evidence anyone is after us, Anna, a lot has happened to you, I'm not saying it hasn't, but maybe you're also just a bit paranoid?'

I didn't know what to say to that. I am paranoid but men have tried to kill me and that does tend to make you paranoid.

Fin mumbled, 'How could anyone get there so quickly? Did you think of that? We only tweeted where we were here a few hours ago.'

'It's not a staff of three, Fin, they have a network of people.'

'A *network?*' He looked at me as if I'd just proved his argument.

'Fuck you.'

We looked at each other. Affection was absent.

'And you know — ' Fin was upset — 'what

would this 'man' do if he caught us?'

'Kill us.' I should have padded that out a bit more, it was pretty scary for him to hear that out loud, and I'm not very good at comforting people.

'Look. It's been fun but maybe we should get away from each other.'

'Yeah, maybe.' I tried to sound confident but I couldn't let him wander off, he was clueless and defenceless. 'Tell you what: we'll split up. I'll go and confront Gretchen Teigler, get this sorted once and for all, and I'll tape it for you.'

He could see the finale to his podcast. I had him back. 'Well, maybe I should come with you.'

'No, Fin, I'll go alone.'

'No, really, I'd like to come with you. Really. Would it mean an end to all of it?'

I wanted to say yes, it definitely would, but I didn't want to lie. I felt the first glimmer of hope I'd had in a long time. I started to mumble something about *maybe*, but it sounded thin. I just sort of trailed off and looked away over the bridge to the sea. As I said, I'm quite bad at comforting people.

I suddenly wanted to talk to someone as flawed as myself. I took my phone out and called Hamish.

He picked up and sighed into the receiver. 'Anna, I'm so sorry. I tried to tell you Estelle was pregnant when we were at the house but you just started screaming and shouting and throwing the suitcase — '

He was such a coward. I loved him again a little bit.

'Hamish, look, I have to tell you something about Sophie Bukaran and then I'll leave you alone. You have to move the girls to safety. Men are chasing Fin and me.'

I could see Fin's eyebrows rising slowly.

'Men are chasing you?'

'Yes.'

'What *men*?'

'Hit men.'

Fin's brows stopped at maximum elevation. He looked out of the window.

'Why? Is it debt? Are you gambling?'

'No, Hamish, it's a long sad story from before we ever met. There's a contract out on me and they know I'm with Fin. They can trace Fin to Estelle and Estelle to Porto. If they come to Porto they'll find the girls. You need to move all of them to somewhere random, somewhere safe.'

There was a considered silence and he said, 'Anna, is this some sort of concocted drama to get my attention?'

It was a low move. A shabby move. I wanted to fume back. We said these things to each other because we were exhausted and ill-suited and disinhibited, I told myself as I looked out of the window and watched the bridge dip, slipping into La Rochelle.

'Hamish, listen to me, OK? I am Sophie Bukaran. Google the pictures and see if I'm lying.'

38

Speedboat taxis were lined up at the exit to Venice airport. The drivers directed us to the boat at the front of the queue and we clambered in gracelessly, sitting in the open area at the back. The driver asked us if we wouldn't rather go inside. I didn't want to. There was something hearse-like about the little cabin in the middle with net curtains drawn across the windows.

We showed the driver the address Hector had given us. The driver asked *really? There?* We assured him that the address was the one we wanted. He gave us a ridiculously high cash-only price and asked if we were still sure? Fin said yes, still sure, but why cash only? Not a tourist area, said the driver. I told him we had cash.

He shrugged and walked along the running board to the front, started the engine and pulled carefully out, heading towards a great expanse of mud-brown water. Wooden posts breached the surface, marking out the waterway. There was nothing much to see.

Brown water, rotting warehouses slumped on islands, more brown water, pontoons with large boats undergoing repair, more brown water, another shabby warehouse. It wasn't quite what I had expected of Venice. I looked at the city map we had picked up in arrivals. We were coming at the city from the wrong angle to see any postcard views, coming in at the back, far away from the

Grand Canal and all the sights. The address Violetta's luggage had been sent to was next to the train station.

The driver was even more bored by the endless flat water than we were. He sped up on the straight until the boat began to skip the surface and judder clumsily. He slowed down, rebuked by the water.

Fog lifted and the horizon split into a jagged line of buildings. We slowed to a gentle putter as we approached and skirted Venice proper. I had expected great palaces of forgotten fortunes rising up out of Canaletto-blue but this looked like a council estate.

The driver turned into a narrow channel and turned again, the canal narrowing, the buildings around us tall and mean, windows fewer, until we reached a slimy stone staircase leading to a dim walled alley. Neither of us wanted to get out but the taxi driver insisted: this is the address we had given him, just through there.

We paid and took the greasy steps up, wary of our footing, into a dark passageway that smelled of stale urine and mildew, keeping our eyes on the open courtyard beyond. We came out into a narrow, damp square of high blank walls. Graffiti was scrawled and half washed from the bare bricks. The clouds parted overhead, bathing the first floor above in bright sun, lighting the square, like prison-break floodlights.

There was only one door in the courtyard. Old, weathered and peeling.

We walked over to it and knocked, heard a lock buzz and the door gave a loud, shrill creak as it opened. Fin pushed and we stepped inside to find ourselves in a ramshackle living room and a thin fug of cigarette smoke.

It was very dark. A high window afforded a little light that only served to deepen the shadows elsewhere. It took a moment for our eyes to adjust.

Damp-blistered walls were painted deep blue. It was sparse. A sagging brown couch was pushed up against the far wall. Two wicker garden chairs sat nearby and a filthy portable electric hob was on a table under the high window. Against the near wall stood a coffee table covered in framed photos. A little girl and a beautiful woman, blonde, slender, pictured at night, in ball gowns, in studios. They didn't look like family photos. They looked as if they had been cut out of magazines.

There was only one other door, at the far end of the room, low and sitting open. Inside, I could see the foot of a sheeted bed with a coverless duvet and damp cardboard boxes stacked against the distant wall.

From the dark of the bedroom came a woman's hoarse voice uttering a complaint. '*Fabrice? Non ancora!*'

I called out, 'Hello?'

Julia Parker shuffled out of the dark and stood in the doorway. She was fifty but looked ancient. She was the beautiful woman in the framed photos, but wizened now. Her nose had caved in, her skin was loose. She was tall, stick-thin, the only meat on her a dowager's hump. Dressed in a long pink smock over blue tracksuit trousers, garish lime Crocs over pink socks, she looked as if a carer had dressed her up for a joke. She would have drowned in a size 42 dress.

'*Chi diavolo sei? Chi vuoi?*' She looked between us, back and forth.

'Julia Parker?'

'*Si.*'

'Do you speak English?'

'Yes.'

'Can we talk to you about Violetta?'

She tipped her chin and looked down on us. 'You are fucking *Dana* tourists?'

'No. Well, kind of. I was a friend of Leon's.'

She looked me up and down. 'From when?'

'About nine years ago. I only heard that he had died a few days ago.'

'Hm. You were his 'friend' friend or his *friend* friend?' She spoke like a posh Londoner, with just the slightest trace of Italian accent, but her voice was gorgeous. Drawling, gruff and clipped. I could imagine her young and cynical, charmingly melancholy in a way only very beautiful girls can be.

'Literally, just his friend. I didn't know him for long. I worked at a hotel in Scotland. He was there with a girlfriend and she was a nightmare. He used to come out to meet me near the bins at night to smoke cigarettes and talk. I think he was bored to death.'

She wasn't sure of me. 'What was her name?'

'Lillie Harkän.'

'Ach, Lillie.' Julia shuffled over to the couch and sat down. 'Always hated that bitch. So boring.'

'Leon left her there. She was furious. They made me pack her bags and I spat in her Creme de la Mer.'

Julia laughed at that, hearty and unkind. She mimed rubbing the saliva-spoiled cream on her face and laughed more, started to cough and choke and went very red. Both Fin and I panicked a little and stepped towards her but she coughed her way out of it and waved us away, telling us to sit down, sit down.

We sat down on the wicker chairs. When she finally caught her breath, she lit a cigarette and smiled at me. 'What do you want?'

'We have some questions. Were you in Saint-Martin with Violetta and Leon when the *Dana* went down?'

'No. I was here. The police had to call my friend to come and tell me. I don't like phones.'

Fin said, 'Can I record this?'

She didn't even look at Fin but spoke to me and shrugged a careless shoulder. 'Sure.'

Fin took out his phone and fitted the mic.

'Julia, people are saying that Leon killed himself and the kids. I don't believe that.'

She waved a care-worn hand. 'Why, darling? You don't know what anyone will do.'

I was a little dismayed by that. I had been hoping for an ally. 'Well, we're working on a different idea about what could have happened. When Violetta's luggage came back from the hotel, did it have a size 42 dress in it?'

'Oh, that's not her luggage.'

'Not her luggage?'

'They send it here to me. I don't know. It's not

Violetta's. It's . . . the hotel send me the wrong bag. The clothes are the wrong size, all wrong, too big. Expensive shampoo, wrong underwear, wrong everything. I would have contacted the owner of the bag but there were no markings on anything. The luggage, so weird, all the labels cut out of the clothes and so on. Weird.' While she said this, my eyes kept flicking to the mic on Fin's phone and she said, 'Actually, I don't think I want this recorded.'

He shot me a filthy look. She wouldn't have remembered we were recording if I hadn't drawn her attention to it. He turned it off and put it down. But she was wary of Fin now. 'You,' she said to him, 'you didn't know Leon. You, I don't know. These people are rich and mean and they hate . . . ' She trailed off.

Fin said, 'I could wait outside if you prefer?'

'Hm.' She nodded.

'I could go to the shop.' Back in duty-free we'd remembered to buy power packs to charge our phones but forgotten to get tobacco and I knew he was anxious to get more. 'Is there anything you need?'

She smiled sardonically as her hand rolled a circle around the room. 'As you can see, I have everything a person can need.'

'Cigarettes, maybe?' suggested Fin.

Julia shut her eyes and scratched the base of her neck. 'Actually, that would be nice. Pall Mall Menthol. Malik's store around the corner gets them for me.'

She waved a vague direction with her finger.

Fin took some cash from me and opened the

270

door. For a moment the room was filled with light and damp air, sounds and smells of the world beyond. He left, shutting the door behind him.

I was looking at the framed photos on the coffee table. Julia when she was gorgeous, Violetta as a child, as a teen, as a tiny girl in a ballet tutu and headdress, holding an arabesque pose. Most were of them were of Violetta.

'I very much like your pants.' Julia was looking at my wide-leg trousers, 'Like Katharine Hepburn.'

'They're Margaret Howell.'

She recognised the brand, smiled as if she hadn't heard the name for a while. 'Wool?'

'Yes.'

'It's itchy?'

'No. They're silk-lined. Was there an M for Missoni dress in the luggage they sent back?'

'*That* I would have noticed.'

I knew she would have.

She said, 'All those clothes were big. Size I-don't-know. Too big though for Vee.' She waved her hand at the cheap room. 'This is temporary. No money so we moved here for a moment, some years ago. It's my friend's. Old boyfriend from Belgrade. He is eighty-seven.' She gave a wry smile. 'He's so fucking demented now, I don't know if he even remembers I am here. I still love that man. He was a fucking god.' She smiled lasciviously, playing her fingers over her bony decolletage.

'Where did Violetta get her money?'

'Vee didn't have any money.'

271

'But she spent a thousand euros on two dresses.'

'Ha! No. Violetta didn't have a thousand euros, that's for sure. Leon, my beautiful Leon, he was broke. We were broke a really long time, Vee and I. Leon came back and helped for a while, then even his money stopped coming. For a year before Vee died it had stopped. Nothing. We had to move here from a beautiful apartment. But it was going to be OK, he said. His new woman, Gretchen, she said she would support us.'

'And did she?'

She laughed and it turned into a rattling cough. 'Do I look supported?'

'She changed her mind when Leon died?'

'Before even. Dauphine Loire, her PA, put a private investigator on to his affairs after they married and found out he was broke. She found out all that and told her. Fucking fat bitch. Violetta was very angry with her. But . . . Gretchen didn't investigate before she married him so — you know — *love?* Maybe? They had prenups but she could have found out he was broke if she cared. Only Loire cared enough to find out. Ask why. Is Loire inheriting? Gretchen could have found out. She supported us for a while, a little money, just enough to irritate.'

'But not now?'

'Humph. Formal letter. Not even from her. From the bitch PA. *Change of circumstances.* Who does that to their friends? She has plenty. When I had plenty I shared with *everyone.*'

'If you were so broke, why didn't Violetta want the diamond necklace?'

'Haw!' She raised her hands. 'That necklace?

What *is* Leon doing, spending like that? He's broke. He is making it worse, buying a fucking necklace *at public auction?* Never pay retail! Twenty per cent to the auction house — fuck! Violetta was too good to say it but I did: You. Are. Broke. Stop spending, Leon! He was making it worse. He was very driven, you know? But we're his girls! We don't give a fuck. Sometimes you have, sometimes you don't have. We're still his girls.'

I knew then that Julia had sent those texts to Leon on Violetta's behalf. It was her style, her tone.

'But Violetta booked the best suite at the hotel in Saint-Martin. She arrived there on a private plane.'

'Really? I thought she flew commercial. Well, maybe a friend paid for her. She was always tricking people into paying for her.'

'How did she do that?'

Julia smiled softly. 'She was so beautiful, graceful, people want her around, you know? She'd just, be friendly, I don't know, flatter a little bit, send them the bill or suggest something, I don't know.' Julia was smiling and squirming in her seat, turning her elegant hands in circles by her ears. She was describing her daughter grifting money out of people as if it was a dance recital. If my girls did that they'd be grounded until they were thirty. But then she stopped. She slumped. Her hands fell to her sides and she clutched the sofa. 'We made allowances for Violetta. You have to understand, she had a difficult time with me, with Leon, you

273

know. She got in trouble sometimes but I was so crazy.'

'What kind of trouble?'

'Huh! Ah! You know . . . ' it pained her to say it, 'taking things from friends. She gave them back! But when Leon left me he also left her. I mean, I was really crazy. She . . . ' Julia cringed and caught herself. 'She had a difficult time. I was . . . you know. You have to make allowances. So, maybe she got a friend to pay for her? She could make people do things, manipulative girl. Maybe Leon paid?' She shrugged. '*Non lo so.*'

'Her half-brother, Mark, flew easyJet and stayed in a cheap Airbnb. Would Leon pay for Violetta and not Mark?'

'No, he wouldn't. Not his style.'

At that, Fin walked back in. He had bought her a carton of two hundred Pall Mall Menthol.

Julia stood up to meet him; she called him darling and thanked him sweetly with a hand squeeze. Then she sat back down on the couch, her cigaretted hand outstretched, the other hand resting on the pack of two hundred as if it were a toy dog. I have never seen anyone more regal.

She reminded me of Leon. They must have been a great couple. Beautiful, fun, charismatic, those special creatures it's hard to envy because, despite their flaws and lies and shallowness, they enhance the world by existing.

Julia saw the awe on my face. She recognised it. She pouted and graced me with a small, wry smile, then dropped her eyes and turned away as if to say, yes, here I am. I am a peerless pearl who has fallen from her setting. I have rolled into the

274

dust under a couch and been forgotten. But, if you can see past the dust and the gloom, you will see that I am still a pearl.

39

We walked past Malik's store, through grimy streets until we reached a wide canal bordered by mean-windowed warehouses. We were both slightly stunned by our surroundings but I knew we shouldn't let our guard down. Citizens of Venice didn't have the bourgeois uniformity of Saint-Martin. Off the main drag everyone looked like potential assassins.

Fin could see how jumpy I was. 'You need to calm down.'

'But they'll know we're here. There's only one flight to Venice from La Rochelle every second day off season. If they get here and ask at the water-taxi stand they'll find us in minutes.'

'Well, honestly, Anna, I think you're overreacting.'

'I'll just take my medication.'

We weren't getting on at this point.

We followed a lane until we came out at the concourse in front of the train station leading down to the absurdly blue Grand Canal. The station building was long, low, vaguely fascistic, with a bronze emblem on its roof like an airline pilot's cap badge. The wide forecourt was full of milling tourists and busy commuters heading home. It was impossible to keep track of all the faces or potential threats.

Persuading Fin he should eat a proper meal, I got him into a water taxi and convinced him it would be better for us to sit inside the cabin. I looked up a list of vegan restaurants on my phone and pointed the driver to one address.

The driver started the engine and drew out into the canal.

Venice is foggy in November. The city was subdued but every so often we would stumble across a famous site — the Rialto Bridge, museums, certain palazzos on the canal — and throngs would suddenly appear as if people were welling up from the ground. These people were all dressed for a different place or for another season, in plastic ponchos or summer clothes, they didn't seem to be in Venice. The taxi driver explained that enormous cruise ships docked nearby and dumped huge numbers of tourists between the hours of nine and five. He said Venetians hated the cruise ships because the passengers ate on board, spent no money in the city and made the best sites impassable. We could see them on the water's edge, following tour guides with raised umbrellas, recording everything on phones but looking at nothing, seeing nothing.

'What did Julia say when I was gone?' asked Fin.

I told him and I said, 'She said Leon was broke. She was relying on Gretchen to support her andVioletta but Gretchen had cut her off. She called Dauphine Loire a 'fat bitch'. Maybe she was the size 42 dress.'

'Forty-two isn't fat.'

'Fin, Julia is a cocaine-addicted supermodel. She probably thinks you're a bit fat.'

I looked behind for motorboats following us but the waterway was so busy and the taxis all looked the exactly the same.

'I suppose if Loire was in Saint-Martin she could have paid for Violetta. She wouldn't have excited a lot of attention in the family, could have been there as Gretchen's proxy and taken the picture. But how would she get off the boat?'

I took out my phone and opened Facebook, sent a message to Adam Ross: '*How would someone get off a yacht in the middle of the Bay of Biscay?*'

And it made me think of the question we had tweeted: '*Any answers to the Mark Parker stationery shop question?*'

Fin looked at his own phone. 'There's so much feedback it's impossible to filter through all the replies. Most of it's about ghosts and me eating chips. Mostly ghosts.' He offered me his phone. 'D'you want to try and see if you can find an answer in amongst it all?'

I didn't know what else I would find on there. I flinched away. 'No. You do it.'

He scrolled through a bit and found one from a Mail Boxes Etc. It had a small scan of a newspaper article attached. The *Southampton Daily Echo* had covered this at the time of the sinking. The article reported that Mark Parker had been in there before he went to France to meet his dad. He'd had a poster from the horror film laminated. Later, when the wreck dive went viral, the story was repeated in the paper and the article suggested it might be the poster that people were seeing in the dive film. The information was already out there, hidden in the noise.

Fin was visibly excited by this discovery. He wanted to do an episode about it right away. I said it was a good idea.

Fin said, 'And, Anna, I've been seeing this image a lot.' He showed me the photo of the cat nailed to my old front door.

I pushed the phone away.

'Vicious.'

I shrugged. 'People . . . '

Fin nodded kindly and said, 'Yup. Sorry about that. Sorry for saying you were paranoid. I can see how you got there.' He didn't say I wasn't paranoid though.

He dropped the phone into his top pocket and turned away, reached out to me and touched my back. He was patronising me, not sympathising. I knew the difference. We ignored each other for a while and looked out of the taxi at the view of the canal. It was eerily quiet. Colourful gondolas were tied up, slapping against each other. Largely empty *vaporetti* motored slowly past.

It slowly dawned on me that we were being followed by another water taxi. We were on a quiet part of the canal now but when our driver slowed, so did that one, it was always there, I knew because the driver was wearing a distinctive green scarf. He was standing at the wheel but kept turning back, taking instructions from someone in the cabin. I couldn't point it out to Fin: we'd just had an argument about my paranoia.

A few hundred yards on our taxi pulled up

into a side canal, went down it for fifty yards and stopped by some steps, pointing us up a lane to the restaurant.

I paid and turned back at the top of the steps and saw the water taxi that was following us pull past the opening very slowly. The curtains were drawn in the cabin. Fin saw it.

I couldn't help myself: 'I think that water taxi was following us. I watched it, it was a bit sinister.'

'It's Venice in November,' smiled Fin weakly. 'Isn't everything a bit sinister?'

We walked up the stairs to a heavy wooden door and stepped into a warm room. The walls were lime-washed, the floor rough stone, there were very few tables. It was quiet, past lunchtime, and all the other diners looked like fellow tourists.

The waiter sat us down near the door and gave us linen menus.

We ordered, and as the waiter was walking away I felt a damp breeze on my ankles. The door had opened behind us. I looked up.

It was the ponytailed woman in the grey cashmere poncho that we had seen in Saint-Martin. She was standing in the doorway, looking straight at me, the light glinting off her glasses, turning the lenses opaque. I don't know why but I nodded. She nodded back and walked up to our table.

Fin recognised her too. He was as surprised as I was.

'Mr Cohen, Ms Bukaran, may I join you?'

She didn't wait for an answer. The waiter

brought over a chair and took her poncho. She wanted to keep it with her but he offered to hang it up. She said no, she would hang it on the chair behind her. While this went on I picked up my phone and I took a photo of her. It was quite dark and I was sitting down, she was standing up. It wasn't a good picture and she was quite nondescript.

She sat down, spoke to the waiter in immaculate Italian telling him that no, she would not be eating, just bring a glass of still water with lemon, quickly please. Then she introduced herself to us. She was Dauphine Loire, assistant to Gretchen Teigler. How do you do. It wasn't a question. She flashed a smile of neat, character-less teeth.

Fin looked worried.

'Are you following us?' I asked.

'I was in Saint-Martin when you were also there, I think.' She showed us her teeth again.

'What do you want,' I said, 'apart from water?'

Her mouth opened and a laugh-type sound came out. Her mouth snapped shut and the noise stopped. 'I am here on behalf of Ms Gretchen Teigler,' she said, 'to speak to you about your audio broadcasts.'

I understood why Trina was afraid of this woman. There was something very cold about her. She was here to perform a task and didn't care what we thought about it. She was so disengaged that she seemed slightly robotic.

'We want you to stop this broadcasting. We are prepared to pay you to do so.' She flashed her teeth again.

This is how the Teiglers had always operated. First bribes, then threats.

I said, 'I believe we have a friend in common: Patricia Hummingsworth.'

She turned her head to look at me. There was no memory of DS Patricia Hummingsworth in her eyes. Nor of the man she had sent to kill me in my mother's kitchen. In fact there was nothing in her eyes, so much nothing that it felt like a warning. I didn't take it.

'DS Hummingsworth gave you advanced warning that the other girl corroborated my evidence. You bribed her.'

'That was disproved in court,' she said, blinking once and wiping the allegation away.

'Nothing is 'disproved' in court. Courts find things proven or not proven but not 'disproved'. There are some advantages to living with a pedantic lawyer.

Dauphine was astonishingly unashamed about what she had done to me. It was almost hypnotic. Some people have no internal ethics, they do what they can get away with, but most will be at least conflicted if they're caught out in a lie. I put my hand on hers and smiled, 'Wow! You look so young for your age!'

She pulled her hand away and I saw a spark of something on her face. She half-blinked and regained her composure. I prodded her again, 'Have you had surgery?'

She blinked again, 'It's amazing what they can do.'

'Isn't it?' I said, too loud, quite rude, pretending to look for scars in her hair line.

'Wow!' Then I pulled out some euros and dropped them on the table. 'You're creepy, d'you know that? Something's missing in you.'

I stood up and Fin followed me. I picked up my bag and phone.

She stood up to meet us. 'We have an airplane waiting on the landing strip at the Lido. We would like to fly you to Paris to meet with Ms Teigler. She will explain everything.'

Fin looked at me. He raised an eyebrow. It was a great chance to speak to Gretchen, possibly the only one we would ever get.

I said, 'Give me your number and I'll call you in an hour.'

She smirked in a way I didn't like and gave me her card. Dauphine Loire, PA to Ms Gretchen Teigler, email, landline and mobile numbers, and an address in Neuilly-sur-Seine, Paris.

We walked out of the restaurant and on to the street. I texted the blurry photo I had taken straight to Trina Keany and asked if it was the woman who threatened her. Fin was freaked out, glancing behind us, looking around as if he expected assassins to jump out at any moment.

'Stop it,' I hissed. 'She'll be watching and know she scared us. Get your head up.'

It is hard to stride confidently in Venice in November. The drizzle makes the cobbles slippery. We tiptoed gingerly in a way that we hoped might convey nonchalance, and followed the pavement over little bridges, heading down to where the canal widened until we came upon an abrupt throng of Chinese tourists gathered around the mouth of St Mark's Square. It was the worst place in the world for two stringy Westerners to hide. We were both freakishly tall in among them.

'She wasn't fat,' said Fin.

'I saw an old photo of her and she was a bit chunky then. Maybe she went on a diet or got lipo or something.'

We talked and walked, working out a plan of action. My paranoia never came up again. We found ourselves in winding lanes of very expensive clothes shops, just the sort of one-percenter flash that Saint-Martin was avoiding. Strappy sandals for two thousand euros, fur coats for twenty. We slowed down and I wondered aloud what it would be like for Violetta to live here and be poor. The contrasts were so pronounced, between Julia's damp room and this ostentation. Fin said it would make you avaricious. I thought it would make me angry. Justified anger is powerful. It can prompt people to do terrible things, like spit in someone's Creme de la Mer because they were rude and you were powerless.

We walked off the panic and came to the edge of a wide expanse of water, punctuated with barbershop poles and moored gondolas, the gondoliers smoking diffidently in groups on the dockside.

I looked left to a row of private yachts. They were huge, dwarfing the *Dana* and the pretty yacht in Saint-Martin.

The one nearest us had lifeboats hanging from harnesses in openings on the lower decks, a helicopter blade peeking out from the top deck. I took out my phone and found that Adam Ross had answered my message.

'*I watched that fucking wreck dive film. You owe me now! There's a ghost! This is the ripcord from a Zodiac.*'

He had sent a screenshot with a hand-drawn red circle around a white ribbon. It was at the point of the film where the diver had just opened the double doors and was about to enter the *Dana's* cabin. A rotting white ribbon was flapping outward.

I googled 'zodiac' + 'yacht'.

'Fin. Fucking hell, Fin, look. Look at this.'

Zodiacs come in different sizes, one-man, two-man, all the way up to sixteen. They are self-inflating life rafts that come in a canister, operated with a ripcord which must be attached to the railings of the craft. Pull the cord and the raft inflates and ejects itself into the water, leaving the ripcord behind attached to the handrail.

Someone had got off the boat once it was at sea. The police had been on the wrong track from the very beginning.

'Who?'

'Creepy drawers back there?' I suggested. 'She might have done it to make sure Gretchen Teigler didn't have to support Leon's extended family. She didn't even leave the diamond necklace on board — she either posted it from there or, more likely, brought it back with her. Perhaps Julia was right:Teigler was leaving her fortune to her and marriage to Leon could have changed that. It must have been galling to be cast aside, especially after the things she's done for her.'

'Look, we have to be very careful,' said Fin. 'We can't imply someone's guilty if we don't have evidence.'

I agreed, there was a lot we still didn't know, but we were creeping closer to the answer.

We were looking at the close-up picture of the ripcord when a text came back from Trina Keany:

'*That's her. RUN.*'

40

I called the mobile number on Dauphine's card.

'We can be there in an hour, if the invitation still stands?'

'Of course. One hour is fine.' She gave me the plane's tail number and told me to ask for it at the airport entrance. 'Do you know where you're going? It's the Aeroporto Nicelli on the Lido.' Her Italian pronunciation was intimidatingly perfect. 'I'll see you there.'

I found myself listening to a dead line.

Fin and I walked to the Giardini della Biennale Arte, a public park by the waterside, and stumbled on a cafe. We ordered ludicrously overpriced drinks and sat outside.

Fin took out his phone.

The first podcast episode was hitting tens of thousands of likes and retweets. The second one had reached a hundred thousand likes. Fin was thrilled. Major newspapers were writing opinion pieces about what we were doing, the ethics of it, mostly denouncing us. The bitchy commentator who 'said what everyone else is thinking' had written an op-ed about how she hated me then and stood by that. She blamed me for the other girl's death. There were profile pieces on Fin and Sophie Bukaran. There were also a lot of side-by-side pictures of Anna-on-the-step and Sophie Bukaran's missing poster, mark-up arrows and circles around the scar on my face.

Sophie Bukaran hadn't been declared dead, she was just listed as missing. Some tweets were from police officers who had worked on the case back then, asking me to get in touch.

We ordered more drinks and moved outside so that lapping water could be heard in the background. He turned on the recorder and I said hello, I'm Sophie Bukaran. This isn't part of the podcast but, just for clarity, yes, I am *that* Sophie Bukaran, the Sophie who was involved in the Soho hotel rape case ten years ago and that's really all I wanted to say about that. Fin recorded a short episode, detailing our flight and arrival, our meeting with Julia. He cut in a little bit of the recording from her interview. It made us both smile to listen to it because her voice was so rich and deep. '*So weird*,' said Julia in the clip. '*All the labels cut out of the clothes and so on. Weird.*'

But he edited it before the next line, when Julia said that she didn't know if she wanted her interview recorded. He didn't see a problem with cutting it just before there, he said that was when she withdrew her consent. I said no, I didn't know, wasn't she referring to all of it? Wasn't she retrospectively withdrawing consent to all of it? No, said Fin, it was fine, don't worry.

But I did worry. I thought Julia was fabulous and it was disrespectful to use her voice when she might not have wanted us to. It didn't sit right with me.

We listened back to the recording and it sounded OK. Just as Fin posted it online his phone rang out. It was his agent calling.

288

'Blimey! I didn't know I still had an agent.' He went away to take the call in private.

I was alone for the first time since Inverness. Was Dauphine Loire a psychopath? I didn't really know what one of those was but it was odd, surely, to meet someone you had tried to kill and display no reaction at all. I thought of lovely, warm Julia and missed my girls. I missed them so badly but knew they would be OK as long as Estelle was there. She liked them and they liked her. I hated her right now but I did trust her with the girls. It felt like a big admission. It took the sting away a little.

As if he had heard my thoughts, my phone rang and it was Hamish. 'I googled. Oh, Anna. I'm so sorry. I didn't know. Are you safe?'

'I'm sorry for all the lying.'

'I keep thinking, if that happened to our girls . . . '

It wasn't sad enough that it had happened to me, apparently. But I was feeling reconciliatory and I said, 'Yes.'

'You were so young. I'm so sorry.'

'It's OK. Will you move them?'

'Yes. Someone broke into the house last night. The cops called me. They didn't take anything. I think they were looking for you.'

There was a frightened pause between us. 'Shit, Hamish, I'm so sorry.' We weren't often sincere with one another any more. All the trust was gone. It felt a bit uncomfortable. 'Were you offended that they didn't steal any of your precious antiquey *objets d'art?*'

'I was a little bit, yes. They must be

modernists.' Hamish can be disarmingly dry. 'I'm going to move the girls, as you said, keep them safe until it's over.'

'Can I talk to them?'

'They're swimming.'

We stayed silent on the line for a moment, listening to each other breathe. 'Keep them safe, Hamish. That's all that matters.'

'OK,' he whispered. 'I just wish this hadn't happened at the same time. Anna, I'm sorry it's such a mess.'

He was feeling guilty, looking for me to make him feel better. I imagine Helen got the same treatment. Like Leon, Hamish was a bit of a lovable shit. Superficial charm, tellers of tales, but selfish to the core. It seems that I had a weakness for such men.

'Anna? I'm sorry?'

He was prodding me for reassurance. I didn't owe it to him, I wasn't his partner any more, but I did because I liked him and thought I probably always would. 'This could have happened at any time, Hamish. It's not because you left, it's because Fin is famous. I'm glad it happened when the girls were away from the house. And with you, even with Estelle, I'm just glad they're safe.'

'I know. Anna . . . ?' His voice was thin, petering out, his breathing ragged. He wasn't good with big emotions.

'Hamish, if something . . . if we don't get to speak again. I loved you very deeply.'

'Anna? I have . . . love.' His voice rose to a high C. He was crying too much to say anything but it was OK. I didn't need to hear it back.

'Goodbye, Hamish.' I hung up and sipped my coffee and remembered drinking coffee in the early mornings in the house, when everyone was asleep and I could read, my favourite memory. I remembered it until Fin came back.

He was smiling, eyes alight, and dropped into the seat.

'What's the agent saying?'

'She still is my agent and she is creaming herself. She's got all sorts lined up for us when we get back. We're being featured in newspapers and magazines, on talk shows and radio shows, our podcast is right up there. And the #MeToo angle is a whole other aspect of it.'

He went on and on, details about the things and lots of money and so on. He was excited about the future, was making plans. I wasn't really thinking about that. I just agreed to everything.

'We've had a big money offer for an advance on a book. I couldn't write a book. How about you do that?'

I said, yeah, sure, why not, I'll write a book.

That is this book, incidentally. What was I thinking? I didn't consider the process of writing a book, the six months of self-doubt, the wrongness of all words, paragraphs strangling each other, civil war on the page, the sheer boredom of writing about myself. I just glibly said, yeah, sure, why not, I'll write a book. I agreed as if I was asked to taste a new flavour of crisp for the first time. Go on then. I'll try it right now if you like, while we're waiting for a bus.

'Anyway,' I said. 'Someone broke into our house in Glasgow last night.'

'Oh my God.'

'I know.'

'Fuck!'

'Yeah. They didn't take anything. Hamish thinks they were looking for me. We should go and see what Loire's planning.'

We found a taxi to take us to the dock for the Lido airport and we sat inside, buttoning up our coats like natives. Soon we were in broad open waters and the temperature plunged. The waters were wide and cold.

We arrived at the Lido and moored at the dock for the airport. We gave the driver a hundred euros to turn the engine off and come inside the cabin with us. We waited, net curtains drawn, watching. Within minutes we saw a boat approaching from the city. Then we saw them getting out. Dauphine Loire followed by a red-faced man in the battered leather jacket.

'He's a heavy,' whispered Fin.

'D'you think?'

'He doesn't belong with her. Look at his big hands.'

The man reached up to grab the railing and we saw a knife sheath inside his jacket. He got into the front of a waiting car, Dauphine got in the back and they drove away in the direction of the airport. Then I told Fin:

'That's the man I made you run from in Saint-Martin.'

41

In a brittle, frightened silence we took the taxi back to the city and got dropped at the train station. We knew Loire would have a plan, that she might have people with her, we knew we weren't getting on the plane, but the sight of the knife in the man's jacket made us both want to run away immediately and completely. We were very scared. I wanted to talk to Gretchen Teigler but it wasn't safe to go through Loire.

In the station I bought two first-class tickets for the next train to Lyon, leaving from Santa Lucia Station in just under an hour, changing at Milan. I didn't think we should wait around at the station. It was small and there was nowhere to hide. We were just five minutes' walk from Julia's address.

It was my idea to go back and see her again. I needed to ask her permission to use the recording of her voice. It was pointless, the episode was already posted, but I felt queasy about it and wanted to ask her formally, as a token of respect. Fin thought I was being stupid but I needed her to know that I cared enough to ask. Beautiful women like Julia have a hard hand to play, so much is projected on to them, they get bulldozed all the time. I think I wanted to say that I cared what she thought and maybe have her admire my trousers again. I think I had a little crush on her.

So we went back.

We found our way through the narrow lanes and warehouses to Malik's store and then it was easy. People get lost in Venice, it's disorientating because the streets are winding and the buildings high so there are few sightlines or landmarks, but we found the courtyard again and saw her door. We didn't notice it was hanging open until we were quite close.

Fin reached forward, pushing it with his fingertips. The door shrieked open into the dark blue room. I had to grab Fin's arm to stop him going in.

We stood in the doorway and blinked into the dark room. I saw Julia's feet. A hole in the sole of her pink sock. One of her Crocs had come off and lay, marooned, ten feet away, towards the bedroom door.

I stepped in front of Fin. He was gagging.

Julia was on her back, her face waxen, her mouth and chin a black bloody mess. The knife must have hit a lung. She had been stabbed so many times that her pink smock had turned a deep red, a glistening wet bloom on her chest. A kitchen knife lay on the floor. It must have taken minutes for her to bleed to death but in that time she had dragged herself across the room to the coffee table of framed photos, her passage marked by a bloody, puddled smear across the floor.

She had dragged herself all the way and was holding the framed photo of Violetta. She was about seven, standing in a ballet pose, her little tummy rounded in her tutu.

Then I noticed that Julia's eyes were open.

The urge to shut the eyes of the dead is, I think, a universal. When my mum died I needed to shut her eyes, to protect her because she couldn't blink, even though she was dead. No one had shut Julia's eyes.

The bedroom had been ransacked, bed tipped over and the contents of the boxes scattered around the floor. An empty box lay on its side, the trail of blood under it.

Was Julia dragging herself across the room as they did that? Or did they wait for her to die, watch it and then search her pitiful belongings afterwards? Julia had nothing. Whoever ransacked the place was looking for something other than money.

'Now we really should call the police,' Fin whispered behind me.

'Christ, no, not the Italian police. They'll hold us here for bloody years. We've got to get out, right now.'

We left and pulled the door closed. We walked back to the station quickly, panting and dizzy.

'Our DNA is all over that room,' whispered Fin as we passed Malik's store.

'Just walk, Fin, just keep walking.'

We walked very quickly. It was a mistake. Now we were lost. I couldn't focus or see properly because my eyes were brimming, heart racing and everywhere looked the same. We were going to miss the train.

'Stop,' I said. He did and so did I. We leaned against a wall. We breathed.

'Our DNA . . . ' whimpered Fin.

'Look: we gave the taxi driver her address, we made him read it three times, then we broadcast an interview with her. DNA traces are the least of our problems.'

'What's going on? Who'd kill her?'

I wanted to believe Julia's murder had nothing to do with us but I knew it did. We were the first people the police would look for when her body was found. They wouldn't let us leave the country. We had to get out right now.

Not daring to ask for directions, we followed the light to the banks of the Grand Canal and walked along with the throng of commuters to the Santa Lucia Station.

Inside, through a glass maze of shops, a passageway led to the open-air platforms. A crowd had gathered around the Orient Express, boarding for Vienna. Our train was on the neighbouring platform and we had to fight through the star-struck mob.

We found our seats at the very front carriage of the train and sat at a table opposite each other. It was quiet, too far along the train for hurried latecomers to join us. A lone business-man slunk in and sat at the other end of the carriage, diagonally across from us, as far away as it was possible to get, which suited us just fine.

I looked up and found Fin weeping into his hands.

'Hey, Fin, hey. Stop.'

He couldn't stop though. 'I don't want to do this any more,' he whimpered. 'I want to go home.'

I felt the same. We didn't know what we were doing. What if that happened to the girls or Estelle or Hamish?

So we sat there, avoiding one another's eye, grieving the lost glory that was Julia, guilty and frightened and miserable.

The train started with a jolt, pulling slowly out of Venice, across the lagoon and into a bank of thick fog.

42

Those of you who followed the podcast at the time or heard it later will have been waiting for this chapter. I'm sorry if this spoils it for you.

The podcast episode, 'We Got Drunk with a Hired Assassin', won a number of awards and broke records for downloads. People thought it was funny and strange and touching and it was easily the most popular episode but that is not what happened. We didn't get drunk with a funny man who told wild stories — at least, that's not all that happened. I've put the text of the episode in italics below. You can skip it if you'd rather not have the memory spoiled.

The real meaning of stories depends on where they're told, when and to whom. The podcast episode was of a drunk with a deep voice and a strange accent telling mad stories. But context alters meaning. This is the context.

We were in shock, wondering what the hell to do. It had been fun but frightening so far, we were reckless with our own safety, but now the podcast was leading to the deaths of the people we were interviewing. We weren't ready for that.

At this point I thought there were two possibilities: either Gretchen Teigler had ordered Julia's death to frighten us off or Julia knew something else and she'd been killed to stop her telling us. But no one could know we would go back and find her so it couldn't have been a warning. What stayed with me was the level of violence. Julia had been stabbed so many times. It was vicious. It was emotional. True crime podcasts will tell you: that's personal. Her eyes were left open; a box was carelessly dropped on the trail of blood she made getting to Violetta's photograph. But what really bothered me, because I was imagining that Julia's last moments were happening to me, was this: the photograph was not held flattened to her heart. She wasn't embracing the picture of Violetta. It was facing outwards, like a final statement to the world, a summation of her life: this was all she loved.

I looked out of the train window. We were slowly crossing the lagoon through thick and swirling fog. Lorries and cars on the road looked faded and ghostly.

We were staring into one another's wet, frightened faces. Fin was still weeping. It reminded me of the trust exercise in couples therapy, when the couples counsellor got Hamish and me to sit knee to knee and make eye contact for what felt like seven hours, during which all I could think was 'I hate you'.

Fin and I took our phones out and tried playing with them for comfort, but there was no reception and Wi-Fi was 'currently unavailable'. I scrolled through photos of the girls to calm myself down but stumbled across a selfie of Estelle and me, hugging each other at a spring concert in the park. Our cheeks were tight and we were laughing. The pretty Victorian bandstand was in the background. I put the phone away.

There were signs for a buffet car through the

carriage doors. I dried my face and went to buy a drink.

Out of the automatic door, past a big wheelchair-friendly toilet, I found myself in a buffet car of red and white plastic, quite new. Tall standing tables were dotted around the carriage. A breakfast bar with seats faced a wide window. Fin came up behind me and stood at my side.

A small Italian man behind the bar called to me, 'Buona sera, signora. Cosa vorresti?'

My Italian is bad. I was embarrassed about it as I tried to order two small bottles of white wine, one for me and one for Fin, but the man serving me said no. Two small bottles were more expensive than a normal-sized bottle of wine. I don't think I agreed but everything was a bit hazy, I was upset and covering up bad Italian.

The man opened a full bottle of wine, put it on the bar with a single plastic cup on top and asked Fin what he wanted.

Fin wanted a vodka but, again, the man advised him in very quick drawling Italian that this was not cost-effective. Fin didn't understand what he was saying so he nodded, moved his hands around, and the man somehow took this as a request for a half-bottle of vodka.

It was very expensive.

Neither of us was thinking clearly. Somehow, Fin also ended up with an egg sandwich and a gigantic bag of crisps called 'Paprika Xtreme'. These would feature later in our adventure, in quite an unexpected way.

Back at our seats, we settled in at the table and began to drink. At first the alcohol soothed and warmed and calmed. It was medicinal. Had we been anywhere else we could have left it there and walked away but we were stuck on a slow train to Milan. It was going to take ten hours and a change at Milan to get to Lyon and we seemed to be stopping at every train station on the way. This is why we continued to drink after the alcohol had done all the good it possibly could.

You may have noticed but there hasn't been much sleeping in this story so far. We had been grabbing a few hours here and there, on planes and in airport lounges, we were running on adrenaline. Fin was terribly underweight and I didn't drink much anyway. Then the heating in the carriage was turned up. I shut my eyes for what I thought was a blink and crashed.

I heard talking very near to me and the sound of Fin laughing. I vaguely wondered what was going on, I wanted very much to know, but I couldn't wake up. I was out for nearly an hour. We were pulling out of Vicenza Station when I woke up with a sticky mouth and swollen eyes.

I was very surprised by what I saw.

Across from me, next to Fin, sat the man from Saint-Martin, the man we saw with Dauphine Loire. He and Fin were smiling, craning forward, listening with rapt attention to a figure seated right next to me.

Fin's half-bottle of vodka was lying empty on the table. They had almost finished another half-bottle. The wine was finished, as was the egg sandwich, but its scent lingered. I lunged forward, trying to shake myself awake and they

301

all turned to me and cheered.

I rubbed my eyes. They were all quite drunk but Fin was utterly meroculous.

'Good morning, princess!' said the big man next to me. 'A toast! To the princess!'

I didn't like the way he hissed 'princess'.

I looked at him. He was ruddy and wearing an old-fashioned brown suit with big shoulder pads and greasy lapels. He smelled of cigarettes and vodka and rose water and stale sweat. Were the two men together? They looked alike. But I was drunk and half asleep and couldn't work out what was going on.

Fin introduced me to the man sitting next to me: this is Demy. Demy this is . . .

I said my name was Anna. I wasn't making a point about my identity. I was so sleepy and groggy that I forgot who I was supposed to be just then.

Demy turned to me and shook my hand. He held it slightly too tight. His hands were like spades and his many rings dug into me. His knuckles were scarred. His hands reminded me of the calloused hand on my neck back in the kitchen when I was Sophie. Was this the man who tried to kill me? I searched his face but it wasn't him. He watched me with rheumy eyes, the whites tinged yellow. His mouth was smiling.

He lifted his glass to me. 'A toast!'

Fin explained that Demy had come over to join him after I fell asleep. He was sitting over there when we came in, remember? Fin pointed back to the seat where the shy businessman had been. I shook my head but Fin didn't notice.

What I meant was that no one had been sitting there when we came in. Someone got on *after* us and sat down where we couldn't see him. But Fin was drunk. He had forgotten this completely.

So, continued Fin, after I fell asleep Demy came over for a chat and drink and then, when the train stopped at Padua, this guy got on! He was pointing to the man next to him. I didn't think Fin recognised him.

'Hey!' said the man. 'I am Zviad!' His English was good. 'I'm so sorry. We ate your sandwich but don't worry. I get more vodka!'

This elicited a cheer from Demy.

'Do you know who he is?' I asked Fin, pointing at Zviad.

They looked at each other and laughed.

'He's the man who's been following us!'

'Hey,' said Zviad, who was very ruddy and broad and spoke with an unexpectedly soft voice, 'Mrs Bukaran, may I say: it is my *honour*. You are a famous lady.' He flattened a hand to his chest and bowed as much as the table would let him.

'Where are you from?'

'Albanian.'

I looked at the man next to me. 'Both of you?'

'No!' said Demy with mock offence. '*I'm* Georgian.'

That got a big laugh. For the rest of the journey, whenever there was a pause or the mood dipped, someone would repeat the punchline and everyone would laugh. This went on until the garrotting in the toilet.

Fin explained that Zviad got on and, well, you know . . .

'No,' I said, 'I don't know.'

'Well,' said Fin, 'obviously, his intention towards you was not honourable.'

'Orders,' shrugged Zviad apologetically.

'But I was already drinking here with my friend Demy.'

Fin and Zviad looked at me. Their eyebrows rose. Was Demy Zviad's boss? He didn't seem to be. He was scarred. He was forty. He looked like the Russian gangsters who sat outside Russian cafes in Swiss Cottage in London, tableloads of men in cheap suits, smoking and drinking coffee. He was Georgian which would make him *vory*, a criminal mafia that stretches back generations, has its own brutal culture and dress. I could see that Zviad knew exactly what Demy was. He wouldn't cause us any trouble while Demy was with us. Even the gutter has a pecking order.

Fin had not noticed that Demy was a gangster. Fin thought Demy was a charismatic passer-by, a protective witness, keeping us safe from Zviad.

'You take orders?' Demy asked Zviad. 'From who?'

Zviad looked ashamed. 'Employer.'

Demy smirked and narrowed his eyes. 'Nice to have a job.'

Zviad blushed to the roots of his hair. I didn't know what was going on. Some gangster shit anyway.

'Another story!' Demy announced, slapping the table. 'More drink!'

When all glasses were full, Demy took a deep breath and began, 'Once upon a time — '

'Can I tape this?' Drunkenly, Fin held out his

304

phone and the mic with two hands.

Demy looked at them. His eyes clouded. He blinked. He was drinking more than the others but was still by far the most coherent. He shrugged and pouted, 'Sure.'

Fin turned the recorder on and sat it on the table. This is where the podcast episode started:

'*There was once this man, let us call him Demy. Ha ha ha ha!*'

Fin and Zviad laughed at the cue.

'*This man Demy grew up in a small town. There was nothing there. Everyone was very poor BUT because everyone was poor no one really knew they had nothing. Hey, I have a stick, you have two sticks, you feel rich, right? It's relative. Nothing but dirt floors, skinny little kids, hungry half the time, running around, no one looking after them.*'

The description was grim but Demy was telling it fondly, half smiling, his voice extra deep because his chin was on his chest.

'*The kids in the village they were all together.*' He drew a wide circle on the table. '*Yeah? Look after each other. But two boys were special close friends. Demy and Yergey. Same age. Both had no fathers. One dead, one in prison. Yergey is a crazy man. He will do anything, very impulsive. But*

Demy, he is more thoughtful, a serious person. Not alike at all.

'So these boys grow up, close, close, close. They grow up and they go to the city to find their fate. Sleep on the streets together, get drunk together, do . . . things. Anyway. They get jobs. Like you, Zviad. In time Demy works for one boss, Yergey same boss but different city. They don't see each other for a long time. Really a long time.'

Demy's voice was velvet soft, his eyes milky. He was reliving it.

'Then one day to Demy comes an order. Someone is stealing our money, someone close, and we know it is one of two men. Needs to be taken care of. So Demy goes to the address and waits, watches, sees the two men he must kill coming out of a bar. Demy rolls down the window on his car and calls to them to come. One of them is Yergey.'

Fin was very affected by that and Zviad's hand rose to his mouth. Demy paused, so overwhelmed with emotion that he struggled to get the words out, but it was a drunk's sadness, fleeting and shallow. I felt he had told this story many times before and knew it worked.

'So these two men get in Demy's car. Yergey in the front. He's so pleased to see Demy. The old friends are catching up — hey, what you been doing, where have

306

you been? They get a bottle out. They smoke and drink in the car and have a good time. Finally, Yergey says, 'Why are you here, Demy?'

'Demy says, 'You know why I'm here.''

He poured a drink and swallowed it.

''You know why I'm here, Yergey.'

'And so now Yergey does know why. They both know why.

'So, Demy turns round and he shoots the other guy in the head, POP. Dead man in the car. Do you know what Yergey says?

'Yergey says, 'Demy. I am glad it is you.'

'That is the sort of man he is. He knows it has to happen and he finds something to be glad about.

'Demy is moved by that. So, they roll the dead guy out of the car, just straight out to the ditch by the road.'

Demy made a rolling motion with his hands, a smile playing on his face. I knew then that this was not a story but a memory and I wondered why he was telling us it.

'So they sit and talk. They tell the stories of their times in the village, when they fished and played and climbed walls and went to school hungry. And when they left together, how they came to the city and became important men.

'They go for one final drink together.

Well, a few drinks actually. REALLY a few,'
he tittered. 'They drink and Yergey tells the
real story of all the crazy robberies he did
and all his wild days, stealing from bosses,
sex with the big boss's wife even! Crazy stuff
— it's a confession, final confession.

'Demy tells Yergey about his killings, sad
things he did, bad things, all his things that
he had done.

'So, at the end of the night they are back
in the car and Yergey says, 'OK. Now it is
time. Now you kill me.'

'But Demy says, 'Yergey. I can't do it.'

'Yergey says, 'You must. This is how it is.
You must kill me or they will kill you.'

'But Demy can't kill his friend. He tries
but he can't. He cries. He says, 'If I kill you,
what am I? I'm an animal.'

'He tells Yergey that he cannot kill him
but he must disappear completely. Demy
makes him go.

'Yergey disappears. Demy tells his boss
that he killed him and put the body in the
river. But no body is found. Time goes on
and still, no body. They become suspicious.
Soon no one believes he did kill Yergey. But
Demy saved his childhood friend. He made
that choice. Yergey disappears. For a while.

'But Yergey is crazy and it's a crazy time.
Civil war, new regime, crackdown, anti-
commerce, all these things and the big boss,
he knows something is not right. He has the
police in his pocket. He tells them — go
find Yergey.

'You know how the police found him? They wrote to his mother and told her that he had won a prize draw. Top prize: a fucking iPad. He comes home to get the new iPad and pthhht!'

Fin and Zviad laughed. You can hear them laughing at Yergey's foolishness on the recording. They both laugh as if they wouldn't be fooled by a cheap trick like that. But they were being fooled by a cheap trick.

I laughed too. It was hard not to but I was watching, surprised that I was laughing, and I saw that Demy's face was laughing but his eyes weren't. They were assessing the relative threat of the men in front of him. Zviad chortled away, his muscles rippling. He leaned over the table and Demy sat forward, glanced into the inside of Zviad's jacket. I saw Demy spot the knife. I saw Demy blink and go back to laughing and telling the story.

'So: the police arrest Yergey when he comes for his iPad. Yergey is an idiot. He's saying, OK, take me in, but make sure Mama gets that iPad!

'The police tell him, we will let you go, Yergey, OK? We don't want you, we want bigger fish. They tell him his friend Demy has been murdered by the boss for not killing Yergey. The boss cut Demy's balls off. The boss boiled Demy alive.

'Yergey is devastated. He didn't know even Demy was dead. He doesn't care what

309

happens to him, Yergey just wants to bring the boss down. So, he tells the police everything Demy was ordered to do by the boss. Who he was sent to kill, which ones he did, which ones he didn't. He tells them everything because he is a good friend and he wants revenge on the boss for killing Demy.

'But Demy is not dead.

'The police were working for the boss. They tricked Yergey to give evidence against him and now Demy is arrested. All because he loved his friend. The police released Yergey. They sentenced him to live with what he had done.'

He poured another drink.

Fin asked, 'What happened to Demy?'

Demy looked up. 'He was arrested for all those murders. All cases closed! Good for the cops, good for the boss. Demy was sent to prison and was killed on his second day.'

The men around the table looked confounded.

Demy yelled, 'Oh! You thought Demy was me? It's a common name, Demy! You thought it was me, that guy?'

Fin and Zviad laughed, raucous with relief and said it was brilliant. They did think it was him! Ha! What a trick! Ha!

That's where the episode ends.

His story was about killing people, about not trusting the police, about the inevitability of death and punishment. No one heard that in it but me.

When the laughter died down Demy leaned in and whispered to Fin, 'I tell you another story, a history story, if you put the recorder off.'

So Fin turned it off as Zviad poured more vodka into his cup and downed it.

'Who here,' asked Demy of the company, 'has heard of Bitch Wars?'

'I have!' said Zviad. 'I've heard of the Bitch Wars.'

'Of course *you* have!' said Demy, waving him away, a salesman dismissing a dependable buyer. 'But Findlay Co-Hen. Do *you* know this story?'

Fin shook his head.

'OK!' said Demy. 'All glasses full? All glasses full!'

He refilled all our glasses. Everyone lifted their cups to their mouths. But Demy and I didn't swallow. We tipped the cups and smacked our lips but we didn't drink. He was getting ready to do something but he wasn't watching me because I am a woman.

Demy began again, holding his arms wide to the table, inviting us in.

'Once upon a time, far away from here, in the East, some men formed a club! This club had rules. So, these men, clever men, brave men, handsome men.' He patted his cheek and batted his eyes and we all laughed because Demy wasn't handsome. 'These clever, handsome men formed a club to help themselves. There were many rules. Most important rule: no collaboration with the authorities. Not even to pass a policeman his cigarettes, not even to pick up a paper in a prison yard or switch on a light. Never aid the authorities. Thieves' code. Vory.'

I looked at Zviad and Fin. They were enthralled by Demy's story. It frightened and flattered the audience, told them that they had a place among such men, living epic lives, that life and death were in their hands. But they weren't hearing what Demy was telling us. This was a forbidden story. He shouldn't even mention *vory* to civilians like us. He shouldn't say the words 'thieves' code' or admit that such a thing existed. He was going to kill us all.

Fin didn't know that but Zviad should have noticed.

'*Vory* ran everything. Trains, agriculture, cigarettes — BUT: come the Nazis! Germans! So the authorities says, you! Handsome men! You can get out of prison if you come fight the Nazis! Come out and join the army. Some did do it. Some hate Nazis. Some lose family in the war and are angry. And some are Jews. Nazis are pretty nasty to Jews, I don't know if you know that . . . '

We all nodded to show that we did know that, actually. Demy continued.

'But so: they left gulag. They fight for the government. This broke the club rules.

'After the war, government take them out of the army and when they go back to their normal lives — boom — send them all back into gulag for new crimes, back they send them. War heroes, Nazi killers. Who cares. Straight back.

'So: once they get back in gulag, the pure *vory* who didn't fight, they call these men *suki* — means 'bitches' — because they cooperated

312

with the authorities. Those *suki* men, they're real tough bastards. They fight all the way to Berlin. You know, four thousand Nazis killed themselves in Berlin at the end because they hear these men are coming. That's how tough. But they broke the code so . . .

'So, the pure *vory* attack the *suki* and they refuse to work with them, they put them out of everything, beat them up. They treat them as low, like informants to the police.

'Think about that. You go to fight the Nazis, maybe you are a Jew.' He shrugged and gestured to Fin. 'Some people are. It is right to fight to protect your people. What else? But afterwards . . . These are the men persecuted in gulag.' He looked at Zviad and addressed him specifically. 'Men are raping you up the ass, other men are mouth-fucking you.'

Zviad was afraid but Demy wouldn't let him break eye contact. Zviad tried dipping his head but when he raised his eyes again there was Demy, waiting for him.

Demy whispered at him: 'Did you know that?'

'No,' said Zviad quietly, 'I did not know that.'

Demy stared hard at him. It was tense. Zviad tried to act casual. He reached forward to the packet of Paprika Xtreme and opened them, trying to seem relaxed, but visibly trembling. We were all frightened now and too drunk to hide it. Zviad ate a crisp but his mouth was very dry and he couldn't swallow. Defeated, he put the packet back down on the table.

'But!' continued Demy, smirking at Zviad. 'So the *suki* they think, you know, OK, fuck this. We

313

just kill all the pure *vory* and take over. Kill them all. So they began to kill them on sight. In prison, in the camps, in the streets, in the clubs. This is the Bitch Wars. *Suki* Wars. Bitch Wars go on for twenty, thirty years. *Suki* kill *vory*, *vory* kill *suki*, on and on. Next generation take over from their fathers, split down the middle. They make separate prisons for us, keep us apart.'

He sat back, and took a long drink of neat vodka.

Zviad caught my eye. He seemed to understand the threat Demy posed now. Fin still hadn't a clue. He was so drunk he wasn't listening.

Demy opened his mouth to pour more vodka in, must have lifted his tongue in a certain way, because a perfect arc of saliva sprayed from his mouth and landed on the table. He saw it and laughed with surprise, pointing at the speckles on the tabletop.

Zviad laughed but it came out weak and wrong.

'Yes,' Demy smirked at him, 'that's Bitch Wars.'

Zviad shrunk in on himself and frowned at the table. The threat he exuded evaporated. We all felt it.

Fin looked at me and widened his eyes with fairground surprise. He was incredibly drunk.

'So where are you two going on this train, princess?' asked Demy.

'Paris,' I lied. 'We change at Milan. Where are you going?'

Fin shook his head a little but he didn't contradict me.

'Paris, same as you, princess. One more hour to Milan.' He toasted me, his eyes dark and mean. 'We need *more* vodka!'

We still had a third of a bottle left but Zviad leapt to his feet. 'I'll go.' He almost saluted. Stiff with fright, he turned and walked out of the carriage to go to the buffet.

Demy stood up and said, 'And I go to piss.'

Zviad wouldn't come back.

43

'That was creepy,' said Fin. 'The thing about prison? Is that true?'

'Fin, he's telling the story to psych Zviad,' I said. 'Demy's a hired assassin.'

Fin was very interested and held his phone up again. 'Could we ask him about that?'

'We have to get out of here. Demy's here for us.'

'No. He was already on the train. He's going to Paris.'

'Fin: he got on *after* us. Do you remember?'

But Fin wasn't sober enough to fit anything together. He blinked slowly and got more confused.

I explained, 'He's a professional criminal. Either he was following us or he happened to spot us and knew there was money in finding me. There's a contract. It'll be a lot of money.'

This was news to Fin. 'He's just a businessman.'

There is a nice way to dispel self-delusion, which is a beautiful thing if you can get it, but this isn't it: 'You fucking idiot, Fin.'

'But he's funny,' he said, as if that was a defence. 'Are you sure?'

It was at this awkward moment that Demy arrived back, walking down the aisle, zipping up his flies and sighing with theatrical satisfaction. He sat back down and poured all three of us all another drink. He didn't refill Zviad's cup.

'A toast!' he said.

And so began another spell of drinking or pretending to drink.

Zviad never came back from the buffet car. Demy mentioned that the toilet had flooded and avoid it if you need to piss.

Over the course of the next thirty minutes Fin's eyes would flicker to the seat next to him, wondering where Zviad was. Sometimes he even wondered aloud where he was, but Demy would say something reassuring or do something distracting, say that the buffet was very busy, or else he would launch off into another gangster story, not scary this time because he didn't consider Fin any kind of threat.

At one point Demy did consider Fin a threat. Fin, very drunk, leaned in too close and whispered. 'Did you kill our friend Julia?'

Demy considered the question. 'Who?'

'Our friend Julia Parker, back in Venice, she was stabbed many, many times.'

I became aware of a noise, a faint, distant banging sound coming from the disabled toilet.

Demy chortled, 'Stabbed? With a knife? Like in a panic?'

Here he pretended to jab Fin with his finger, giving off little frightened screams. It was funny, the way he did it, but he could see it was inappropriate. Fin laughed uncomfortably: don't judge him for that. When frightening men make a joke people laugh.

The banging noise was getting louder. A guttural sound, like a low growl or groan, caught

Demy's attention and his eyes flicked to the carriage door.

'Men don't stab,' he said. 'Why you ask me this? Where did your friend get killed?'

But his attention was on the toilet door.

'In Venice,' said Fin.

'Very sad!' Demy nodded. 'A toast!'

A sudden loud thud from down the corridor made Demy flinch. It sounded like someone falling against a wall. Fin didn't hear it. He put his head down on the table and fell asleep.

Demy stood up clumsily, knocking over and spilling the last of the vodka on to the table. He said oh! Don't worry! He would go buy more, don't worry. I said OK and shut my eyes, making sure Demy saw me fall asleep. He walked away and I watched through my lashes, saw him walk away, out of the carriage, and then saw the toilet door open. Demy slid in and shut it behind him.

We were drawing into a deserted concrete platform. The train slowed. The station signs slipping past the window read 'Brescia'. Fin was asleep on the table.

'Get up, Fin!' I shook him but he was out cold. I tried to lift him but, thin as he was, I couldn't. He was a dead weight. He slithered from my arms to the floor, slipping under the table. The train stopped in the empty station. I tucked his arms in under the table, pulled all our stuff underneath to make it look as if we had left the train. I hurried along the carriage to the toilet.

The door was locked. I could hear faint banging against the inside wall, a head being slammed hard. I put my ear to the door and heard a grunt.

I opened the door to the platform and waited, listening as the banging slowed down, getting softer and softer and then still.

I threw the bag of Paprika Xtreme on to the platform, aiming for the exit, and it emptied as it flew, scattering crisps in a long arc, making it look as if we had dropped them as we ran away from the train.

I hung out of the carriage door and shouted at the outside of the toilet window, 'FIN, HURRY!'

I bolted back through the carriage and clambered under the table, tucked myself tight in around Fin.

I could see along the dirty carpeted floor to the bottom of the toilet door. It opened. Zviad's legs lay still on the floor. Demy stepped over him, kicking the feet behind the door and locking it from the outside with a coin. Then his feet disappeared in the direction of the exit. He must have been looking out on to the platform.

The doors beeped a warning but Demy was still on the train. The beeping ended.

I closed my eyes. The carriage doors slid softly shut and the train took off.

44

As the train jolted away I looked up and Demy caught my eye. It was only for a moment. I unfurled from under the table and he watched me through the glass, wind whipping his hair up as the train pulled away.

I stood in the aisle, hands trembling, heart cantering in my chest. I thought I would be sick but then I wasn't and then I thought I might be sick again. This went on for some time while Fin snored sweetly on the floor.

I sat down.

Twenty minutes later the train pulled languorously into Milan. I didn't know how often the trains ran from Brescia. Demy could already be here.

I dragged Fin out from under the table, stood him up and half carried him off the train. We staggered along the platform and into the main hall. I swear he fell asleep on his feet as I was reading the departures board. I found the platform number for a fast train to Lyon and made Fin run.

We caught the train by a hair, boarding as the doors were shutting, working our way through the carriages and sitting in the middle this time. I don't think I'll ever sit at the end of a train again, or in any carriage with only one way out.

It was a six-hour unbroken journey. The chairs were uncomfortable. The carriage reeked of chemical toilet. I have never been more pleased to be anywhere. We slumped and I passed out, waking with a start twenty minutes later, clammy and shaking. Fin was wide awake, still quite drunk but happily playing on his phone. SNCF did have Wi-Fi. It was while I was asleep, I should say, that Fin tweeted the podcast episode with Demy's story in it. I didn't tell him what had happened to Zviad until afterwards.

'Why did you think he was going to kill us?'

'He was telling us.'

'No he wasn't.'

'He told us, Fin. The story about Yergey? The Bitch Wars.'

Fin blinked hard. 'They were just stories.'

'There's no such thing.'

I told him about Zviad in the toilet. Fin insisted that we call the Italian police, Zviad might still be alive, we didn't know, but a decade of avoiding the authorities makes you skittish. So Fin called, spoke for a bit, louder and louder, looked increasingly exasperated and then handed me the phone.

The operator didn't speak English or attempt to moderate his heavily accented Italian. I didn't even try to use my broken Italian. I knew the call would be recorded and it would show us trying to inform the police of the murders of Julia and Zviad but failing. It was good. We could use it later to prove that we were innocent. I kept the call going for as long as possible and then hung up. I didn't know they had CCTV on all train carriages and had film of Demy dragging Zviad into the toilet.

I don't think I have ever been so tired in my life. Every cell felt depleted but I was too wired to sleep. I lay my head on the window and watched the mountains glide by in the grey dawn and missed my girls as Fin played on his phone.

'Oh,' he said. 'Anna . . . '

He showed me the Twitter feed. The Demy episode was already raking in the RTs, but one comment came in every thirty seconds. It was bot-generated. Untraceable. It was a photo of my girls.

I had never seen this photo. It was the girls in Halloween fancy dress costumes they'd worn to the school. It must have come from someone else's Facebook post. They were grinning in front of the gates with their arms around each other. Lizzie had no front teeth. Same photo over and over again.

The picture was captioned 'Call me, DL x'.

45

At Lyon we checked into a bland corporate hotel a mile or so from the station. We got one room. Neither of us felt safe enough to be alone. Or sleep. Or even lie flat, actually. We were both, in the parlance of the street, fucking terrified.

I ate all the complimentary biscuits, stared out of the dirty window and drank watery hot chocolate. When I couldn't take any more and had to walk, we went out. We went to find Sabine's bakery.

We walked fast for an hour. It felt good. We were in a posh clothing street off the Place des Jacobins when I saw Fin turn to look in a shop window and the skin on his neck folding in five straight lines. He was thinner than he had been when we set off. God, I missed Hamish. I missed his beautiful hands and his flaws and his uncomplicated selfishness. I missed fighting with him about Candy Crush. I missed my face buried deep in his faithless chest and my nose brushing his hair.

'Here.'

Fin was staring into a shop window full of beautiful cakes.

'Really?' I said, stupidly thinking he was hungry.

'This is Sabine's bakery.'

'Oh.'

He took out his phone, fitted the mic and

turned on the voice recorder. Then he smiled at me, slipped the phone into the top pocket of his tweed jacket, mic sticking out, and walked boldly into the shop.

It was a sombre room of bare pink plaster with brightly coloured tiny cakes, pink and green, brown and blue, tiny éclairs and millefeuilles, all the classics, done in miniature. They were little works of art. Behind the counter were two women, both in white chef jackets. Sabine was blonde and looked remarkably like Amila. We knew it was her immediately, even though we had never seen a photo of her, because she knew us.

She crossed her arms and spoke to us in English. 'Get. The. Fuck. Out.'

'Oh,' said Fin, surprised by the level of aggression. Awkwardly, he raised a hand as if he was waving hello to her on a bridge a mile away. 'Um. Hi.'

'Out!'

She lifted the counter and came out, arms wide, shepherding us towards the street. It was a bit frantic. She was moving very quickly, having been in a hot kitchen, and we were sloping about like a pair of hipster bums who hadn't slept, were hungover and felt sorry for themselves. Somehow there was a consensus that if she got us as far as the street we would never have the chance to speak to her again. We resisted.

I stood on her foot. She narrowed her lips and turned to me, wide-eyed. Sabine was tiny, I should say, so she was looking up at me at quite an acute angle. She could have bitten a chunk out of my shoulder if she had been so inclined.

'Amila is innocent,' I said. 'Don't you want her free?'

She shook with anger. 'Amila is ill. Amila is very ill and was misdiagnosed in prison. Now it's too late. They can't treat her without killing her but you don't care about that because it's not in your story.'

She tried to wiggle her foot out from under mine but I pressed it harder. 'What if we can get her out?'

She stopped. 'Like, a jailbreak?'

'Like, prove it was someone else.'

She snorted not once, but twice, and whispered, 'You don't know these people.'

'Gretchen Teigler?'

She looked at us, one to the other, and smirked. 'She'll kill you.'

'She has tried.'

That got her attention. I softened my hold on her foot.

'When?'

'Just now on a train. Two assassins. And before.' I lifted up my fringe to show my scar and she looked confused.

'*Elle est Sophie Bukaran,*' said the woman behind the counter.

Sabine knew the name. She nodded at me, impressed. 'You *do* know her then?'

'I do.'

Fin blurted suddenly, 'How could you afford to open a bakery?'

Sabine blinked.

'I know you didn't have the money before

Amila's conviction but suddenly you do. How did that happen?'

'Are you accusing me of something?'

Fin was too tired to couch it. 'I am, yeah. I wonder how it is that you've suddenly got money and Amila decides not to appeal against her conviction.'

Sabine laughed bitterly, staring into the street beyond us, standing very still. She snapped back and looked at us. 'Come in,' she ordered. 'Come in here.'

She turned away, looked at my foot and I released her. She walked back through the space in the counter and waited at the side for us to follow her through to the kitchen.

It was spotless, full of new stainless-steel appliances and worktops. The sound quality would be tinny and awful. Too many hard surfaces. She waited until we were standing with her and then she said, 'I was paid by Gretchen Teigler, in cash by her secretary. She came here with the money in a bag and told me that Amila should serve her sentence and not appeal and I could have all that money. She opened the bag to show me it. It was a lot. She didn't know it was already too late. We were dealing with bigger things than her appeal.'

'You took the money?'

'I did. It made no difference. It was already too late for Amila. She's dying but at least now, when the courts decide she's nearly dead and release her, I can afford good palliative care. So I took the money, signed a non-disclosure and opened this bakery. She wanted this. We both wanted this. So now I visit Amila once a month and I send her photographs of the bread every day, so that she can see the morning's work. When I visit her, if it's one of the days when she can talk, we talk about the bread, about the bakery and the cakes.'

'If she can talk?'

Sabine hung her head. She braced herself and her voice became a whisper. 'Amila's headaches, the reason she left the *Dana* in Saint-Martin, were caused by a brain tumour. She is dying. They have operated twice but it keeps growing back. An appeal will take years. She wouldn't live long enough to go to court. If she was free she could have had better treatment, she could have travelled for the operation, it might have gone better. But she isn't. She's in prison and this — ' Sabine motioned to kitchen — '*this* is what she wants me to do. So you — ' she prodded me in the chest — 'you tell people. Tell them I took blood money from that bitch and let her think I betrayed Amila, that her money was enough for me to do that. I let everyone think that. I don't care what you think of me because I have one thing to do for my Amila. I get up at three thirty every morning and make beautiful bread, and I make it with love, for Amila. I take a photo of the bread every day and I print it and, before we open the doors to our customers, I put that picture in an envelope and I post it to Amila because she can't read any more. But she can see pictures. And every morning I stand at the postbox. And every morning I kiss her envelope and I whisper her name. My Amila is worth ten of Gretchen Teigler and my Amila is dying and I am dying too. Now get out of our shop and don't you fucking come back here.'

We did.

Outside Fin took the phone out of his pocket, pulled the mic out and put it into its little bag and drew the string. He put it in his pocket.

'I don't know if we should use that recording,' he said.

I think we both felt very humbled. 'Yeah. Best scrub that. We can tell it ourselves.'

We walked for a bit. I thought about Sabine, how she was prepared to have people believe her low, the constancy of her love. She could have been lying, but I didn't think she was.

Teigler wielded her power so ruthlessly. She had warped all of our lives. She might have spies here, she might know we'd been to see Sabine. We could have put her in terrible danger just by talking to her, like Julia.

Out of nowhere I said, 'I can't fucking stand this any more. I'm going to Paris to confront Gretchen Teigler face-to-face.'

'But Demy's in Paris,' said Fin.

'I'm expecting Demy to be there.'

We walked on. I expected Fin to say he'd stay or go to his friend's in Clermont-Ferrand. He stopped and nodded and said, 'OK. I'm coming too.'

On the Paris train I sent a text to Dauphine Loire.

'*I'll be at the Neuilly villa tomorrow. Tell Gretchen I'll only talk to her.*'

She didn't reply.

46

We got drunk again, on a train again, but this was more melancholy because Demy wasn't there to tell stories. We were scared and being drunk helped.

We were still quite drunk when we got to Paris.

I don't honestly know how we ended up in a hotel as expensive as that. I don't know if we took a taxi or what happened. It seems too far to have walked from the station. But maybe we did. I just don't know. There are gaps.

But we got there and we saw it was a hotel because a big sign outside said 'HOTEL' and so we went in.

We were drunk, we were exhausted and dishevelled. We staggered over to the reception desk. No one asked us to leave. I have a vague memory of a smirking beautiful woman explaining the breakfast times to Fin as he rocked softly on his heels next to me.

She told us all she had was a suite. I thought maybe she had confused us with some important dishevelled drunks but she took our passports, photocopied them and gave them back. She called Fin by his proper name, welcomed him, and we were escorted up in the lift by a man. I think it was a man.

The suite had a living room with a very big television and sofas with a lot of cushions. The dominant colour was beige. Off the living room was a dining room and then a door led into a bedroom with a gigantic and inviting bed, a headboard of grey silk, crisp white linen sheets and too many pillows.

Fin tried to tip the man who had brought us here but he refused to take the money.

'I loved it,' he said, apropos of nothing.

'Wha'?' Fin tried to tip him again.

'The train podcast. Demy. Brilliant. Thank you.' And he walked out and shut the door.

We slept for ten hours. I can't make that interesting. Of note was the fact that we were in separate beds, I on the couch, Fin on the bed. I had a bath at one point. Later he had a bath. It's quite boring to hear about but the experience was glorious. It was lovely to be clean.

During the night a number of things happened without us.

The podcast went stratospheric. Most of it was Demy telling the story of Yergey and a lot of Fin and Zviad giggling. I've heard that episode since and I admit that it is compelling.

Also: Zviad's body was found in the toilet. He had been strangled. Zviad was thirty-one and had a wife and a seven-year-old son in Durres. The CCTV from the train was viewed and Demy was found and traced to Pigalle a few hours later. He was arrested and charged with Zviad's murder. He was not charged with Julia's murder. His real name was Yergey.

This was all unknown to us as we woke up the next morning, late, about ten, and ordered breakfast in our room. A trolley arrived with coffee and fresh croissants and jam, muesli and almond milk. We opened the windows in the dining room and ate with our feet on the table, looking out of the window at the Paris rooftops. If we stood on a chair and bent sideways we could see the Eiffel Tower. We both felt hung-over, but calm, until our predicament sank in.

I was nervous. Fin could see that. 'What are you going to say?'

'I'm going to tell Gretchen what happened to Leon.'

'Don't you think she knows already?'

'I have to believe she doesn't.'

I looked at him. He was eating cereal with almond milk. The bowl was small but it was his second portion. I could tell that he was enjoying it. I smiled.

'Are you smiling because I'm eating?

'No, I'm smiling because I care. It's that addict vortex, isn't it? Everyone around gets sucked in. Two weeks from now I'd be crying and banging on the bathroom door and begging you to eat a cracker.'

He laughed at that, covering his mouth to keep the cereal from going everywhere.

He finished his food. He picked up his phone and started to scroll. 'Fucking hell. This is out of control.'

He showed me the numbers. They were ludicrous, in the hundreds of thousands. This had to be the peak of it and there would never be a better time to expose Teigler.

'I'm coming with you,' said Fin.

'No, you're not.'

'Yes, I am. I'm coming.'

I didn't think Fin should come with me. It could go very wrong. The plan was thin and had three different factors that could easy fail. We argued for a bit but he wasn't even open to a discussion about it. 'I'm coming,' was all he would say. He didn't need to. I thought of Julia lying on the floor, eyes fixed on the ceiling.

'It might not work, Fin. I'm walking into a very dangerous situation. There's no real reason for you to come. If I'm there alone and they kill me it'll be over, you'll be clear.'

'I'm coming,' he said, 'I won't let them hurt you.'

'What are you going to do? Faint at her?'

'I saved you in Skibo. I'm coming with you,' and he got up and locked himself in the bathroom.

That was fair. He had saved me. All I had left to do was talk to my girls. I called Hamish and we had a curt, in-front-of-the-kids conversation.

'How are you?'

'Very well, Anna, how are you today?'

'Did the move go OK?'

'Actually better than could be expected. We got an upgrade so it was worth doing.'

'Oh, I'm in mortal danger but you save a buck. Well done.'

'Yes, tens of euros so, in the end, it's all been worthwhile.' As I said, he can be quite dry.

We both instinctively knew not to say where they were, just in case. But Hamish mentioned the journey and a flight and I assumed they were far away from Porto.

I could hear the kids watching TV in the background. He put them on to talk to me.

It was all the usual stuff. You don't need to hear that. We were pretending things were OK so it was all pretty banal, even while it meant the world to me. I kept telling them I loved them and how happy I was that they were having a good time. Jess was talkative. I think she was trying to reassure me that I was still number one. She didn't want to mention Estelle or say anything positive about her to me. I didn't want their future to be all about me vs Estelle. I didn't want that for them.

I asked Jess to put Estelle on. She asked if I was sure. I said, yes, of course, we're friends. I was friends with Estelle before Daddy even met her, you remember?

She gave the phone to Estelle.

'Estelle?'

'Yes?'

'You know the situation?'

'Yes.'

'If anything happens I want the girls to remember us being friends. Can you cheer it up a bit?'

'Oh, yes, of course! Of course, Anna, don't worry about a thing.'

Estelle has the same weaknesses as me. Maybe that's why we liked each other. She said, 'The girls have made holiday diaries to show you, so you know what happened each day. They'll talk you through them when they get back.' There is no word for the realisation that a step-parent cares for your children almost as much as you do, it's a very strong feeling, a great, hot soup of gratitude and relief and love.

'I didn't hit him, Estelle. I want you to know that. And it was over between us. He's not lying about that. We were struggling.'

'OK then!' She said it for the audience, not for me. 'So, where is Fin?'

Fin was still in the bathroom. He'd been running the water in the sink for a suspiciously long time.

'Fin is pretending to wash his hands in the sink but I think he's actually throwing up his cereal.'

She snorted at that and I laughed along with her. The bathroom door opened and out came Fin.

'Can I speak to him?'

I caught Fin's eye. 'I don't know if he wants to speak to you, to be honest, Estelle . . . '

But he did. He reached forward and took the phone and went into another room. He whispered to her. I don't know what they said. When he came back he had hung up and his eyes were red.

'What did you say to her?'

'Goodbye.' He looked at me. 'It's hard to be alive sometimes. Don't you find it hard?'

I was worried he meant he didn't care if we were murdered today. 'I do, until my life is threatened and then I'd fight the world.'

He smiled. 'Fuck it, let's go to Gretchen's house.'

'Fin, you are planning to come back out of there, aren't you?'

'Yes.' But he didn't sound unconvinced. I felt he was planning to do something heroic.

'Stick to the plan.'

'I will.'

I knew he was depressed and reckless, I knew he was losing weight and I should have left him in the hotel. I let him come with me because I was afraid to go in alone. I'm a coward and a bad friend.

We went downstairs.

We did not belong in that hotel. The other guests wore dress-down cashmere sweaters and couture frocks. As we crossed the lobby to the front door I saw, on a tiny plaque on the wall behind reception, the room tariff. Our suite was six grand a night. It almost made me hope we didn't come back. We'd be washing dishes for a century.

47

The Teigler villa was set back from the street, obscured by a row of trees and an eight-foot-high wall with broken glass twinkling on top. Cameras were perched on high poles at either end. The gate was grey metal, tall and barred, with matching sheet metal behind it blocking the view of the house.

Fin took his phone out, put the mic in and turned on the recorder. 'We are at the gate of the villa,' he said solemnly. 'We're going in to meet Gretchen Teigler. It's a pretty serious gate, three big bolt locks, cameras everywhere.'

He nodded me to the button. I took a deep breath, raised my hand and pressed the bell. We heard nothing.

The intercom was a grey metal box with a speaker on it and a small glass eye. We had to assume we were being watched. Fin nodded me to it and I raised a hand to press again just as the heavy lock on the gate snapped open. Fin pushed it with his shoulder and we slipped into the grounds.

From a drab Parisian street we found ourselves in another world. Combed white gravel chips framed twin square lawns on either side of a path leading up to curved steps to the door. The building was a nineteenth-century villa, two storeys and modest in scale, pale yellow with stucco plaster leaves painted green running diagonally across the facade. They were lush and bushy at the bottom, trailing to sparse and detailed at the top. It was quite lovely.

The lock on the gate snapped shut behind us. We were trapped.

We looked at each other. I hoped I didn't look as scared as he did. Fin took a step forward on the gravel and we discovered that it was not just ornamental. Every movement of our feet echoed around the yard, the sound amplified by the sheet metal gate.

We waited.

I don't know what we were expecting, dogs or snipers, but nothing happened.

Fin's voice was very low as he muttered into his phone mic, 'We are trapped in here. The gate is locked behind us and we're approaching the front of the house now.'

We crunched up to the stairs, our steps ridiculously loud in the vacuum of sound. We stopped at the bottom. Nothing happened. We walked up the steps to the front door.

'We are at the door,' whispered Fin.

I knocked. We could hear steps approaching inside and the front door opened. A Filipino maid in her sixties, wearing a black uniform under a white starched pinny, invited us in without looking at our faces.

We stepped into the hallway.

From the outside it looked like a grand nineteenth-century villa but inside it was pure San Diego, as if the inside had been scooped out and remodelled as an ugly Californian hotel from 1987.

The hallway was shallow and wide, three small rooms knocked into one, black-and-white-tiled floor and very little furniture. A white marble statue of a headless naked woman stood between two sets of double doors. There were no seats.

The Filipino lady shut the front door behind us, bolting it top and bottom. She turned back and pointed at the phone in Fin's hand.

'Non.'

She watched him take the mic out and put it in the drawstring bag. She watched him turn off the voice recorder and ceremoniously put the phone away in the top pocket of his suit jacket.

'Is it recording?' she asked in unexpected English.

'No,' said Fin, patting his pocket.

She looked at the centimetre peeking out of his pocket, unsure whether to believe him.

Fin told her the microphone fitting was at the bottom, in the mouth piece. 'It can't pick up sound as long as it's in my pocket. That's why I have this.' He showed her the detachable mic and dropped his phone back into his breast pocket.

She looked, reassured herself that it was pointing the wrong way, and then turned and walked away through a side door.

We waited. The renovations must have included soundproofing because we heard nothing, no muffled steps or radio burbles, no sounds of car engines from the street or jets overhead. It was quite disconcerting.

Fin leaned his back against the wall for a moment. He was very pale.

338

Suddenly one set of the double doors in front of us opened.

Dauphine Loire stood there, smiling coldly, dressed in a white wrap dress, patent nude shoes, steel-framed glasses and a silver belt.

'Hello,' said Dauphine. 'Thank you for coming to see us. Come with me, won't you?'

She turned and walked down the stairs, inviting us to follow with an imperious wave of her hand.

Her accent was no longer Venetian. Now her inflection was fluent Southern Californian. As an observer of accents, she was very good, I'll give her that.

We followed her down into a large airy room with wall-to-wall cream carpets. There was no one in there, just a big TV on a wall and a giant cream sofa. The far wall was a sheet of glass looking out on to a long stretch of lawn. At the end of the lawn I saw the roof of a glass tourist boat sliding slowly along the Seine.

Dauphine walked over to the right-hand wall, pressed three fingers into a square and a door swung open on the wall. We followed her through it into a stone corridor. It led down and along the back of the house. It must have been subterranean, the geography of the house was quite confusing, but we came through a door into a Victorian sunroom attached to the side of the house. It had been stripped of shelves and seedling pots and redecorated as a sterile space. It was eye-wateringly bright.

And there, in the bright blaze, sitting in the centre of a white-and-yellow-striped sofa, was a small woman in a blue dress, steel-framed glasses, her hair up in a blonde chignon.

She stood to meet us as we came in. Hands clasped in front of her, a signal that she would not be shaking hands.

'Hello,' she said. 'I am Gretchen Teigler.'

48

We were being offered tea and cakes by both
Dauphine and Gretchen. Fin said no, that we'd
rather just get on with it, thank you. They agreed
that yes, tea and cakes would be nice, yes, I'll call
the maid. It was as if they couldn't hear him
speaking. That's how I knew that they were
almost as nervous as we were.

Dauphine pressed a button on an intercom on
the wall and told someone to bring tea and
macarons.

A voice crackled back, '*Oui, madame*'.

They were dressed alike but there was no
physical similarity between them. Dauphine was
slim and tall, her legs were long, Gretchen was
short and stubby and wide across the hips.
Dauphine sat down next to Gretchen and her
pose exactly mirrored Gretchen's. She crossed
her legs, clasped her hands around her knees, it
was extraordinary to watch her smile and
respond to Gretchen's every gesture, mimicking,
reflecting. When Gretchen looked at me,
Dauphine followed her gaze to my face and all
the Gretchen-inspired warmth drained from her.
I could have been a tree or a table.

'I hear — ' Gretchen's accent was Californian,
her voice soft — 'that you are investigating my
husband Leon's death?'

I nodded.

'In a 'podcast'?'

'Yes.'

'And that you actually met him some years ago?' She seemed to speak exclusively in questions.

I nodded. My mouth was so dry I didn't trust myself to speak.

'Well — ' she gave me a cold smile — 'that's nice.'

We looked at each other, Gretchen Teigler and I. She had done such awful things to me, brutal things, when I was young and vulnerable, but she looked at me unflinchingly. I wondered how she dared. And she kept looking at me, sternly, as if I were the offender of the piece. What mental processes did she use to justify what she had done? I couldn't imagine.

She seemed to be having similar thoughts about me though because we were glaring at each other now. Dauphine interjected and I knew it wasn't to spare me. 'We have crossed paths before, you and I,' she said. 'I believe you used to call yourself 'Sophie Bukaran'?'

'I didn't *used to call* myself that. It's my name. People change their names though, don't they, Dauphine?'

It was as if Dauphine saw me for the first time. She looked at my face, her head tipped, her cheek twitched a curious smile. 'Huh!' she said, suddenly interested.

Gretchen was not interested. My teaser didn't pique her curiosity at all. She just wanted this to be over. Her mouth turned down at the corners. 'I have someone here who knows you.'

She glanced at Dauphine, nodding an order.

Dauphine stood up and pressed the button on the wall again before sitting back down. They looked expectantly at a door in the back wall. I think I knew who was out there. Why wouldn't they? He was the only person I was scared of.

The door opened and the man stepped into the room, presenting himself to the company. He was big, dressed for a fight, badly scarred on his neck and jaw. I would have known him without the white squares of grafted skin on his cheek and jaw. Dark hair, long lashes, narrow chin. For a moment I was back in my mum's kitchen, oil spluttering in the pan behind me, flinching from the sight of Patricia's name on the face of my ringing phone.

I think he expected me to scream or something. He had been waiting for this moment. He had probably thought about me more than I had thought about him. Every time he had an operation, when his scars ached, when anyone flinched at his scars. He had been waiting to meet me again and I spoiled it for him by not reacting at all.

'Do you know me?' he said.

'You're that oily boy,' I said and shrugged. 'So what? Second time lucky?'

He tried a threatening scowl but it didn't take. What he didn't know was that I wasn't going to get scared. I was already scared and had been for a long time. My blank reaction annoyed him. He scanned the room for someone to frighten and saw Fin, skinny, effete. He turned square to him, expecting at least a cower.

But Fin sauntered over to him, stepping

343

protectively in front of me, holding out his hand. 'Good afternoon,' he said pleasantly. 'Very nice to meet you. I'm Fin Cohen.'

Perplexed, Scarface smiled and took Fin's hand, squeezing tight. I noticed he planted his feet carefully, as if he was expecting Fin to try a throw or a punch. But Fin didn't do any of that. He just shook the man's hand and stared into his face.

All the women watched them shake hands for too long. It was a peculiar moment but Fin knew what he was doing: he was getting a good, clean look at his face. When Scarface finally realised that there would be no bouts of wrestling or judo, just a whole lot of handshaking, he let go and shuffled back to the wall, cupped his hands in front of himself, waiting.

I said to him, 'You and Ms Teigler have known each other for a long time. Where did you meet?'

He looked at Gretchen, who gave a non-committal roll of her shoulder. She didn't really care what anyone said now. We were coming to the end of it.

'London?' I said. 'When the rape case was going on?'

They looked at each other. Gretchen gave a little head shake.

'The rape case,' I said. 'The court case against the men who raped me.'

No one said anything. I could see Gretchen losing patience and squirming. I liked it.

I asked Scarface, 'Did you kill the other girl and set fire to her house?'

He gave a slow blink.

'Never mind,' I said. 'Let's assume you killed her after you tried to kill me. Your blood was all over my kitchen, wasn't it? Bet the police kept some of that.' I turned to Gretchen. 'I heard you're pawning the stadium in Fulham.'

She curled her lip. 'I don't know what you're talking about.' She turned towards Scarface, opened her mouth and drew a breath, on the brink of telling him to get me out of here, but was interrupted by the sound of rattling china outside the door.

'Ah!' Dauphine clapped her hands together. 'Tea!'

The maid, it turned out, was the Filipino woman who had opened the front door. She arrived with a tea trolley carrying an elaborate china tea service and a plate of multicoloured macarons, set out in circles of red, green, yellow. I think Gretchen and Dauphine had been on a diet or something because they were mesmerised by the sight of the cakes.

The maid rolled the trolley into the middle of the room, picked up the teapot to pour, but was ordered to leave, which she did.

Dauphine stood and poured. Fin and I both realised at the same time that there were only two cups. We were not expected to be here for very much longer.

Fin went for it. 'We really came here to ask you about the sinking of the *Dana*, if possible, Ms Teigler. It should only take a few minutes.'

Gretchen looked from the cakes to Fin's phone in his pocket. 'You're not recording this?'

Fin said, 'There wouldn't be any point, would

there? I think we all know how this ends.'

Gretchen shrugged, dispassionate to the brink of bored.

Fin ploughed on. 'We all know Amila Fabricase is innocent,' he said. 'That someone else was on board the *Dana* that night and got off. You have the necklace that should have gone down with the ship. That story about it being posted is tissue-thin. There are traces of a Zodiac ripcord in the wreck dive film. We know someone flew Violetta into Saint-Martin, paid for her hotel suite, bought her two dresses in different sizes. There was someone else there and that person cast the *Dana* off from the dock. They drugged the Parkers and then left on the Zodiac lifeboat before it sank. They had the necklace with them. They couldn't stand to leave it. But they didn't keep it. They gave it to you.'

Gretchen gave a sickly smile. 'You don't believe in ghosts then?'

Fin gave her one back. 'You don't seem very surprised by any of this. I mean — ' He stepped forward and did a strange thing: he picked up a bright green pistachio macaron and took a big bite. 'Why aren't you surprised?' He spluttered bits of green powder on to the floor. 'You know all of this already, don't you?'

She gave an incredulous lady laugh from deep in her throat. 'Whatever can you mean?'

I hated her at this point. I loathed her faux innocence, her decor choices, her bringing Scarface back to frighten me. Leon was no hero but how could he marry her? How could he stand her? Maybe he needed cash to support his families but there must have been less disgusting billionaires in his social circle, someone with a bit of panache or style or a bit of something. Gretchen was revolting.

'Leon was broke, wasn't he?' I said loudly. 'Did you know that when you married him?'

Gretchen sniffed and pursed her lips. 'He covered it well.'

'You were angry when you found out.'

'Well, I had already married him by then.'

At this point I thought fuck it and stood up to take a raspberry macaron without being offered. 'But you were angry enough to withdraw all financial support to Julia?'

I took a bite. Christ, it was gorgeous. So sweet and acid, lemon and raspberry, soft and crunchy, that I almost didn't hear Gretchen mutter, 'I didn't withdraw Julia's financial support.'

She looked at Dauphine who leaned towards her and explained softly, 'The lawyers had a problem with Julia's papers. She wouldn't sign the contract. They're sorting it out now. It's just temporary.'

Gretchen grumbled, 'I didn't hear anything about that.'

'They're sorting it out now.'

Fin said, 'You could have sent her a suitcase of cash,' and waved his half-eaten macaron at the fancy room.

Gretchen smiled bitterly. 'Yes, well, other people's money is always infinite, isn't it?'

'Dauphine is lying,' I said. 'It's not temporary. Julia hasn't had any support for two years.'

Gretchen frowned, in as much as she was able.

'What's she living on?'

'She's fine,' said Dauphine dismissively. 'She has a house that an old boyfriend lets her live in.'

'It's two damp rooms,' I said.

Dauphine raised a shoulder and told Gretchen, 'She's happy there.'

'No, Julia is not happy there. Julia is dead. She was murdered. Two days ago she was stabbed repeatedly in the chest. She dragged herself ten feet across the room, bleeding out, drowning in her own blood, to get a photograph of Violetta. She was clutching it, face out, on her chest when we found her.'

Gretchen was genuinely shocked. Her hand began to shake. Dauphine put a protective arm around her shoulder. 'Don't upset yourself, darling.'

'Do you feel bad about that?' I said to Dauphine.

She was wary. 'Of course. It's terrible.'

'No, I mean, just leaving your mother lying there like that? You killed Julia, didn't you, Violetta?'

Violetta stood up suddenly and her plate crashed to the floor. Her lemon macaron shattered like a yellow dust bomb. She looked at it, moved to say something but stopped. She looked at Gretchen. A warm, loving smile broke out on her face. But this time Gretchen didn't reciprocate the warmth. She shrank away from her and whispered, 'What did you do?'

Violetta ignored her and nodded Scarface to me but Gretchen held up a staying hand.

'Violetta,' she whispered, 'what did you do?'

Violetta turned to her and tried the loving smile again. 'Protecting *you*, Gretchen, that is all I want to do.' Her accent was Italian now. She sounded like an off-echo of Julia's gorgeous drawl.

They looked at each other, Gretchen cowering and horrified by what she had heard, Violetta's expression happy and loving, like a mother on a Christmas card. Her reaction to Gretchen's shock was wrong, so wrong that it was clear Violetta was fluently expressing emotions she wasn't feeling. I remembered the restaurant in Venice, the eerie sense that she could eat soup or stab me in the face and feel nothing much about either.

I carried on, trying not to look straight at Fin. 'Julia dragged herself across the room to get to a photograph of you. Did you watch her? Did you watch her die? Or were you already busy raking through her belongings, looking for the luggage from Hotel Toraque. You couldn't believe she still kept the luggage the hotel sent back, could you? She kept it all that time. But you needed it back because it proves Dauphine was there. Her DNA is all over it. It wasn't even your size. That's Dauphine's body rotting in the *Dana's* dining room. You got her to take you to Saint-Martin in Gretchen's plane, to hire the hotel suite for you — '

'They were great friends!' said Gretchen.

I couldn't stop myself. 'You are a fucking mug, lady! Violetta has been playing you all along. Was Dauphine a bit needy? Was she friendless? Isolated because she worked for you, was she?'

Gretchen flinched.

'Of course she was. And she was blown sideways when beautiful Violetta wanted to be friends with her. She couldn't believe it. Violetta made the overtures, didn't she? *We've got so much in common!* Think about it.'

I could see her rolling through the history, realising how Violetta had played her chubby sidekick Dauphine before she turned all that charm on Gretchen.

'Violetta, did you pick the dresses and charge them to her? She probably thought it was a friendly gesture. Familial. But she was a size 42, and you're not.'

'Look, Dauphine never meant to harm them.' Gretchen was on her feet. 'She was a good person. She was a *good* person.'

'*Dauphine* never meant to harm them?' I couldn't believe we were back here. 'What is wrong with you?'

Gretchen was not only fooling herself, she was weeping with the strain of denying it all. 'Dauphine was so protective of me. Yes, she loved Violetta but she didn't want me supporting them *all*. She was worried for me. She went crazy, it was so out of character: she poisoned the champagne. She killed them all. Vio was only trying to protect me.'

'Why is everyone trying to protect you? You're a spoiled-shitless billionaire.'

She didn't like that at all. 'Yes, Violetta took the *Dana* out and sank it. She did it for me and I am grateful. She knew I couldn't live through another public scandal. I can't — ' At that

Gretchen sank to the sofa, covered her face and sobbed. Violetta sat down next to her, head tilted, rubbing Gretchen's back sympathetically.

'Darling, no,' murmured Violetta, 'don't cry, please. If you cry, I'll cry, *please.*'

I watched them and I knew that Gretchen was crying because, deep down, she knew. The real Dauphine didn't poison anyone. She knew it was all Violetta and she helped to cover that up because it suited her better than confronting Violetta, calling the police, sitting through a tawdry, exposing investigation and a court case that asked humiliating questions about her relationship with Leon, about his money.

I spoke up. 'None of it was Dauphine. Violetta did it all. You know that.'

Gretchen sobbed louder, trying to drown me out. She cried open-faced, her hands limp on her knees. Violetta leaned towards her, holding her hands, nodding encouragingly. I saw now that Gretchen thought I was victimising her by telling a truth she didn't want to hear. It made sense of the way she behaved during the rape case and why she felt OK about trying to shut me up. Even now, even after the other girl and her attempts on my life, Gretchen still felt that I was attacking her. Self-pity makes tyrants, it's the defining characteristic of brutal regimes, but it was more than that with Gretchen. It was laziness too. Violetta suited her, flattered her, coddled her, and Gretchen would harbour Violetta until it no longer served her to do so.

'Poor Gretchen,' I said. 'You won't get to choose.'

She looked up at me, her face wet and red. 'Choose?'

'Choose when it ends. With Violetta. She'll choose.'

Gretchen looked at Violetta's hands cupped around hers. 'I think you should shut up.'

I didn't. 'Does your will leave everything to Dauphine?'

Gretchen flinched and shut her eyes Violetta's back straightened and she looked at Scarface, trying to catch his eye, but he was looking to Gretchen and didn't see her. I carried on.

'Violetta is Dauphine now. You vouched for her, she has Dauphine's passport, her identity, her life. You know what she's planning, don't you?'

Gretchen stood up and snarled at me, 'You disgust me, you know that? Drunk in a hotel room with four men? What do you *expect* to happen?'

She was trying to shock me, to stop me saying it out loud, but I've heard much worse. 'She's going to kill you, you stupid, self-indulgent bitch.'

I saw a flicker of terror in Gretchen's eyes. She knew I was right.

She raised a hand and Scarface came for me. I was so shocked by the speed with which he moved that I spat in his face. Pink saliva and raspberry pips dripped off his scarred chin.

Then I saw the gun in his hand. He was holding it by the barrel and he raised it over my head.

One word, over and over again. That was all I

heard before the blackness. It was Fin's voice and he was screaming.

'NOW! NOW! NOW!'

49

I woke up. My head was so sore I couldn't open my eyes. I moved my fingers first. Then my bare feet. Soft. A cool breeze brushed hair on to my cheek. I opened my burning eyes one at a time.

The bed board above me was grey silk. I was in the big bed, in crisp linen sheets. I was alone. The windows were open to the rooftops of Paris. I was back in our hotel suite.

I tried to sit up but an electric pain shot through my head, back to front, making me cry out and lie still. My eyes throbbed with pain.

'Hello.' Fin was standing in the door.

'God — how long have I been here?'

'A day.' He sat on the edge of the bed. 'Awake some of the time.'

'A whole day?' I felt my head. There was an egg-sized lump on my scalp above my right eyebrow; it was hot to the touch.

'You've been scanned for a haematoma but they'll have to do it again. He left pills for the pain. They're worried about a concussion.'

'Did it drop?'

Fin slid his phone out of the breast pocket of his jacket and looked into the lens. 'No. The live-stream stayed up the whole time. We got everything. Scarface in vivid close-up, Violetta's confession, everything. But,' he said seriously, 'it's not all good news: we lost a lot of numbers during the wait in the hall. They picked back up when you called Violetta out. Went stratospheric then. The cops were watching and, obviously, when Scarface came in they were mobilised. He's already wanted by police forces in a number of territories. The police were waiting outside.'

'Outside?'

'Well, the maid wouldn't open the gate because they didn't have an appointment. They had to climb over the wall.'

'What happened?'

'Gretchen and Violetta were arrested by the French police for conspiracy to murder us but the Italians want to interview Violetta about Julia. They've got CCTV of her passing Malik's store. The board of the football club have issued a statement saying the allegations about the stadium sell-off are unfounded but the press are all over them. They're reopening the *Dana* investigation. I told them what Albert did at Skibo but they said we'd need more evidence of a crime. You can't arrest someone for being a turd.'

'That seems unfair. What are the numbers like?'

'*Millions.* Trina Keany's second. She wants to do a crossover podcast.'

'Let's do it. I like her.'

I was slowly becoming aware of noises in the living room, hissing and whispering and the distant growl of a TV.

Fin saw me look towards it and smiled. 'So, anyway . . . '

Then he got up and walked out. Didn't even shut the door.

But I was glad he didn't shut the door because I heard him say something and I heard squeals. I knew who it was. Jessica and Lizzie ran into the room and got into bed with me.

They touched my lump and said it felt hot. I held on to them. I was crying so much that I made their little chubby hands wet. Lizzie thought I was crying because my head hurt and they took turns kissing my bump better, jabbing it with passionate little kisses, taking turns. It was incredibly painful and I never wanted it to stop. With each kiss I thought of Sabine's love for Amila, of my mum's love for my dad, and how close I came to suicide. Trina was right. It is a passing impulse, a signal that change is needed. If I had done it I wouldn't be here, in a giant bed in Paris, having my sore face kissed by tiny lips. I was in the afterwards, it was glorious, and a lot of people didn't make it here.

That is all I'm saying about that. There's been more than enough emotional stuff in this story, crying and despair and so on.

Hamish was out there as well, with Estelle. I was still angry, I was, but there are times in this life for hating and this wasn't one of them. I was grateful to have such lovely people to be angry with. Maybe it was the bang on the head.

The doctor was called back to the hotel room and his technicians used a portable scanner to check me for brain bleeds or clots. No sign of long-term damage but we were to call if there were any changes.

It was an amazing day. A day of amnesty.

Fin ate, my girls were there, Hamish and I

talked about all my lies and sadnesses, about my mum. She was kind and tall and her face was mostly a glorious Persian nose and she was terribly proud of it. She liked gardening, and omelettes, and taught at the School of Oriental and African Studies in London, and she wrote books on genre and Middle Eastern poetry. She was amazing. I think part of the reason I ran away and never came back was that I couldn't deal with her death. And the attempt on your life, said Hamish, and the court case. I said, yes, that too. We sat on the bed together and talked about the court case, what was said, what they asked me. Hamish cried. He's a lawyer and he cried over how they treated me in court. I found that very moving.

He didn't mind that I had lied about everything. I apologised for thinking about killing him so much. He apologised for telling Estelle that I hit him. He said it was to excuse himself and malign me. He was sorry, he'd been angry with me. He would come clean to Estelle. I still don't know if he has, though.

You know, Hamish sounds like a prick in this book but he isn't. He's the father of my children. He's a good father and he has been a dear friend to me. We're both flawed. If he told this story I might sound like a prick, or maybe a bigger prick than I already do.

Fin went out for a walk with Estelle and when they came back he spent some time lying on the bed with me and we talked. He said she still loved him but couldn't live with his illness. She wanted more from life and he thought that was honest. I think his heart was broken and I took his hand and told him kindly lies: it would be all right. The feelings would pass. He was 'still an attractive woman'.

We talked about Dauphine Loire and poor Mark Parker, both dead, and Leon. I didn't think Leon was my friend any more, I knew he was dishonest and grasping, but he was also charismatic and charming, superficially lovely and I like shiny things. But mostly we talked about the other girl, who she might have been, the astonishing courage it took for her to stand up when she'd witnessed what happened to me. What a hero she was.

'I think we should find out who she was,' said Fin. 'We should honour her.'

I didn't know. I liked to think of her as an unknown soldier, a symbol of all the girls who stood up, all those brave bold girls who saw the girls before them crucified and spoke up anyway. Many were felled and she stood for all of them.

We watched cartoons on TV, ignored calls. We didn't need to speak to anyone else. We spent the evening all together. Everyone that mattered was in that hotel suite and we knew it and were grateful for each other. Most people never get an hour like that.

About ten o'clock, the medication started to lift, the fog cleared and I suddenly realised my situation: oh Christ.

I had not been murdered. I was still alive. A doctor with a portable brain scanner and two technicians had examined me in a suite in the most expensive hotel in Paris. We were all staying here. I'd left Hamish's car in an airport short-stay car park for five days and I had spent all of my cash running around Europe, making a podcast, something with no discernible market value whatsoever.

That could mean only one thing: I was going to have to write this fucking book.

Acknowledgements

For any number of reasons, this book had a long, complicated gestation. The best editor is a good friend who'll give you the bad word. It could not have happened without the guiding hands of Jade Chandler and Emily Giglierano. They insulted my baby with kindness and patience and understanding and I cannot thank them enough.

Many thanks are also due to Peter Robinson and Henry Dunow, Reagan Arthur and Liz Foley.

For the times they were and the reason I wrote a whole book about getting lost in someone else's story to save your life, thank you Fergus.

For the time it was and people in it: Stephen Evans, Jane Scoular, Edith Mina, Monica Toner, Owen Evans, Brian McNeill, Eve McNeill and Ellie Dowling, thank you.

We do hope that you have enjoyed reading this large print book.

Did you know that all of our titles are available for purchase?

We publish a wide range of high quality large print books including:
Romances, Mysteries, Classics General Fiction Non Fiction and Westerns

Special interest titles available in large print are:
The Little Oxford Dictionary Music Book Song Book Hymn Book Service Book

Also available from us courtesy of Oxford University Press:
Young Readers' Dictionary (large print edition) Young Readers' Thesaurus (large print edition)

For further information or a free brochure, please contact us at:
Ulverscroft Large Print Books Ltd., The Green, Bradgate Road, Anstey, Leicester, LE7 7FU, England. Tel: (00 44) 0116 236 4325 **Fax:** (00 44) 0116 234 0205

Other titles published by Ulverscroft:

THE LONG DROP

Denise Mina

The 'trial of the century' in 1950s Glasgow is over. Peter Manuel has been found guilty of a string of murders and is waiting to die by hanging. But every good crime story has a beginning, and Manuel's starts with the murder of William Watt's family. Watt is an ordinary businessman, a fool, a social climber — and the police are convinced he's guilty. Desperate to clear his name, Watt turns to Manuel, a career criminal who claims to have information that will finger the real killer. As Watt seeks justice with the cagey Manuel's help, everyone the pair meets has blood on their hands, as they sell their version of the truth . . .